Frog is Sad

009

Frog is Sad

Max Velthuijs

Andersen Press • London

Copyright © 2003 by Max Velthuijs
This paperback edition first published in 2005 by Andersen Press Ltd.
The rights of Max Velthuijs to be identified as the author and illustrator of this work
have been asserted by him in accordance with the Copyright, Designs and Patents Act, 1988.
First published in Great Britain in 2003 by Andersen Press Ltd., 20 Vauxhall Bridge Road, London SW1V 2SA.
Published in Australia by Random House Australia Pty., 20 Alfred Street, Milsons Point, Sydney, NSW 2061.
All rights reserved. Colour separated in Switzerland by Photolitho AG, Offsetreproduktionen,
Gossau, Zürich. Printed and bound in Italy by Grafiche AZ, Verona.

10   9   8   7   6   5   4   3   2   1

British Library Cataloguing in Publication Data available.

ISBN 1 84270 427 3

This book has been printed on acid-free paper

Frog woke up feeling sad . . .

. . . he felt like crying, but he didn't know why.

Little Bear was worried. He wanted Frog to be happy.
"Please smile, Frog," he said.
"I can't," said Frog.
"But you could *yesterday*," said Little Bear.

But Frog couldn't smile today.
And he couldn't be happy.
And he wanted to be on his own.
So Little Bear went away.

Rat came by. "Cheer up, Frog!" he said.
"I can't," said Frog.
"But it's such a beautiful day!" said Rat. "You're not sick,
are you?"
"No," said Frog. "I'm not sick. I'm just sad."

"Shall I make you laugh?" said Rat.
And he began to dance madly about.
But it didn't make Frog laugh.

Then, Rat walked on his hands . . .
but it didn't cheer Frog up.

Then he balanced a ball on his nose,
just like in the circus!

Frog didn't even smile.

Rat was disappointed. He didn't know what else to do.
And then he had an idea . . .

He rushed off to fetch his violin . . .

. . . and he started to play a beautiful tune,
a tune so beautiful that Frog began to cry.
He cried until the tears streamed down his cheeks.

And the more Rat played his violin, the harder Frog cried.
"But Frog, why are you crying?" asked Rat.
"Because you play so beautifully," wept Frog.
He was overcome with emotion.

At that, Rat burst out laughing.
"Oh, you are *silly*, Frog," he said. He laughed and laughed.
Frog just stood there . . .

Then, suddenly, he began to smile.
His smile grew and grew . . .

. . . until he was laughing and singing and dancing with Rat,
all his sadness gone.

They made such a happy noise that Duck came running . . .

. . . and Pig and Hare . . .

. . . and Little Bear last of all.
They all fell about, roaring with laughter together.

"Oh!" gasped Frog. "I have never laughed so much in my whole life, ever!"

"Dear Frog," said Little Bear. "I'm so glad you can smile again. But why were you so sad in the first place?" "I don't know," said Frog. "I just was."

PEACE AND ME

ALI WINTER • MICKAËL EL FATHI

 Lantana

ALFRED NOBEL invented a substance that helped countries go to war, but he is best remembered for his amazing contribution to world peace. How did this happen?

As an ambitious young man from Sweden, Alfred moved to Paris in the 1840s to study chemical engineering. There he met an Italian chemist who had invented a liquid called nitroglycerin that exploded when it got hot.

Experiments with this dangerous liquid had killed and injured several people. Alfred was determined to make it safe to use. He did lots of experiments until he found a way to turn the liquid into a solid form that could be blown up safely. He called his invention dynamite.

Dynamite sold like hot cakes! It could blast through rock and was used in building projects all over the world. Alfred built over ninety factories in twenty countries and became a very rich man. But all his newfound wealth didn't make him happy. He realised that his invention was also being used as a weapon of war, and this worried him a great deal.

But then he had an idea.

When Alfred died, he left behind a set of instructions in his will. The money he had made would be given out as prizes each year to the person who had achieved something of "greatest benefit to mankind". The prizes would be in Physics, Chemistry, Medicine, Literature and Peace.

It is this final prize that has inspired this book. Turn the page to discover some of the amazing men and women who have been awarded the Nobel Peace Prize, and the inspirational peace ideas they have left behind...

Alfred Nobel was born in 1833 and died in 1896. The first Nobel Peace Prize was awarded in 1901.

For my little nephew, in the hope that he will inherit a world of peace
— *Ali*

For Zélie, my peaceful daughter (except when we want her to sleep at night)
— *Mickaël*

Martin Luther
KING Jr.
UNITED STATES

Jane
ADDAMS
UNITED STATES

Rigoberta
MENCHÚ TUM
GUATEMALA

John Boyd
ORR
UNITED
KINGDOM

Fridtjof
NANSEN
NORWAY

Jean Henry
DUNANT
SWITZERLAND

Wangari
MAATHAI
KENYA

Desmond
TUTU
SOUTH AFRICA

Nelson
MANDELA
SOUTH AFRICA

Shirin
EBADI
IRAN

Malala
YOUSAFZAI
PAKISTAN

Mother
TERESA
INDIA

Peace is...helping those in trouble

Inspired by the life of Jean Henry Dunant

JEAN HENRY DUNANT was born in Geneva, Switzerland, into a wealthy family that cared for the poor.

When he was thirty-one, he thought of a plan to make his fortune and went to meet the French president Napoleon III to ask for his help. Napoleon was in a small Italian town called Solferino, leading his army in a battle against Austrian troops.

When Jean arrived, there were thousands of wounded and dying soldiers lying among the dead on the battlefield. He was horrified. He forgot his own money-making ideas and set about helping the soldiers.

He set up a hospital inside a local church and bought supplies to help the wounded. He asked women in the town to nurse the injured from both sides of the battle—friend or foe. His motto was *Tutti Fratelli*, which means *All Are Brothers*.

When Jean returned home, he wrote a book about his experiences. He had an idea that an organisation should be set up to care for wounded soldiers, whichever side of the battle they were on. Many important people read his book and were impressed by his ideas.

In the years that followed, an international organisation was formed to help people in crisis. It was named the Red Cross. Over a hundred years later, wherever there is conflict or disaster, the Red Cross can still be found.

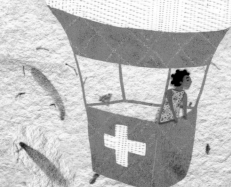

Jean Henry Dunant
(1828-1910) won the Nobel
Peace Prize in 1901

Peace is...
making sure everyone has a home

As a child, **FRIDTJOF NANSEN**
loved spending time outdoors and
camping in the forest near his home in
Norway. He was so good at sport that he broke
the world speed skating record when he was only
eighteen years old.

Fridtjof decided to study zoology at university because he thought
this subject would keep him outdoors rather than in stuffy lecture halls.
Soon he was invited to join a ship sailing to Greenland. The voyage lasted
many months and sparked a lifelong spirit of adventure.

From then on, Fridtjof set sail whenever he could. He led a team across Greenland on
cross-country skis, and came closer to the North Pole than any other person before him. He had
become the most famous explorer in the world!

After World War I, the newly-formed League of Nations asked Fridtjof to help nearly half a million
prisoners of war make their way home. The skills he had learned from his years of exploring made his
efforts a success. Next, he turned his sights to finding homes for several million refugees.

One of the biggest hurdles Fridtjof faced was that many refugees lacked identity papers to prove their
nationality. He invented the "Nansen passport", a certificate that allowed them to travel freely
across borders between countries. It was approved by over fifty governments.

The great explorer who was always leaving home to travel the world became even
more famous for helping refugees find homes of their own.

Fridtjof Nansen (1861-1930) won
the Nobel Peace Prize in 1922

Inspired by the life of Fridtjof Nansen

Peace is...giving people the skills to thrive
Inspired by the life of Jane Addams

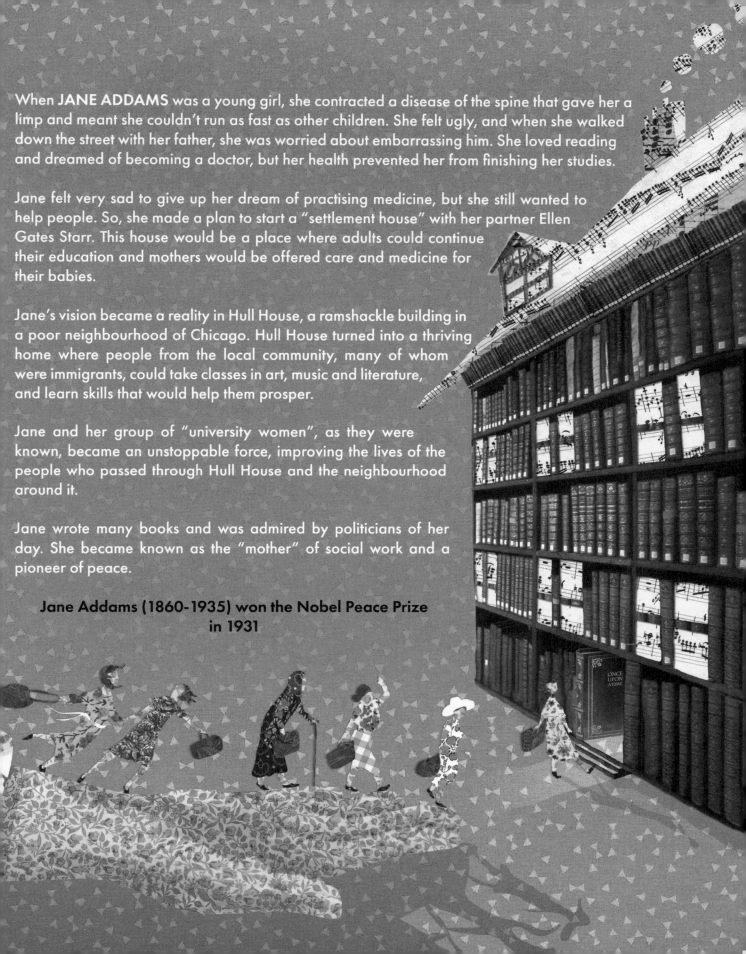

When **JANE ADDAMS** was a young girl, she contracted a disease of the spine that gave her a limp and meant she couldn't run as fast as other children. She felt ugly, and when she walked down the street with her father, she was worried about embarrassing him. She loved reading and dreamed of becoming a doctor, but her health prevented her from finishing her studies.

Jane felt very sad to give up her dream of practising medicine, but she still wanted to help people. So, she made a plan to start a "settlement house" with her partner Ellen Gates Starr. This house would be a place where adults could continue their education and mothers would be offered care and medicine for their babies.

Jane's vision became a reality in Hull House, a ramshackle building in a poor neighbourhood of Chicago. Hull House turned into a thriving home where people from the local community, many of whom were immigrants, could take classes in art, music and literature, and learn skills that would help them prosper.

Jane and her group of "university women", as they were known, became an unstoppable force, improving the lives of the people who passed through Hull House and the neighbourhood around it.

Jane wrote many books and was admired by politicians of her day. She became known as the "mother" of social work and a pioneer of peace.

Jane Addams (1860-1935) won the Nobel Peace Prize in 1931

Peace is...making sure no one goes hungry

Inspired by the life of **John Boyd Orr of Brechin**

JOHN BOYD ORR was born in a small village in Scotland and grew up to be a teacher. He noticed that lots of his poorer pupils couldn't concentrate in class because they were hungry. This observation stayed with him and, after a few years, he left teaching and went back to university to study biology and medicine.

During World War I, John used his skills as a surgeon to treat wounded soldiers and won medals for his bravery. He gave his men fruit and vegetables from the deserted fields and gardens they marched through, and his soldiers became the healthiest in the army.

When the war was over, John returned to Scotland to continue learning about better diets. He found that giving children milk to drink made them healthier and helped them grow taller. Decades later, many children still receive free milk at school because of his research.

During World War II, John was asked to advise the British government on food. Britain was suffering severe food shortages but John's clever planning meant that many women and children were healthier at the end of the war than they were at the start.

One of the unsung heroes of the war effort, John Boyd Orr helped millions of people avoid starvation during the conflict and in the difficult years that followed.

John Boyd Orr (1880-1971) won the Nobel Peace Prize in 1949

Peace is...treating all people as equals

Inspired by the life of Martin Luther King Jr.

MARTIN LUTHER KING

JR. grew up in Atlanta, Georgia. When he was six years old, he was told that he couldn't go to school with the white children he liked to play with in the street. Their school was for white children, and his school was for black children.

Slavery had ended, but there were still rules that separated people by the colour of their skin. Black people didn't just go to separate schools, they also had separate libraries and even separate water fountains.

When Martin grew older, he became a Baptist minister. He heard about Rosa Parks, a brave black woman in Alabama who was arrested when she refused to give up her seat on the bus to a white man. Martin led a boycott against the bus company that lasted over a year. Eventually, the courts decided that the bus company should end segregation on public buses.

Martin had become famous for his role in the bus boycott. His call for peaceful protest in the campaign for racial equality made him the voice of the civil rights movement.

Martin's best-known speech persuaded the government of the United States to make changes to its laws. In this speech, he said, "I have a dream that my four little children will one day live in a nation where they will not be judged by the colour of their skin but by the content of their character".

At the age of thirty-nine, Martin was assassinated. Forty years later, when Barack Obama became America's first African American president, he paid tribute to the bravery and courage of Martin Luther King Jr., who had sacrificed his life for a brighter future.

Martin Luther King Jr. (1929-1968) won the Nobel Peace Prize in 1964

Peace is...
caring for those who are less fortunate

Inspired by the life of Mother Teresa

MOTHER TERESA was born in the city of Skopje in eastern Europe, and her parents named her Agnes. When she was only a girl, she decided to devote her life to the Catholic Church and to helping the poor.

At eighteen, she bravely left her family and travelled to a convent in Ireland where she learned to speak English. After a few months' practice, Sister Teresa, as she had renamed herself, set sail for India.

Sister Teresa became a teacher and was loved by her students, but she was saddened by the poverty around her. She moved out of her Calcutta convent to live among the local people. Wearing a simple white cotton sari with three blue stripes, she found ways to offer love and support to those who needed it, particularly the homeless children whom she loved like a mother.

Sister Teresa became known as Mother Teresa and the Pope permitted her to set up an organisation of nuns who would live among the poor. In this organisation, called the Missionaries of Charity, the nuns would care for "all those people who feel unwanted". Her organisation grew from a handful of women to thousands of volunteers around the world.

The woman who had waved goodbye to her family when she was only a teenager gained a global family by spreading her message of love. After she died, Mother Teresa was declared a saint by the Catholic Church.

Mother Teresa (1910-1997) won the Nobel Peace Prize in 1979

Peace is...finding ways to forgive

Inspired by the life of Desmond Tutu

DESMOND MPILO TUTU was born in a gold-mining town in South Africa and moved with his family to Johannesburg when he was still a boy. His family was not rich, and Desmond earned pocket money by selling peanuts at railway stations.

Desmond earned a place at medical school but his parents couldn't afford the fees, so he accepted a scholarship to study teaching. He was an inspiring teacher but became frustrated by an education system that helped white pupils get ahead in life and held black pupils back.

Desmond decided to study theology and became an Anglican minister. After travelling abroad to study some more, he became the first black Dean of Johannesburg. He went on to become Bishop of Lesotho, Bishop of Johannesburg and Archbishop of Cape Town—the first black minister in each position. He used his achievements to speak out bravely against the South African political system, known as apartheid, that treated black people as second-class citizens.

When Nelson Mandela came to power, Desmond encouraged those who had committed violence during apartheid to apologise to their victims and their victims' families in the hope of forgiveness. It was a revolutionary approach by an extraordinary man and contributed greatly to peace in South Africa.

Desmond Tutu (1931-) won the Nobel Peace Prize in 1984

Peace is...respecting all communities

Inspired by the life of Rigoberta Menchú Tum

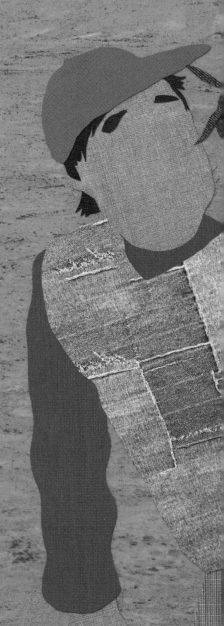

When **RIGOBERTA MENCHÚ TUM** was eight years old, she was sent to work in the fields to harvest coffee, sugarcane and cotton. She came from a family of Mayan peasants in Guatemala. Although they were very poor, Rigoberta's mother taught her to be proud of her ancient Mayan heritage.

At that time, a brutal civil war was raging in Guatemala that destroyed hundreds of villages and made a million people homeless. Rigoberta stood by helpless as her father, mother and brother were all killed by the Guatemalan army for opposing the government.

While her sisters escaped into the mountains, Rigoberta stayed in the countryside to campaign for political change. She taught herself Spanish and a number of Mayan languages so that she could pass on her message of resistance to her fellow peasant workers.

At the age of twenty-one, she was forced to flee from Guatemala and seek safety in Mexico. From there she travelled the world speaking out against the oppression of indigenous peoples, and particularly women, in Guatemala and other countries.

She became known for her fearless voice, calling out for respect and fair treatment, and inspiring men and women around the world to do the same.

Rigoberta Menchú Tum (1959-) won the Nobel Peace Prize in 1992

Peace is...valuing the things we have in common

Inspired by the life of Nelson Mandela

ROLIHLAHLA MANDELA was born into the Tembu tribe of the Xhosa people in South Africa. At school, he was given the English name "Nelson", which was easier for white people to say.

When Nelson was expelled from university for joining a protest, he travelled to Johannesburg. There he joined a political party that opposed apartheid. Apartheid was a legal system imposed by the white government based on the colour of people's skin. It took away the rights of black citizens and gave white citizens unfair advantages.

Nelson began to promote armed resistance against the government. He was arrested and sent to prison for almost thirty years. At his trial, he made a speech calling for racial equality and finished with the famous words, "It is an ideal for which I am prepared to die".

All around the world, people called for Nelson to be freed from his prison on Robben Island. When he was finally released, he had so much support that he was elected president of South Africa. He worked tirelessly to unite the black and white citizens of his country through peaceful means, and never tried to take revenge on the people who had put him in prison.

For his determination to mend the deep rifts in his country, Nelson Mandela was heralded as a truly inspirational leader.

Nelson Mandela (1918-2013) won the Nobel Peace Prize in 1993

Peace is...letting silenced voices be heard

SHIRIN EBADI was born in Iran to a well-educated family. From a young age, she had a keen interest in the law and worked hard to receive a law degree before becoming Iran's first-ever female judge.

All this was to change after the Islamic Revolution. The new government said that women could not be judges and Shirin was forced to give up her job and become a clerk in the same courts she had once ruled over. She resigned in protest and sought instead to become a lawyer. For many years her application was refused, but finally she was given permission.

Shirin set up her own law firm and never shied away from difficult cases. She represented the families of murder victims and fought for the freedom of political prisoners. She spoke up for the rights of women and children even when others wouldn't. And she often didn't charge any fees.

One day, while attending a conference abroad, the government seized everything she owned and threatened her with prison if she returned to Iran. Shirin made the difficult decision to stay abroad, not because she was afraid of prison, but because she knew that she wouldn't be able to continue speaking out against oppression if she was behind bars.

Shirin Ebadi has inspired people around the world by bravely standing up for the rights of those whose voices have been silenced, even at great personal cost to herself.

Shirin Ebadi (1947-)
won the Nobel Peace
Prize in 2003,

Inspired by the life of Shirin Ebadi

Peace is...
protecting our environment

Inspired by the life of Wangari Maathai

WANGARI MAATHAI grew up in a town in Kenya where children played amongst the trees and a natural spring provided water for the people.

Wangari became the first woman in East and Central Africa to earn a doctorate degree. But when she returned to her village after her studies, she was horrified to find that the trees had all been cut down, the spring had run dry and the countryside was turning into a desert.

Wangari decided to plant a group of native trees in her backyard. Then she encouraged other women to start planting trees, and before long thousands of women all over Kenya had come together to plant seedlings, enough for one tree for every person in the country. The women received a small fee for each seedling that grew, which helped them feed their families. This mass tree planting effort became known as the Green Belt Movement.

Wangari's movement believed in democracy and freedom of speech, and she often came into conflict with the government. But she was firm in her belief that planting trees would improve the quality of the soil, increase food production, provide more firewood for cooking, and create jobs. Soon these ideas spread to other African countries and Wangari was celebrated around the world for her work.

And it all started with a single seed.

Wangari Maathai (1940-2011) won the Nobel Peace Prize in 2004

Peace is...
making sure
every child gets
to go to school

Inspired by the life of Malala Yousafzai

MALALA YOUSAFZAI was born in a valley in Pakistan at the foot of the mountains. Her father promised her an education, but a political group known as the Taliban took control of the valley. The Taliban banned music and television. Worst of all they banned girls from going to school. Life changed a great deal for Malala and her family.

Malala vowed to tell the world what was happening in her small village. At the age of eleven, she started blogging for the BBC using a false name. Soon, newspapers all over the world had picked up her story and, despite the danger it put her in, Malala began to speak publicly about how important it was for girls to have the chance to be educated.

After a few years, the Taliban were forced out of the valley and Malala was overjoyed to go back to school. However, when she was fifteen, a masked gunman from the Taliban boarded her school bus and shot her. She was badly wounded and taken to a hospital in the United Kingdom where she spent many months recovering from the attack.

Since then she has supported the education of girls in countries around the world. Her courage and determination earned her many prizes and awards. She has become a voice of inspiration for young people everywhere and the youngest person ever to win a Nobel prize.

Malala Yousafzai (1997-) won the Nobel Peace Prize in 2014

PEACE IS...

...helping those in trouble
...making sure everyone has a home
...giving people the skills to thrive
...making sure no one goes hungry
...treating all people as equals
...caring for those who are less fortunate
...finding ways to forgive
...respecting all communities
...valuing the things we have in common
...letting silenced voices be heard
...protecting our environment
...making sure every child gets to go to school

WHAT DOES PEACE MEAN TO YOU?

AMNESTY INTERNATIONAL

Amnesty International endorses this book because it shows how standing up for other people makes the world a better, more peaceful place.

VEGETARIAN MEALS IN

30 minutes

MORE THAN 100 DELICIOUS RECIPES FOR FITNESS

ANITA BEAN

BLOOMSBURY SPORT

LONDON · OXFORD · NEW YORK · NEW DELHI · SYDNEY

BLOOMSBURY SPORT
Bloomsbury Publishing Plc
50 Bedford Square, London, WC1B 3DP, UK

BLOOMSBURY, BLOOMSBURY SPORT and the Diana logo are trademarks of Bloomsbury Publishing Plc.

First published in Great Britain 2019.

Copyright © Anita Bean, 2019
Illustrations and design by Louise Turpin
Food photography by Clare Winfield
Food styling by Jayne Cross
Photographs of Anita Bean by Grant Pritchard
Getty photographs on pages 16, 31, 35, 44 and 46

Anita Bean has asserted her right under the Copyright, Designs and Patents Act, 1988, to be identified as Author of this work.

For legal purposes the Acknowledgements on page 211 constitute an extension of this copyright page.

Bloomsbury Publishing Plc ma ... ufacture of our books are natural, recyclable products made f ... ring processes conform to the

To find out more abou ... gn up for our newsletters.

CONTENTS

INTRODUCTION

Welcome to *Vegetarian Meals in 30 Minutes*, my second collection of fitness-inspired vegetarian recipes. It's for everyone who enjoys eating delicious, healthy food – not just for vegetarians – and being active, whether that's working out in a gym, playing competitive sport, or simply taking a daily walk. It's for you if you have a busy life but don't want to spend hours in the kitchen or shopping for lots of specialist ingredients.

When I wrote my first cookbook, *The Vegetarian Athlete's Cookbook* (Bloomsbury, 2017), I wasn't sure whether vegetarian cooking would appeal to many athletes, or whether the myths about needing meat to compete would prevail. Well, I couldn't have been more wrong! I was truly overwhelmed by the enthusiastic response the book received from vegetarians and non-vegetarians, athletes and non-athletes alike, and I was inundated with requests for more veggie recipes.

My aim with *Vegetarian Meals in 30 Minutes* is to show you how to make delicious vegetarian meals in less than half an hour that will support your sport or active lifestyle. It's a collection of my best recipes and the culmination of 25 years of experience working with athletes and teams from many different food cultures. It is also the product of cooking for my own (vegetarian) children during their competitive swimming years. As any swimming parent will know, feeding teenage swimmers is particularly challenging, as they train between two and four hours each day, mostly early in the morning or late in the evening, so they are always hungry. Needless to say, my kitchen frequently resembled a food factory!

I have my Hungarian parents to thank for my love of vegetarian food. They raised me as a vegetarian from birth. We had a big garden in rural Essex, where we grew lots of produce, and I have vivid memories of picking apples, harvesting sweetcorn and shelling peas. As a child, I was always helping my mum cook in the kitchen, whether it was stirring a vegetarian goulash, chopping onions for a lecsó (a Hungarian vegetable stew) or rolling out lángos (a type of flatbread). By the time I started secondary school, Mum allowed me free rein of the kitchen to cook vegetarian meals by myself. As there weren't many vegetarian cookbooks around in the 70s, I created lots of my own recipes using produce from the garden and inspiration from home economics lessons at school. And that's really where my passion for food and nutrition began. I went on to study Nutrition and Food Science at the University of Surrey.

In my career as a registered nutritionist, I have never preached a vegetarian diet nor tried to stop people eating meat, as I respect the right for everyone to have the freedom to eat the way that best fits their set of beliefs. While I choose to exclude meat from my diet for ethical, moral, health and environmental reasons, I appreciate that a vegetarian diet may not be for everyone. However, I do think that eating less meat is healthier, more compassionate, sustainable and better for our environment. As a lifelong vegetarian I have never tasted meat, so I do not know how difficult it feels to stop eating it. But, vegetarian or not, I believe that everyone can enjoy vegetarian food and benefit from eating less meat and more plants.

Growing up as a vegetarian in the 60s and 70s wasn't easy, as I was very much in a minority. Vegetarianism was practically unheard of in those days and people assumed either that something was 'wrong' with me or that I must be part of a religious cult. They couldn't understand why I wouldn't eat a hamburger! When I told them I was vegetarian, the reaction I usually got was 'What do you eat then?' or 'Don't you miss meat?' Having never eaten meat, I certainly didn't miss it, and the answer to the first question comprised a very long list of foods. I enjoyed watching their jaws drop. Nowadays, when I get asked the same question (yes, still!), that list of foods has grown even longer, and I can just point people to this book.

Thankfully, attitudes to vegetarianism have changed enormously since my childhood. I am no longer thought of as 'cranky' or 'weird', nor do I have to explain endlessly at dinner parties why I don't eat meat. I no longer struggle to find a vegetarian option on restaurant menus; nowadays, thankfully, the choices usually extend beyond an omelette or pasta. In fact, cutting out or eating less meat has become a hugely popular lifestyle choice for lots of people, and I'm relieved that vegetarianism no longer raises eyebrows. There are now entire supermarket aisles devoted to vegetarian food, trendy cafes and even Michelin-starred vegetarian restaurants. Vegetarianism has certainly come a long way.

Barely a week goes by without vegetarian or veganism hitting the headlines, whether it's a supermarket launching a new range of products or a report about the environmental damage farming does to the planet.

According to a 2018 survey by supermarket chain Waitrose, a third of UK consumers say they have deliberately reduced the amount of meat they eat or removed it from their diet entirely. One in eight are now vegetarian or vegan, and a further 21 per cent say they are flexitarian – where a largely plant-based diet is supplemented occasionally with meat.

An emerging food trend is the rise in popularity of fake meats, with plant-based meat substitutes designed to look and taste like meat. These include vegetarian 'steaks', 'bacon' and 'duck' made from soya and wheat protein; vegan 'pulled pork' and nuggets made from jack fruit; beef, chicken and pork substitutes made from seitan (processed wheat gluten); vegan burgers oozing with beetroot juice; and all kinds of meat look-alikes made from Quorn. While such innovations hold zero appeal for me (I think it is counter-intuitive to eat products mimicking meat), they are satisfying a growing number of people who want to cut down on their meat intake but still have the experience of eating a similar product without the moral, health and environmental dilemmas. You won't find any meat substitutes in this book, but I believe anything that contributes to a reduction in global meat consumption has to be a good thing.

However, several myths about vegetarian diets still persist, particularly when it comes to sports and fitness. Two of the biggest myths are that you can't perform at a high level on a vegetarian diet, and that you can't build muscle without eating meat. Well, to dispel the first myth you only have to look at the growing number of high-profile sports stars like Venus Williams, Tom Daley, Adam Peaty, Lizzie Deignan, David Haye and Lewis Hamilton, who have adopted a meat-free diet. They are testament to the fact that you don't need meat to be successful in sport. Then there's my personal experience as a vegetarian bodybuilder: I trained with weights for 10 years without eating meat, won successive bodybuilding titles, including the United Kingdom Bodybuilding and Fitness Federation (UKBFF, formerly the EFBB) British Championships in 1991, and finished twice in the Top 10 at the IFBB World Bodybuilding Championships. Anecdotes aside, there is plenty of scientific evidence to support the efficacy of vegetarian diets for both strength and cardiovascular fitness (see p. 16).

I also want this book to help clear up the confusion and misunderstandings about nutrition. In Chapter 8, I bust some of the most common nutrition myths and provide science-backed facts behind them. I believe that social media has created a culture of fear around food and it concerns me to see that vegetarianism and veganism are often caught up in the sphere of dieting and disordered eating, especially in young people. I've seen so many people cut out foods unnecessarily and without medical reason just because they've read something on a website. This can leave them deficient in crucial nutrients or with an unhealthy obsession with food. The internet is full of non-evidenced based food fads and supplements, so it's easy to fall prey to poor nutritional advice, whether it's keto diets, clean eating, or the latest miracle superfood.

We've entered an era of reductionist thinking around nutrition, where foods are often categorised as 'good' or 'bad'. For example, people often speak of butter or sugar as being 'bad' for you without any consideration of the amount consumed or what it is eaten with. Similarly, avocados and hummus are regarded as 'good', but that doesn't mean you can eat limitless quantities – anything in excess isn't good for you!

I believe that all food can be part of a healthy diet and that eliminating or restricting any food fosters an unhealthy relationship with it. Finally, I believe that food is more than fuel and nutrients. What we eat and the way we eat it says a lot about our values, and choosing to eat vegetarian food embraces compassion, gratitude and kindness. Being able to choose what to eat, to have the means to buy what we eat and enjoy meals with others is a privilege.

In Part 2 you'll find more than 100 delicious recipes that take 30 minutes or less to prepare and cook. They are packed with maximum nutrition, perfect for fuelling your workouts and promoting speedy recovery. I love making food and hope that this book will help you develop a passion for good food, too, however busy your life.

I also hope that the recipes in this book will bring you much enjoyment.

Bon appetit!

PART 1
NUTRITION

CHAPTER 1

HOW TO USE THIS BOOK

○ ○

This book is divided into two sections: Part 1 is a guide to vegetarian nutrition, and Part 2 is a cookbook.

If you're thinking about switching to a vegetarian diet or you simply want to find out more, then dive straight into Chapter 2 for a quick read about the health and environmental benefits of eating less meat.

Chapters 3–7 provide a wealth of evidence-based advice, tips and tricks on planning a vegetarian diet to help you perform better and live a healthier life. You'll find features on key sports nutrition topics such as pre-exercise nutrition, recovery, hydration and sports supplements. There's also plenty of practical guidance on calculating your calorie, protein, carbohydrate and fat requirements that you can use straight away, as well as cutting-edge science on topics such as gut health and low-carbohydrate diets. If you're fed up with all the fake news and misinformation out there, then head to Chapter 8. Here, I bust some of the most popular food myths and answer popular questions that I've been asked since the publication of *The Vegetarian Athlete's Cookbook* in 2017. If you want to delve further into the science, you'll find references for all of the studies mentioned in this book on pp. 212–214.

The second section of this book, the cookbook, includes more than 100 simple recipes that can be made in 30 minutes or less. They are delicious, nutritious and quick to make, and have been created to support health and performance. You'll also find lots of nutritional and cooking tips interspersed with the recipes. I strongly believe that cooking should be a pleasure, not a chore, so I have endeavoured to make the recipes as easy to follow as possible. I hope these recipes will help you to embrace and enjoy eating healthy meals, and discover how tasty and easy vegetarian cooking can be.

CHAPTER 2

THE BENEFITS OF A VEGETARIAN DIET

One in eight people are now vegetarian or vegan, according to a 2018 survey by Waitrose,[1] and a further 21 per cent are flexitarian, which means a third of people in the UK have stopped or reduced eating meat.

Nowadays, people use lots of different terms to describe the way they eat – vegetarian, semi-vegetarian, vegan, plant-based, flexitarian, meat reducer – but vegetarianism is typically used to describe a diet that excludes meat and fish but includes dairy produce and eggs. Veganism refers to a diet that excludes all foods of animal original, including honey. The term 'plant-based' is very much on-trend and, although there's no universal definition, it is often used interchangeably with vegan or, increasingly, to refer to a flexitarian style of eating that includes mostly plants, but with small amounts of meat or fish. What is clear, though, is that eating less meat is a strong lifestyle trend that's here to stay. More and more people are cutting down and limiting how much meat they eat, or giving it up altogether in favour of a vegetarian or vegan diet.

Interestingly, this trend away from meat isn't just about health, although there is compelling evidence that vegetarian diets are associated with less risk of chronic diseases, such as heart disease and a longer lifespan (see p. 14). For many people, it's more about helping the environment and reducing their carbon footprint. For many people, the environmental benefits of a plant-based diet are the biggest motivator to cut back. Even seven-time Mr. Olympia champion, Arnold Schwarzenegger, has declared cutting his consumption of meat for environmental reasons.[2]

ENVIRONMENTAL BENEFITS

It's no secret that we'd solve a lot of problems if everyone switched to a plant-based diet. Plant-based foods have much less impact on the environment than meat. The agricultural industry is one of the biggest contributors to climate change and accounts for 15 per cent of all greenhouse gas emissions (GGE) that heat up our planet. This is because livestock produce large quantities of methane. Raising livestock also requires huge amounts of water and grain, results in pollution of our water supplies and leads to deforestation in many regions of the world. For example, producing beef results in six times more GGEs and uses 36 times more land than growing plant protein.

According to research from the World Resources Institute,[3] switching to a vegetarian or vegan diet would roughly halve total emissions, and significantly reduce agriculture's pressure on the environment. If enough of us did it, eating less meat could go a long way towards solving the global problem of scarce environmental resources and global warming. It would help free up the land and water needed to feed a growing population and preserve vital natural resources. Even small changes would have big impacts. A plant-based diet requires far less energy, land, pesticides, fertiliser, fuel, feed and water than a meat-based diet and does less environmental damage, which makes it unquestionably more sustainable.

Scientific research published in The Lancet Planetary Health in 2018 used computer modelling to compare a range of diets across more than 150 countries to determine the relationship between diet, health and environmental impact.[4] The researchers concluded that for people in high and middle income countries, flexitarian or vegan diets which met healthy eating guidelines had positive benefits for health as well as on the environment. They could markedly reduce GGEs, fertilisers, freshwater and global farmland use and still feed the world's population.

With a growing global population, food sustainability is now a major concern. A further report from the EAT-Lancet Commission in 2019 argued that we need to cut dramatically the amount of meat we eat in order to feed the world's population in the coming years.[5] Its 'planetary health diet' recommends we get most of our protein from pulses (such as beans and lentils) and nuts, with smaller amount from dairy products and eggs. According to the report's authors, eating this way will also help prevent diet-related diseases, cut GGEs, and mitigate climate change.

Modelling work has shown that reducing the amount of animal foods in our diet will make a critical contribution to climate change mitigation and keep global warming below 2°C, the threshold beyond which dangerous climate change is thought to occur. A landmark report from the Intergovernmental Panel on Climate Change (IPCC) in 2018,[6] warned of the huge risks of extreme heat, drought and floods if global warming passes even the 1.5 °C mark. It claims that the world is well off-track at keeping below this level. Limiting warming is possible but only if we change the way we eat and switch to a more plant-based diet with less meat (along with changes to power generation, industry and transport).

HEALTH BENEFITS

Eating a vegetarian diet or simply less meat is associated with numerous health benefits. A comprehensive analysis of 96 previous studies at the University of Florence, Italy, in 2017 found being a vegetarian or vegan was associated with a significantly lower risk of heart disease and cancer.[7] Other studies have shown that populations that eat less meat tend to have less cardiovascular disease, type 2 diabetes and certain cancers (particularly bowel, breast and prostate cancers), lower blood pressure, lower body weight, increased longevity. We also know that colorectal cancer is more common among people who eat lots of red meat and processed meat.

IS MEAT BAD FOR YOU?

A 2018 report by the World Cancer Research Fund (WCRF) concluded that there is strong evidence that consumption of either red or processed meat are both causes of colorectal cancer.[8] Processed meat is meat that has been salted, cured, fermented, smoked or blended to make ham, bacon, beef jerky, corned beef, salami, pepperoni and hot dogs. It has also been linked to other cancers, including breast, pancreas and prostate. According to an analysis of data on more than one million women by Harvard University researchers in 2018,[9] women who eat large amounts of processed meat are 9 per cent more likely to develop breast cancer. The WCRF recommend cutting processed meat altogether and eating no more than 500 g of unprocessed red meat a week. Currently, the NHS recommends eating no more than 70 g of red and processed meat a day.[10]

The increased cancer risk among meat eaters may be due to a number of factors including a lack of fibre, a lower intake of plant foods, less exercise, or to certain chemicals found in the meat itself. One theory is that, haem iron found naturally in red meat is broken down to form carcinogenic (cancer-causing) N-nitroso compounds in the bowel. Another theory is that cancer-causing substances are formed when meat is preserved by smoking, curing or salting, or by the addition of preservatives to make processed meat. In addition, cooking meat at high temperatures produces chemicals called heterocyclic amines (HCAs) and polycyclic aromatic hydrocarbons (PAH) and these may trigger cancer.

According to the largest UK study of vegetarians, the EPIC-Oxford study,[11] vegetarians are 32 per cent less likely to develop heart disease than non-vegetarians, as well as having a significantly lower risk of cancer, obesity, type 2 diabetes, high blood pressure and high LDL-cholesterol. In 2016 a study by US scientists,[12] monitoring more than 130,000 people for 30 years, found that every 3 per cent increase in calories from plant protein reduced the risk of dying from heart disease by 12 per cent

The health benefits of vegetarian diets may be partly due to the absence of meat and partly to the higher consumption of plant foods, such as fruit and vegetables, whole grains, beans, lentils, chickpeas, nuts and seeds. Eating a more plant-based diet gives you more fibre, unsaturated fats, polyphenols and phytochemicals (plant substances that have beneficial health properties), all of which are linked to improved gut health (see p. 23) and lower risk of chronic disease. Vegetarian diets also tend to be lower in saturated fat, added sugar and ultra-processed foods, which goes some way towards explaining the health differences between vegetarians and non-vegetarians. It is possible that other lifestyle factors may also play a role – vegetarians typically exercise more and are less likely to smoke and drink excessive alcohol, all of which may account for some of the reduction in disease risk.

But for many people, like myself, choosing a vegetarian or vegan lifestyle is very much an ethical and moral decision. I see eating meat as a form of exploitation and cruelty to animals. Over 2 million land animals are slaughtered daily and almost 600,000 tonnes of fish are killed each year in the UK. Many animals farmed for meat are kept in filthy and cramped factory farms and never experience a natural life out in the open air. By not eating or cutting down on meat, you are helping to prevent this exploitation and being compassionate to animals. The truth is we don't need to eat meat to live or to be healthy. According to the British Dietetic Association,[13] well-planned vegetarian diets have many benefits and even vegan diets can 'support healthy living in people of all ages'.

CHAPTER 3

VEGETARIAN DIETS AND SPORTS PERFORMANCE

It's a common misconception that, as a vegetarian, you cannot get enough protein in your diet or that you need to eat meat to build muscle and perform well in sport. The truth is you can easily obtain all the protein your body needs from many sources other than meat, including milk, yogurt, cheese, eggs, beans, lentils, chickpeas, peas, tofu, whole grains, quinoa, nuts and seeds. The key is to include a wide variety of these foods in your diet and ensure you include one or more of them in each meal.

While a vegetarian diet may not turn you into an Olympic athlete, it certainly won't put you at any disadvantage when it comes to fitness training. According to a 2016 review by Australian researchers,[1] there's plenty of evidence that a well-planned and varied diet does not hinder athletic performance. What's more, a review of studies by Canadian researchers found that vegetarian diets can provide more than enough protein and other nutrients to support the requirements for athletes.[2] And a 2016 study at Arizona State University found that vegetarian athletes had the same aerobic fitness and strength as those who ate meat – in fact, the female vegetarians were fitter aerobically than the meat-eaters.[3]

Plant proteins, such as beans, lentils and nuts, can still provide you with all the essential amino acids if you eat them in sufficient quantities and/or combine more than one source. They don't always need to be eaten at the same meal either, just over the course of the day.

A study published in the *American Journal of Clinical Nutrition* found that the muscle mass and strength of people who ate mostly plant proteins were no different to those who ate animal proteins.[4] As long as they were eating enough protein, the source of protein – plant or animal – didn't matter. In other words, plant proteins are as good as animal proteins when it comes to building muscle strength.

HOW MANY CALORIES DO I NEED?

You can estimate your daily calorie needs by working out your resting metabolic rate (RMR) and multiplying it by your physical activity level. Your RMR is the number of calories your body requires to maintain itself at rest. There are numerous online calculators that determine your daily calorie needs based on your height, weight and age. Alternatively, here's a quick method that will give you a good estimate.

1 Estimate your RMR. As a rule of thumb, RMR uses 22 calories for every 1 kg of a woman's body weight per day and 24 calories per 1 kg of a man's body weight. Estimate your RMR by multiplying your body weight (kg) by 22 (for women) or 24 (for men).
For example, a 60-kg woman will have a RMR of 60 x 22 = 1320 cals

2 Multiply your RMR by your Physical Activity Level (PAL), which is a rough measure of your lifestyle activity (see table).
For example, a 60-kg active woman will require 1320 x 1.5 = 1980 cals

This is roughly how many calories you burn a day. Consuming this number of calories will allow you to maintain your weight, or at least prevent weight gain.

If you want to lose weight, reduce your daily calorie intake by 15 per cent (i.e. multiply by 0.85). For example, to lose weight, an active 60-kg woman would need to consume 1980 x 0.85 = 1683 cals.

If you want to gain weight, increase your daily calorie intake by 20 per cent (i.e. multiply by 1.2) and include at least two or three sessions of strength training in your weekly training programme.

Physical Activity Level (PAL)	Multiplier	Description
Mostly inactive	1.2	Mainly sitting
Fairly active	1.3	Sitting, some walking, exercise once or twice per week
Moderately active	1.4	Regular walking, or exercise two to three times per week
Active	1.5	Exercise or sport more than three times per week
Very active	1.7	Physically active job or intense daily exercise or sport

FUEL FOR YOUR WORKOUT

The body uses different fuels for energy depending on the intensity of your workout. Fuelling for your workout involves matching your calorie and carbohydrate intake to the requirements of your workout. Minimising carbohydrates before low-intensity workouts encourages the body to become more efficient at using fat for fuel. Suitable pre-workout meals or snacks before low-intensity workouts include an omelette, an avocado salad, or hummus with vegetables. During longer or high-intensity workouts the body uses more carbohydrate as fuel. This means you'll benefit from eating a carbohydrate-rich meal before exercising. Good options include porridge, rice with beans, or sweet potato curry.

CHAPTER 4

MACRONUTRIENTS

PROTEIN

WHY DO I NEED IT?

Protein makes up part of the structure of every cell in your body, including the muscles, bones, skin, hair and organs. It is needed for building and rebuilding the muscle fibres that are damaged during exercise, as well as for the repair of all body cells, and for making enzymes, hormones and antibodies.

WHAT TYPES ARE THERE?

Protein is made up of building blocks called amino acids that are combined in different ways to make hundreds of different proteins. There are 20 amino acids, of which eight are essential for adults, which means they can't be made by the body, but must be provided by the food and drink you consume. Foods that contain all eight essential amino acids in proportions closely matched to the body's requirements are sometimes called 'complete' proteins. For vegetarians, these include dairy products, eggs, soya products, quinoa, buckwheat, chia and hemp seeds. Most plant-based protein sources are 'incomplete', meaning they lack one or more essential amino acid, but that's not a difficult hurdle to overcome. Incomplete sources can still provide you with all the essential amino acids if you combine more than one protein source (see p. 20). They don't always need to be eaten at the same meal, just over the course of the day.

HOW MUCH SHOULD I EAT?

The Recommended Daily Allowance (RDA) for the general population is 0.75 g per kg of body weight per day. So, a 60-kg person would require approximately 60 x 0.75 = 45 g a day. Regular exercise increases your protein requirement, so you'll need between 1.2 and 2 g per kg of body weight per day, depending on the type, intensity and duration of your activity, according to the latest recommendations of the American College of Sports Medicine.[1] This extra protein helps to repair and rebuild muscle cells damaged during intense exercise. For example, a 60-kg person who regularly works out would need between 72 and 120 g protein. If you do mostly endurance activities, stick to the lower end of the range. For mostly strength training, an intake at the upper end of the range would be more suitable. However, distributing your protein evenly throughout the day will promote better muscle recovery, mass and strength gains than consuming it unevenly across meals. In other words, you should aim to include similar amounts of protein for breakfast, lunch and dinner. Research suggests a minimum of 0.25 g/kg of body weight at each meal for most athletes,[2] which equates to 15 g for a 60-kg person, although an intake between 0.4 and 0.55 g/kg per meal is now thought to be optimum for muscle building and strength.[3] In practice, somewhere between 15 and 25 g of protein will cover the needs of most active people. Older athletes may need slightly more than younger athletes, around 0.4 g/kg of body weight due to the reduced anabolic response that occurs as we get older.[4]

IS MORE PROTEIN BETTER?

Eating more protein than you need won't make you stronger or give you bigger muscles. Your body can only use a maximum of 0.25–0.4 g protein per kg of body weight per meal for muscle building. If you consume more, the surplus protein is broken down and used as a fuel source. Contrary to popular belief, excess protein isn't harmful and does not cause kidney damage or bone loss in healthy people.

HOW CAN I GET ENOUGH PROTEIN WITHOUT MEAT?

It's a popular myth that vegetarians can't get enough protein. You can easily obtain all the protein your body needs from many sources other than meat, such as milk, yogurt, cheese, eggs, beans, chickpeas, hummus, lentils, soya milk or yogurt alternative (see p. 44), edamame beans, tofu, tempeh (fermented soya beans), soya mince, whole grains (including wholegrain bread, oats, bulgur (cracked) wheat, brown rice, teff, freekeh, spelt), quinoa, amaranth, Quorn, nuts, nut butters, seeds and tahini (sesame seed paste) and seitan (wheat protein). That's quite a long list of foods! The key is to include a wide variety of these foods and ensure you include at least one source in each meal.

Although many plant sources – with the exception of soya, quinoa, buckwheat, chia and hemp seeds – don't contain all the essential amino acids in as large quantities as animal sources, provided you eat a variety of foods containing protein, any shortfall of amino acids in one food is compensated by the higher amounts found in another. For example, rice with lentils will provide more than enough essential amino acids. The key is to combine more than one plant protein source, ideally within each meal, although this isn't essential. Here's how to do it:

- Pulses with grains (e.g. Puy lentil bolognese with pasta, p. 138)
- Grains with dairy (e.g. Performance porridge, p. 52)
- Soya with vegetables (e.g. Thai green curry with tofu, p. 127)
- Grains or pulses with nuts or seeds (e.g. Falafel with tahini dressing, p. 107)
- Dairy or eggs with vegetables (e.g. Green Spanish tortilla, p. 155)

ARE PROTEIN SUPPLEMENTS NECESSARY FOR VEGETARIANS?

Protein supplements, such as powders, drinks and bars, are more popular than ever – you'll find them in practically every supermarket, shop, leisure centre and petrol station, and everywhere on social media. Despite the attractive claims for them, protein supplements will not automatically make you stronger, and are unnecessary if you already get enough protein from food. There's no evidence that consuming more protein than you need will lead to bigger muscles or greater strength gains. On the other hand, protein supplements may be helpful if you find it difficult to meet your protein quota from food alone. Their main advantage is convenience – they're portable, easy to pop in a gym bag or handbag, and handy to consume on the go. But there is nothing magically muscle building about protein supplements compared to protein from food. Studies have shown that food sources, such as dairy or soya milk, are just as effective for muscle recovery as protein supplements.[5]

CARBOHYDRATE

WHY DO I NEED IT?

Carbohydrate in the form of glucose provides a fuel source for every cell in the body, including your muscles. It's the preferred fuel for the brain, nervous system and heart. Any glucose that's not needed immediately for energy is stored as glycogen in the liver and muscles. However, these stores are very small (around 500 g, or 2000 cals) compared to our fat stores, enough to fuel 90–120 minutes' worth of high-intensity exercise. When glycogen stores are depleted, fatigue develops, and you will need to slow your pace. Exercise feels harder and your endurance will be reduced as you run out of readily available fuel.

WHAT TYPES ARE THERE?

Carbohydrates are traditionally classified as simple (sugars) and complex (starch and fibre) according to the number of sugar units in the molecules. Simple carbohydrates consist of either one sugar (monosaccharide) or two-sugar units (disaccharides) and include glucose, fructose, sucrose (glucose and fructose) and lactose (glucose and galactose).

Complex carbohydrates are much larger molecules, consisting of between 10 and several thousand-sugar units (mostly glucose) joined together. They include starches (such as amylose and amylopectin) and fibres (such as cellulose, pectin and inulin).

In practice, many foods contain a mixture of both simple and complex carbohydrates, making the traditional classification of foods into 'simple' and 'complex' very confusing. For example, cakes contain both complex (flour) and simple (sugar) carbohydrates; bananas contain a mixture of sugars and starches depending on their degree of ripeness.

Nowadays, carbohydrates are more often classified by their nutritional quality or nutrient density. This refers to the presence of other nutrients in the food, such as vitamins, minerals and fibre, and gives you a better idea of the food's overall nutritional value. Examples of nutrient-dense carbohydrate foods include oats, wholemeal bread, brown rice, beans, chickpeas, lentils, fruit and vegetables. Aim to get most of your daily carbohydrate from these foods, while minimising refined carbohydrates. These include sweets, cakes, biscuits, sugar-sweetened drinks, sports drinks, gels, white bread, pasta and rice. While not devoid of nutritional value, these foods generally contain less fibre and fewer vitamins and minerals. You don't have to avoid them completely – simply balance them with nutrient-rich foods.

Some people demonise carbohydrates and any food that contains them. The truth is there is a huge difference in nutritional terms between carbohydrates in whole grains or fruit (both of which come with a package of other nutrients) and those in refined grains or fizzy drinks (which contain fewer nutrients). Categorising foods this way and avoiding whole food groups isn't helpful – we need to remember that we eat foods, not nutrients.

HOW MUCH SHOULD I EAT?

Your carbohydrate needs will vary day to day depending on how active you are, but the table below gives you a rough guide. You'll need to eat more carbohydrate on days when you're more active or before high-intensity workouts, fewer on days where you are less active or before low-intensity workouts. The key is to adjust carbohydrate to your training requirements. In other words: *fuel for the work required.*

HOW MUCH CARBOHYDRATE DO YOU NEED?	
Activity level	**Recommended daily carbohydrate intake**[1]
No training (rest)	3 g/kg body weight
Very light training (low-intensity or skill-based exercise)	3–5 g/kg body weight
Moderate intensity training (approx. 1 h daily)	5–7 g/kg body weight
Moderate–high-intensity training (1–3 h daily)	6–10 g/kg body weight
Very high-intensity training (> 4 h daily)	8–12 g/kg body weight

ARE LOW-CARBOHYDRATE DIETS SUITABLE FOR ATHLETES?

Low-carbohydrate high-fat (LCHF) diets have become popular with a lot of athletes. The idea behind exercising with low-carbohydrate stores (glycogen) is to force the body to burn a higher percentage of energy from fat and less from carbohydrate. This has been shown to enhance endurance training adaptations, such as increasing the number of mitochondria and fat-burning enzymes in the muscles, so they become less reliant on glycogen during competitions. While this may suit low-intensity workouts, like long, slow runs, it won't suit high-intensity workouts, such as fast running, cycling or swimming, weight training or HIIT (high-intensity interval training), nor competitions. Those longer, harder efforts need more carbohydrates.

One of the main problems with following a LCHF diet every day is that it reduces the muscles' ability to burn carbohydrate during high-intensity exercise, resulting in a lower power output. Exercise feels much harder and you'll almost certainly need to reduce your pace. Constantly 'training low' will reduce your training gains and performance too. The most definitive evidence comes from a 2017 Australian study of 21 elite race walkers.[6] Those following a LCHF diet for 12 weeks were slower in a 10k race than those who consumed more carbohydrate.

ARE 'NATURAL' SUGARS BETTER THAN REFINED SUGAR?

So-called natural sugars, such as honey, maple syrup, agave and coconut sugar, are often touted as healthier substitutes for standard sugar, but there is no evidence this is the case. They contain the same calories and have the same effects in the body. Although they contain other nutrients, like potassium and iron, the amounts are so tiny that you would need to eat excessive amounts of these sugars to gain any health benefit from the other nutrients.

SUGAR – IS IT ADDICTIVE, TOXIC AND FATTENING?

Despite the hype about added sugar being toxic, addictive and uniquely fattening, the research tells a different story. Such claims have no scientific basis, yet they have produced a culture of fear and anxiety around sugar. Clinical trials have not shown toxicity at any level that could realistically be consumed.[7] Claims suggesting that sugar is addictive relate to studies carried out on mice, not humans, who were given enormous amounts of sugar. Such research cannot be extrapolated to humans. Sugar is certainly not uniquely fattening. Although it makes our food and drink taste good, which makes it easier to over-consume, it's eating too many calories overall, from any kind of food, that will result in weight gain. A 2016 systematic review of evidence concluded that sugar is only harmful to health when consumed in excess, otherwise there is no evidence that it increases the risk of cardiovascular disease, obesity or type 2 diabetes.[8]

Overly restricting foods under the guise of health can lead to obsessive behaviour, food preoccupation, guilt, anxiety and food worry. Worrying about every gram of sugar in your food can be stressful, which is not healthy. You need to remember that food should be pleasurable; a little sugar (within the recommendations) can make food taste better and our diet more enjoyable.

The World Health Organisation recommends limiting sugar intake to 10 per cent of total calories,[9] while the UK government recommends 5 per cent of total calories, or about 30 g per day if you eat 2000 calories a day.[10] This recommendation refers to 'free sugars', or those which are added to foods and drinks by manufacturers, plus those present in honey, syrups and fruit juice. It does not include sugars found naturally in milk, fruit and vegetables. The reason we are advised to limit our sugar consumption is because sugar causes tooth decay and makes our food hyper-palatable, encouraging us to eat more food than we need. Eating too many calories, not necessarily sugar, over long periods of time may result in weight gain, which in turn can lead to insulin resistance and type 2 diabetes. Whether or not you should cut your sugar intake depends on your overall diet quality, activity and lifestyle. Chances are, if you already eat mostly minimally processed foods, you have little to worry about when it comes to enjoying foods with added sugar.

FIBRE

WHY DO I NEED IT?

Fibre is the term used to describe the complex carbohydrate found in plants that the body cannot digest. Unlike other types of carbohydrate, it provides no calories because it is not absorbed into the body. Fibre helps to keep the gut healthy by encouraging the smooth passage of food through the digestive system as well as feeding the population of healthy microorganisms (microbiota) that live in your large intestine (bowel). A high-fibre diet can help reduce the risk of obesity, type 2 diabetes, heart disease, stroke and constipation. Fibre-rich foods are especially beneficial for weight control as they are more filling, take longer to digest and increase satiety.

WHAT TYPES ARE THERE?

Traditionally, fibre was classified as insoluble and soluble. Most plant foods contain both, but proportions vary. Good sources of insoluble fibre include whole grains, such as wholegrain bread, pasta and rice, and vegetables. These help to speed the passage of food through the gut and prevent constipation and bowel problems. Soluble fibre, found in oats, beans, lentils, nuts, fruit and vegetables, reduces LDL cholesterol levels and helps control blood glucose levels by slowing glucose absorption. However, these terms tell us very little about the effects of different types of fibre in the body. Nowadays, scientists also talk about the viscosity and fermentability of different types of fibre, which influence the diversity of the gut microbiota (see box opposite: 'Gut Health').

HOW MUCH SHOULD I EAT?

The UK's Scientific Advisory Committee on Nutrition recommends 30 g of fibre a day for adults,[10] which is quite a bit more than the average of 19 g per day.

GUT HEALTH

Fibre feeds your gut microbiota. These comprise the trillions of bacteria, viruses and yeasts that inhabit your lower intestines and produce chemicals (such as short-chain fatty acids) that help increase immunity and lower inflammation. The latter is a key factor in the development of heart disease and other diseases like type 2 diabetes. These chemicals influence almost every aspect of health: your weight, immunity, cardiovascular system, mental health and your susceptibility to acne, allergies and cancer. Regular exercise increases the number of 'good' gut microbes but there's also some evidence that our gut microbes affect our exercise performance and recovery. In one 2014 study,[11] athletes who took a probiotic supplement for four weeks were able to exercise longer before reaching fatigue than those who took a placebo.

The best way to increase the diversity of your 'good' gut microbes is to eat a wide range of foods rich in fibre, polyphenols and probiotics. These provide 'food' for them, enabling these microbes to multiply. There are many types of fibre and the more types you eat, the greater the benefit.

- **PLANT-BASED FOODS** Try to get as many different kinds of fruit, vegetables, whole grains, pulses, nuts and seeds in your diet as possible. The American Gut Project suggests we should try to eat at least 30 different types of plant each week.[12] Variety is key because each contains different nutrients that the gut microbes thrive on.

- **BERRIES, NUTS, RED WINE AND DARK CHOCOLATE** contain polyphenols that encourage the growth of 'good' microbes.

- **FERMENTED FOODS CONTAINING PROBIOTICS** These include yogurt, sourdough bread (see p. 61), unpasteurised cheeses, sauerkraut (fermented cabbage), miso (a fermented soya bean paste), tempeh (fermented soya beans), kefir (a fermented milk drink), kombucha (fermented tea) and kimchi (fermented Chinese cabbage), and will have a short-term beneficial effect on your gut microbiota.

- **EATING PREBIOTIC FOODS** will help promote 'good' microbes. These include inulin and fructo-oligosaccharides that are found in onions, garlic, leeks, chickpeas, beans and lentils.

- **AVOID HIGHLY PROCESSED FOODS** They contain ingredients that either suppress 'good' microbes or increase 'bad' microbes.

FAT

WHY DO I NEED IT?

Fat provides fuel for the body. It also forms part of every membrane of every cell in the body, our brain tissue, nerve sheaths, bone marrow and the fat cushion lining the eye socket. Fat helps the body absorb and transport the fat-soluble vitamins A, D, E and K in the bloodstream and is a source of the essential omega-3 and omega-6 polyunsaturated fatty acids that cannot be made in the body. It is also needed for making the hormones oestrogen and testosterone and ensuring normal menstrual function in women.

WHAT TYPES OF FAT ARE THERE?

There are three main types of fats: saturated, unsaturated and trans.

SATURATED FATS

Saturated fats are solid at room temperature and are found mostly in meat, butter, lard, milk, cheese, coconut oil and palm oil, and products made with these fats.

UNSATURATED FATS

These can be divided into two types: monounsaturated and polyunsaturated fats.

Monounsaturated fats are thought to have the greatest health benefits as they can reduce total cholesterol, particularly 'bad' low-density lipoprotein (LDL) cholesterol, without affecting the beneficial high-density lipoprotein (HDL) cholesterol. The richest sources include olive, rapeseed, groundnut and vegetable oils, avocados, olives, nuts and seeds. Diets that are moderate to high in total fat but rich in monounsaturated fats (such as the traditional Mediterranean diet) are associated with a lower risk of heart disease and stroke.

Polyunsaturated fats are found in most vegetable oils and oily fish. Like monounsaturated fats, they reduce LDL cholesterol levels, but they can also lower HDL cholesterol slightly, making them less beneficial than monounsaturated fats for health. It is a good idea to replace some with monounsaturates, if you eat a lot of them.

Two types of polyunsaturated fats, the omega-3 and omega-6 fats, are called essential fats, meaning that you need them in your diet because the body cannot produce them.

Omega-3 fats are necessary for normal brain function, immunity and regulating hormones and normal blood vessel function. They are linked to a lower risk of heart disease and stroke and may also help prevent Alzheimer's disease and treat depression. They also play a role in reducing inflammation, so may help reduce post-exercise soreness, promote recovery and reduce joint stiffness. There are two main types: the short-chain fatty acid alpha linolenic acid (ALA) found in plant sources (flax, hemp, chia and pumpkin seeds and walnuts) and the long-chain fatty acids, eicosapentaenoic acid (EPA) and docosahexaenoic acid (DHA), both found in oily fish. Vegetarians can obtain long chain fatty acids from the conversion of ALA that takes place in the body as well as taking vegetarian algae supplements (see p. 34).

Try to include at least one tablespoon of ALA-rich nuts or seeds in your diet each day (flax, hemp, chia or pumpkin seeds and walnuts) – these foods provide the omega-3 fatty acid, alpha linoleic acid (ALA), which can be converted to EPA and DHA in the body. However, this process isn't very efficient as the body can only convert around 5–10 per cent of the ALA you eat into EPA and 2–5 per cent into DHA. So, unless you include plenty of ALA-rich foods in your diet, it's easy to fall short on EPA and DHA. **Omega-6 fats** are widely found in vegetable oils, such as sunflower, safflower and corn oil.

TRANS FATS

Small amounts occur naturally in meat and dairy products, but most are formed artificially during the commercial process of hydrogenation when vegetable oils are converted into hardened hydrogenated fats. Nowadays, trans fats are found in fewer foods as manufacturers have replaced hydrogenated fats with other fats, but you may find them in takeaway and fast foods, certain hard margarines, pastries, biscuits and cakes. They are harmful to health as they increase blood levels of 'bad' LDL cholesterol while lowering 'good' HDL cholesterol, which increases your risk of heart disease. Trans fats may also encourage fat deposition around your middle and increase the risk of type 2 diabetes.

HOW MUCH SHOULD I EAT?

The UK dietary guidelines recommend a maximum intake of 35 per cent of total daily calories from fat – equivalent to 70 g a day for an average person consuming 2000 cals – with less than 11 per cent (20 g) coming from saturated fat. Most scientists now advocate a Mediterranean-style diet, which contains fat mostly from unsaturated sources such as olive oil, nuts and fish. This way of eating is regarded as one of the healthiest in the world and has been shown to have remarkable benefits, including greater longevity and a lower risk of heart disease, type 2 diabetes, hypertension and certain cancers.

When it comes to reducing your health risk, the type of fat you eat is more important than the amount. A high intake of saturated or trans fats is associated with a high heart disease risk, so you should try to get most of your fat from foods rich in unsaturated fats, such as olive oil, rapeseed oil, avocados, oily fish, nuts, seeds and nut butter.

Breakfast burrito, page 70.

IS SATURATED FAT BAD FOR YOU?

There has been ongoing debate among scientists as to whether saturated fat is good or bad for you, resulting in contradictory headlines in the media. Some people claim that reducing saturated fat doesn't cut heart disease and we can eat as much as we want. This view is not supported by the majority of the evidence, which shows that eating too much saturated fat is linked to increased cardiovascular disease and mortality. The 2019 report by the UK government's Scientific Advisory Committee on Nutrition (SACN) recommends the current UK dietary guidelines remain unchanged, and that we should continue to limit our intake of saturated fat to no more than 10 per cent of our overall calorie intake.[13] This will help reduce the risk of cardiovascular disease, as well as total and LDL-cholesterol. This advice is in line with the 2018 World Health Organisation's and the 2017 American Heart Association's review of the evidence.[14, 15]

The problem with issuing blanket advice on saturated fat is that it isn't just one nutrient: there are several different types of saturated fats, which we now know to have different effects on the body. Some types (such as those found in meat and butter) increase blood cholesterol, while others (such as those found in milk, yogurt and cheese) do not have this effect and are associated with a lower overall heart disease risk. Milk, yogurt and cheese are associated with a reduced risk of heart disease, stroke and type 2 diabetes (see p. 39).

CHAPTER 5

SIX NUTRIENTS YOU MAY BE MISSING ON A VEGETARIAN DIET

Lots of people worry that cutting out meat may leave them short on certain nutrients and increase their risk of nutritional deficiencies. The good news is that it's entirely possible to obtain all the nutrients you need without eating meat. Knowing where to find them, and which foods you should be substituting for meat, is key. Of course, if you removed meat from your diet without substituting other foods, then you would not be getting a balanced diet. For example, pasta with tomato sauce or avocado on toast may sound healthy but, on their own, don't qualify as balanced meals.

There are lots of foods that provide the same nutrients found in meat. The main nutrients that you need to be mindful of when planning a vegetarian diet are protein, iron, zinc and omega-3s (see pp. 18–20 for practical guidance on protein). Vegans also need to consider calcium, vitamin B_{12}, and iodine, as these are harder to obtain without dairy products and eggs.

IRON

Iron is needed for making haemoglobin, the oxygen-carrying protein in red blood cells. Low levels of iron in your diet can result in iron-deficiency anaemia. Early signs include persistent tiredness, pallor, light-headedness and above-normal breathlessness during exercise.

Good plant sources of iron include whole grains, quinoa, nuts, seeds, beans, chickpeas, lentils, leafy green vegetables and dried apricots. For vegetarians, egg yolk is also a useful source. Although iron from plants is harder for your body to absorb than iron found in meat, you can get around this by always consuming foods or drinks rich in vitamin C, such as red peppers,

broccoli, oranges or berries, at the same time. Citric acid found naturally in fruit and vegetables also promotes iron absorption. Fortunately, the body adjusts absorption according to its iron needs, so if your diet contains only small amounts of iron, then a higher percentage of it will be absorbed. Interestingly, studies have shown that iron-deficiency anaemia is no more common in vegetarians than meat-eaters.[1,2,3] Haemoglobin levels are very similar between non-vegetarian and vegetarian female athletes.

VITAMIN B12

Deficiency of vitamin B_{12} is a particular risk for vegans, as it isn't found in plant sources. Lack of B_{12} can result in anaemia and impact adversely on endurance performance. The Vegan Society recommends taking a supplement containing 10 micrograms of B_{12},[4] or including vitamin B_{12}-fortified non-dairy milk alternatives, yeast extract or breakfast cereal in the diet. Vegetarians can get vitamin B_{12} from eggs and dairy products.

OMEGA-3 FATTY ACIDS

Omega-3s are vital for heart health and brain function but can also help reduce inflammation and promote recovery after intense exercise (see p. 30). The main source of the long-chain omega-3s, EPA and DHA, is oily fish, so vegetarians and vegans will need to get this elsewhere. Certain plant foods provide the short-chain omega-3 fatty acid, alpha linoleic acid (ALA), which can be converted to EPA and DHA in the body (albeit inefficiently). You'll find ALA in walnuts, flax, hemp, chia and pumpkin seeds. Try to include at least one tablespoon of these in your diet each day or take a vegetarian omega-3 supplement made from algae oil (see p. 34).

CALCIUM

Obtaining enough calcium can be a little trickier if you don't consume dairy products. The best solution is to substitute a non-dairy milk or yogurt alternative with added calcium. Mainstream brands contain similar amounts to dairy milk. Tofu made with calcium sulphate (check the label), beans, chickpeas, kale, spinach, broccoli, sesame seeds, tahini (sesame seed paste), dried figs and almonds are other good sources. It's worth knowing that calcium in green leafy vegetables is not absorbed as well as calcium from other foods. This is due to the high content of oxalates in vegetables that binds some of the calcium, preventing its absorption. So, ensure you get your calcium from a variety of different foods.

IODINE

Iodine is needed to make thyroid hormones, which help keep cells and the metabolic rate healthy. It's especially important during pregnancy as it is essential for normal foetal brain development and for growth in young children. Having low levels can lead to a lower metabolic rate and weight gain, and in pregnant women is linked to lower IQ and reading scores in their children. There are very few sources of iodine in the diet, so if you don't eat dairy, you should take a multivitamin supplement containing the daily requirement for iodine, 150 micrograms. Although seaweed and kelp contain iodine, levels can be extremely high, which carries a risk of excessive intakes.

ZINC

Zinc is needed for growth and also plays a role in the proper functioning of the immune system, hormone production and fertility. A deficiency may impair your performance. The best plant sources of zinc include whole grains, beans, lentils, nuts, seeds and eggs. However, the phytates found in the bran layer of whole grains can reduce the amount of zinc that can be absorbed from food, so you'll need to consume a variety of different sources to ensure you get enough.

VITAMIN SUPPLEMENTS – YES OR NO?

Vitamins and minerals are essential for our health but there is no evidence that consuming more than you need results in better health or performance. A review of 26 studies concluded that vitamin supplements provide no significant health benefits and a study of 160,000 women found multivitamins did nothing to prevent cancer or heart disease. If you are healthy, you should be able to get all the nutrients you need by eating a varied, balanced diet. Over-supplementation of certain nutrients can lead to unwanted side effects, so only take them if you are deficient. However, Public Health England recommends everyone takes 10 micrograms (mcg) of vitamin D between October and April when sunlight (the best source of vitamin D) is in short supply.[5] The NHS also advise 400 micrograms of folic daily if you're trying to conceive (and up to the 12th week of pregnancy) to reduce the risk of neural tube defects in your baby.[6]

CHAPTER 6

FUELLING YOUR FITNESS

Eating the right foods before exercise will help give you the energy to perform to your full potential. You also need to pay attention to your fluid intake before, during and after exercise to avoid dehydration and early fatigue. After exercise, good nutrition will help the body refuel and recover faster before your next workout.

BEFORE EXERCISE

WHY?

The purpose of fuelling before exercise is to keep hunger at bay and raise blood glucose. This will help delay the onset of fatigue and increase your endurance and performance. How much and what you eat depends on how much time you have between eating and the start of your workout.

WHEN?

Ideally, try to schedule your pre-exercise meal two to four hours before your workout. This will give you enough time to digest the food but not too long an interval to cause this energy to be used up by the time you begin exercising. Eating a meal too close to exercise will almost certainly result in stomach discomfort, as the blood supply diverts from your digestive organs to the muscles. On the other hand, leaving too long a gap means you may feel hungry, light-headed and lacking energy during exercise.

HOW MUCH?

The closer your pre-workout meal is to your workout, the smaller it must be. For example, if you have only one to two hours before a workout, then eat a small meal or snack of 200 to 400 calories. If you can eat four hours before your workout, then have a larger meal of 400 to 800 calories. If you prefer training fasted (such as first thing in the morning), then that's fine provided you're doing low- or moderate-intensity exercise (as you'll be burning relatively more fat and less carbohydrate). However, if you plan to do high-intensity exercise for longer than an hour, then having a high-carbohydrate snack 30–60 minutes beforehand will help increase your endurance (as you'll be burning relatively more carbohydrate and less fat).

WHAT?

Your pre-exercise meal should include foods rich in carbohydrate along with some protein and fat. Avoid excessive amounts of fat, though, as this can slow digestion and result in stomach discomfort. A mixed meal will produce a more gradual and sustained rise in blood sugar than a high-carbohydrate meal. Suitable pre-training meals include porridge with fruit; tofu and vegetable stir-fry with noodles; Puy lentil bolognese (see p. 138) or Turkish-style chickpea pilaf (see p. 141). But if you have less than one to two hours before your workout, opt for an easy-to-digest, high-carbohydrate snack. Suitable options include yogurt with granola, bananas, peanut butter on toast, Fruit and nut energy bars (see p. 179) or a smoothie.

WILL FASTED TRAINING HELP?

The theory behind fasted training is to encourage the muscles to burn more fat for fuel and less carbohydrate (see p. 17). This is true up to a point but it doesn't necessarily mean you'll lose weight or that you'll end up losing weight quicker. To lose weight, you need to be in a calorie deficit – that is, you must consume fewer calories than your body needs over the course of several days, not a single workout. Sometimes, fasted training may leave you so hungry that you overeat after the session. Additionally, it may cause you to fatigue sooner or to drop your pace (intensity), resulting in a lower overall calorie expenditure.

DURING EXERCISE

WHY?

If you're exercising longer than 60–90 minutes, your performance may be limited by the depletion of glycogen in the liver and muscles. The purpose of fuelling during exercise is to maintain blood glucose levels within an optimal range and supply additional fuel to your muscles. This reduces the rate at which the muscles burn glycogen and thus helps delay fatigue. Result? Better performance and endurance.

WHEN?

Start fuelling before your glycogen stores are depleted and you feel fatigued. There are no hard and fast rules, but most athletes benefit from refuelling after approximately 45–60 minutes, depending on the exercise intensity and their hunger. The key is to consume carbohydrate little and often; don't over-eat, but don't forget to eat either. Plan to refuel at frequent regular intervals, say every 15–30 minutes, although you may be limited by practical constraints.

HOW MUCH?

The optimal amount of carbohydrate is 30–60 g carbohydrate per hour. The exact amount you need depends on how hard you're exercising and your workout goals. If you're exercising at a high intensity, you'll be burning more carbohydrate and therefore need to consume more. When exercising at a low intensity, you won't need as much carbohydrate as your body is able to burn more fat for fuel. It's a matter of fuelling for the work required. For high-intensity workouts or races longer than two to three hours, further benefits may be gained by consuming 90 g carbohydrate per hour in the form of energy drinks containing a mixture of glucose (or maltodextrin) and fructose.

Rice cakes, page 182.

WHAT?

Carbohydrate can help maintain blood glucose concentration and delay fatigue by providing a source of quick energy to the muscles. You can get 30 g carbohydrate from the following:

- 500 ml sports drink (6 per cent carbohydrate)
- Two Medjool dates
- 40 g dried fruit
- One oat bar or two small fruit and nut bars
- One energy bar
- Two small bananas
- Four energy chews
- Six jelly babies
- One energy gel

For long workouts or races, it's a good idea to take savoury as well as sweet options to avoid flavour fatigue and reduce the risk of tooth damage, e.g. peanut butter or cheese sandwiches, rice cakes (see p. 182), cheese and nuts.

AFTER EXERCISE

WHY?

The purpose of refuelling after exercise is to promote recovery. Consuming carbohydrate will replenish glycogen stores in your muscles and liver, while consuming protein repairs damaged muscle fibres and supports the formation of new muscle tissue.

WHEN?

If you have longer than eight hours between workouts then there's no urgency to consume food straight after training. Protein is not essential in the immediate post-exercise period but plays an important role in long-term recovery and muscle building. Be guided by your hunger and eat your post-exercise snack or meal when you feel hungry for it. Provided you consume enough calories, carbohydrate and protein over a 24-hour period, your muscles will recover before your next workout. However, if you plan to train or compete twice a day, then take advantage of the two-hour 'recovery window', when the glycogen recovery rate is faster than normal.

HOW MUCH?

For rapid recovery after endurance training, aim to consume 1.0–1.2 g of carbohydrate per kg body weight (60–72 g for a 60 kg runner) each hour for four hours after exercise to maximise glycogen synthesis. This way you will ensure your glycogen stores are restored as fully as possible before your next workout.

Caffeine also promotes glycogen storage during the immediate post-exercise period so having a cup of coffee, though not essential, may be a good idea. However, if you have 24 hours or longer to recover before your next workout, then consuming carbohydrate immediately after exercise is less crucial. You should be able to restore glycogen by including carbohydrate in your normal meals. Your post-workout meal or snack should, ideally, include 0.25–0.4 g protein per kilogram of body weight, depending on the type and intensity of exercise you've done. You'll need more following a strength or whole-body workout than following an endurance workout, but generally, an intake between 20–40 g will be suitable for most workouts. As muscle recovery continues for several hours after a workout, try to include a similar amount of protein in each meal.

WHAT?

The two most important macronutrients that you need to consider after exercise are carbohydrate and protein. Recovery meals and snacks should contain carbohydrate to refuel the body's glycogen stores, protein to repair damaged muscle and plenty of fluids and electrolytes to replace sweat losses. Ideally, you want a 'high quality' or complete protein – one that contains all 8 essential amino acids – and one that's rich in the amino acid leucine. Cow's milk and soya milk are near-perfect recovery drinks as they contain fluid along with protein and carbohydrate (as well as other nutrients) to promote rehydration, glycogen replenishment and muscle building. They have been shown to be more effective than sports drinks for promoting rehydration. Other recovery options include smoothies made with milk, yogurt, fruit and vegetables (see Banana and oat breakfast smoothie, p. 73), yogurt (see Yogurt bowl, p. 55), Fruit and nut energy bars (see p. 179), flapjacks and bananas with nuts. Suitable recovery meals include pitta bread with hummus, Bean and sweet potato tortilla (see p. 156), or Lentil, chickpea and spinach dahl (see p. 128).

DO LEUCINE SUPPLEMENTS PROMOTE MUSCLE RECOVERY?

Leucine is beneficial for muscle building – it stimulates protein synthesis and reduces protein breakdown – but it isn't necessary to take supplements. It is found widely in foods such as eggs, milk, yogurt, meat and fish as well as whey protein drinks. So if you're already eating these foods then there's no benefit in taking extra leucine. The optimal dose for muscle building is about 2–3 g, which can be obtained from 500 ml milk (cows or soya) or 250 g strained Greek yogurt, 3 eggs or 170 g tofu.

HYDRATION

WHY?

Starting your workout, match or race properly hydrated as well as drinking to thirst while you exercise will prevent you from getting dehydrated. Dehydration can negatively affect your concentration, stamina, speed and performance, and cause early fatigue, headache, nausea and dizziness. You can get a good idea of your hydration status by checking the colour of your urine: it should be pale straw-coloured, not deep yellow, and should not have a strong odour. A darker colour indicates that you are under-hydrated and need to drink more.

WHEN?

If you are dehydrated, make up for any previously incurred fluid deficits by consuming 5–10 ml/kg body weight, equivalent to 350 to 500 ml, about four hours before training, then continue to drink little and often during exercise, according to thirst.

HOW MUCH?

Previously, athletes were advised to drink ahead of thirst or as much as possible. We now know that this practice increases the risk of over-drinking and developing hyponatraemia (see above, 'Is it possible to drink too much?') Nowadays, the official advice is to drink when you are thirsty. For most endurance workouts and climates, drinking 400–800 ml per hour will prevent dehydration as well as over-hydration. The maximum you can absorb is 800 ml – any more will just slosh around your stomach and won't provide any immediate benefit. Aim to consume fluids at a rate that keeps pace with your sweat rate; you'll sweat more in hot and humid conditions and when working out harder. Drink at regular intervals but do not drink excessively.

    Replacing lost fluid after exercise takes time and is best achieved by drinking little and often. Drinking a large volume in one go stimulates urine formation, so much of the fluid is lost rather than retained. The exact amount you need to drink depends on how dehydrated you are after your workout. Weigh yourself before and after training. For optimal rehydration, aim to replace each 1 kg of your weight (sweat) loss with 1.2–1.5 l fluid.

IS IT POSSIBLE TO DRINK TOO MUCH?

Drinking excessive water dilutes the concentration of sodium in the blood and can result in a condition called hyponatraemia (low blood sodium concentration). Symptoms include stomach discomfort, dizziness, bloating, water retention and, in extreme cases, can prove fatal. The condition is rare but those competing in long endurance events, such as marathons, are at risk. It's most frequently seen in very slow runners who over-estimate their water deficit and over-drink, as well as elite athletes who experience excessive sodium losses through sweating in hot, humid conditions. For this reason, athletes are advised to drink only to the point at which they are maintaining, not gaining, weight. Athletes who sweat heavily (or produce very salty sweat) are advised to consume additional sodium, either in the form of an electrolyte drink or salty foods (such as pretzels) with water.

WHAT?

For workouts lasting less than an hour, water is the best choice. If you're exercising longer than an hour, consuming extra carbohydrate in the form of a sports drink or diluted squash or cordial will not only hydrate the body but also help maintain blood glucose levels. Alternatively, you may prefer consuming water plus food (e.g. bananas, raisins or gels). Drinks containing electrolytes (see 'What are electrolytes?', below) are recommended only when sweat losses are high as they help the body absorb and retain fluid more effectively than water.

WHAT ARE ELECTROLYTES?

Electrolytes are mineral salts that control the fluid balance of the body and play a key role in muscle contraction and energy production. They include sodium, chloride, potassium and magnesium. An excessive loss of sodium through sweat during exercise can negatively impact performance. Generally, the more profusely you sweat, the more sodium you lose, although some people – and men in particular – simply produce more salty sweat than others.

WHAT IS CARBOHYDRATE LOADING?

Many athletes increase their intake of carbs before a big match or race to improve their performance. This fuelling process is known as carbohydrate loading and the aim is to maximise your carbohydrate (glycogen) stores. High-intensity exercise is fuelled mainly by carbohydrate and we know that the body can store only enough glycogen for around 90–120 minutes of exercise. After this time, your glycogen stores become depleted, resulting in the famous feeling of 'hitting the wall' in running or 'bonking' in cycling. So, if you'll be competing longer than 90 minutes, it makes sense to begin your event with full glycogen stores.

This is achieved by tapering training during the pre-competition week and increasing your carbohydrate intake for the final two or three days to 7–10 g/kg bodyweight (that's 490–700 g/day for a 70-kg person). Don't increase calories, though – just tip the balance of calories so you eat more carbohydrate and less fat. Carbohydrate loading doesn't mean eating as much as you can! Eating little and often can be an easier strategy than consuming big meals the day before the race. Focus on carbohydrate-rich foods such as pasta, potatoes, sweet potatoes, rice, noodles, bananas, bread and porridge (see also p. 28 for advice on what to eat prior to an event).

Puy lentil bolognese, page 138.

COMPETITION PREPARATION

THE DAY BEFORE

Your goals are to top up your glycogen stores, stay well hydrated and avoid any pitfalls that may jeopardise your performance.

- Stick to familiar foods and don't experiment with anything new.
- Include a portion of carbohydrate with each meal to maximise glycogen storage.
- Eat plain and simple meals; choose only foods that you know agree with you and eat normal-sized portions.
- Beware of the gas! Steer clear of any foods that may upset your gut. Common culprits include pulses (beans, lentils and chickpeas), brassica vegetables (cauliflower, sprouts and broccoli), spicy dishes and high-fibre cereals.
- Avoid feasting: it's not a good idea to overload the night before a competition, as this can play havoc with your digestive system and keep you awake at night.
- Drink plenty: keep a water bottle handy so you remember to drink regularly throughout the day – your urine should be pale straw coloured (see also p. 31).
- Avoid alcohol: alcohol is a diuretic, so it's better to avoid it completely. Even a small amount can leave you feeling below par the next day.

RACE DAY

Your muscle glycogen stores should be fully stocked and you should feel ready to go. All that remains to be done before the race is to top up your liver glycogen stores at breakfast (these are normally depleted overnight) and replace fluids lost overnight.

- Eat two to four hours before competing. A carbohydrate-rich pre-event meal means you will start the competition fully fuelled. Stick with what you're used to: porridge, overnight oats or granola are suitable options.
- If you can't eat because of nerves, have a milkshake, smoothie or yogurt. This will be digested faster than solid food.
- Drink – but not too much! Two to three hours before the event, drink 350–500 ml fluid. You can then sip small amounts, just enough to quench your thirst, closer to the start time.

CHAPTER 7

SPORTS SUPPLEMENTS

There is a huge array of sports supplements on the market promising greater muscle gains, fat loss and performance. However, the vast majority of them have little scientific evidence to back their claims and are, at best, unnecessary or, at worst, harmful or illegal. I advocate a food first approach and believe that a well-planned healthy diet should be the foundation of any training programme. However, if you do decide to take supplements, then the International Olympic Committee consider the following supplements to have sufficient scientific backing to have a performance or health benefit without causing you harm (see 'Anti-doping', p. 35).[1]

VITAMIN D

Low levels can result in impaired muscle function, weak bones and depressed immunity. Your GP should be able to test your vitamin D level; if it's less than 50nmol/l, then you will benefit from supplements (100 micrograms/day is the upper limit). However, if testing is not available to you, Public Health England recommends taking a daily 10 microgram supplement during autumn and winter.[2]

WHEY PROTEIN

Whey protein contains a high concentration of essential amino acids, which support muscle recovery, including the amino acid leucine, an important trigger for stimulating muscle building after exercise. However, it is not essential for muscle building as vegetarians should be able to get enough protein from food (see pp. 18–20). Choose protein supplements only if you aren't getting enough protein from your diet or as a convenient post-workout option to food (see p. 30). Whey and vegan protein supplements contain similar amounts of protein and are both good sources of essential amino acids. If you decide to use a vegan protein supplement, opt for one containing a mixture of protein sources, such as soya, peas, brown rice, quinoa and hemp, rather than a single source, as they contain a higher concentration of essential amino acids.

CAFFEINE

Low doses (1–3 mg/kg body weight) taken with food or higher doses (3–6 mg/kg body weight) of caffeine without food improve alertness, concentration and reaction time, enhance performance in both high- and low-intensity exercise and reduce the perception of effort during endurance exercise. Levels peak approximately 60 minutes after consumption, so caffeine may be taken before or during exercise, and the effects last several hours. Individual responses vary (due to our genes) and not everyone performs better with caffeine. Potential side effects include sleeplessness, trembling, increased heart rate and raised blood pressure.

NITRATE AND BEETROOT JUICE

Beetroot juice (a rich source of nitrate) can improve endurance performance and reduce the oxygen cost of submaximal exercise lasting 12–40 minutes. It also enhances repeated sprint performance and increases levels of nitric oxide in the body, which helps to dilate blood vessels, increase blood flow and allows oxygen in the blood to reach the muscles faster. The ideal dose is 300–600 mg nitrate, equivalent to one or two x 70-ml beetroot 'shots', taken two to three hours before exercise. Alternatively, you may prefer to consume nitrate-rich foods, such rocket, spinach and lettuce, or 'beetroot load' for three to seven days before a big race.

BETA-ALANINE

Beta-alanine is an amino acid that may enhance sprint performance and benefit efforts of 30-second–10-minute duration or activities involving repeated sprints, such as football. It increases carnosine (a protein) concentration in the muscle, which in turn increases buffering capacity and helps offset the build-up of lactic acid during high-intensity exercise. The optimal dose is 0.065 g/kg body weight/day, or about 3 g/day, but is best utilised when taken in several smaller doses (e.g. four x 0.8 g/day) over a 10- to 12-week loading period, followed by a maintenance dose of 1.2 g/day. It may cause paraesthesia (skin tingling), which is harmless and transient, and can be avoided by using smaller doses.

CREATINE

Creatine supplements may help increase strength, power and muscle mass. By increasing the muscles' content of phosphocreatine, an energy-rich compound made from creatine and phosphorus that fuels muscles during high-intensity exercise, they can help you sustain maximal exercise for longer and recover faster between sets. Vegetarians may experience greater benefits from creatine supplements than non-vegetarians because they obtain none from their diet; creatine is found only in meat and fish. There are several forms of creatine, but creatine monohydrate is the most effective and well-researched form. It can be taken as a five-day loading dose (four x 5 g per day) or 2–3 g per day for four weeks, followed by a maintenance dose of 2 g/day.

IRON

If you have been diagnosed with iron deficiency, then you'll benefit from iron supplements. Symptoms include persistent tiredness, fatigue, above-normal breathlessness during exercise and loss of endurance and power. Your doctor can carry out a simple blood test (measuring ferritin, haemoglobin, iron and haematocrit) and will prescribe supplements if you need them. However, if you're not deficient, you should not take supplements above the Recommended Dietary Allowance as high doses cause side effects such as constipation.

OMEGA-3S

Consider taking omega-3 supplements if you don't get food sources of omega-3s regularly (e.g. walnuts, pumpkin, chia, hemp and flax seeds). These foods contain the omega-3 fatty acid, ALA, which the body converts to EPA and DHA (see p. 24). Supplements made from algae oil contain high levels of EPA and DHA and are more potent options than those made from flaxseed oil. A US study showed that people who took omega-3 supplements for seven days had less muscle soreness and stiffness after high-intensity exercise compared with those taking a placebo.[3]

ISOTONIC SPORTS DRINKS

The sugars in these drinks provide fuel, which may be useful for maintaining blood sugar levels during high-intensity exercise longer than 60 minutes (see p. 17). They have a similar concentration to body fluids (hence the term 'isotonic'), which means they can be absorbed relatively rapidly. They also contain electrolytes such as sodium, which help stimulate thirst and promote water retention, and may be beneficial when sweat losses are high, such as during and after prolonged high-intensity exercise or during hot, humid conditions (see also p. 17). However, consuming sports drinks will provide no performance advantage if you're exercising at a low or moderate intensity for less than 60 minutes.

ENERGY BARS

Energy bars comprise mainly sugar and maltodextrin (carbohydrate made from corn/corn starch). Like sports drinks, they may be useful for maintaining blood sugar levels during high-intensity exercise longer than 60 minutes. The main benefit of packaged products is their convenience; they come in wrapped portions that fit neatly into jersey pockets, are easy to eat while exercising and deliver a known number of calories and carbohydrate. However, there is no evidence they boost performance more than conventional foods, such as bananas, dried fruit and Fruit and nut energy bars (see p. 179).

ENERGY GELS AND CHEWS

Like bars, the main advantage of gels and chews is convenience as they are easy to carry and consume while exercising. They may be useful during high-intensity activities longer than 60 minutes, when rapid carbohydrate delivery is required. You might need to experiment with different brands and flavours to find which ones you can tolerate. Alternative options include jelly babies, jelly beans and honey.

ELECTROLYTE SUPPLEMENTS

Excessive losses of sodium during exercise can result in hyponatraemia (low blood sodium concentration), a potentially dangerous condition (see 'Is it possible it drink too much?', p. 31). Electrolyte replacement in the form of drinks or tablets is not necessary when your sweat losses are relatively small but could be useful when sweat losses are high and prolonged, e.g. during marathons or endurance events longer than two hours, or when exercising in hot humid conditions. They promote rapid water uptake by the body and aid fluid retention so may help avoid hyponatraemia as well as promote rapid rehydration after exercise. However, you can also get electrolytes from food (e.g. bread, cheese and salted nuts) and drinks (e.g. milk).

ANTI-DOPING

There is not a 100 per cent guarantee that any supplement or product is free from banned substances. If you are subject to anti-doping testing and decide to take a supplement, make sure it comes from a reputable company that provides a certificate to prove it has been batch tested for banned contaminants by a recognised sports anti-doping lab. Look for the Informed-Sport logo on the label and check the batch number on the Informed-Sport website.

Under anti-doping rules, an athlete is totally responsible for any banned substance found in their body, regardless of how it got there. Currently, there is no systematic regulation of supplements (unlike prescription medicines), which means there's no official check on their quality or safety. Supplements may be contaminated or not contain what's on the label. A 2013 survey of 114 products in 12 European countries found that one in 10 contained illegal steroids or stimulants.[4] If you are in doubt as to whether to take supplements or not, seek the advice of a UK Anti-Doping (UKAD) Accredited Advisor.

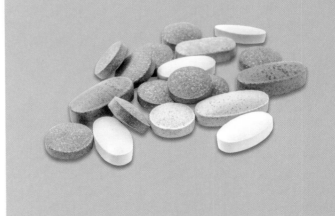

CHAPTER 8

NUTRITION MYTHS

In my practice, I see an increasing number of people who have adopted unnecessarily restrictive eating habits, cutting out certain foods and even food groups in their quest for better health or to optimise their sports performance. This is invariably the result of misguided advice they have read or received from people who are not qualified in nutrition. As a result, many have become confused about nutrition, out of touch with their body's natural hunger cues, and feel guilty about eating certain foods they deem to be 'bad', all of which is damaging their mental and physical health.

Despite the huge amount of information available on the internet, people are more confused about nutrition than ever. The problem is that much of the information we see and hear is contradictory and conflicting, making it hard to tell what is credible. Should you cut carbs? Is soya good or bad? Are gluten-free foods healthier? As the internet is unregulated, it means that anyone can write, blog or post about nutrition. Social media is a particularly thriving breeding place for these people who communicate poor quality and potentially dangerous information. It has become a place where pseudoscience flourishes and fearmongering reigns.

There's no simple solution but you should always check the credentials of the person offering advice, and whether they are a member of a professional organisation such as the Association for Nutrition (AfN) or the British Dietetic Association (BDA). Look out for initials RNutr or RD after their name. To clear up some of the confusion about healthy eating and help you navigate your way around the confusing world of nutrition, this chapter looks at the science behind some of the most popular nutrition myths and separates fact from fiction.

CLEAN EATING

There's no clear definition of clean eating but it loosely means eating natural, unprocessed foods and avoiding anything processed, although there's a big grey when it comes to categorising foods like bread and cheese. The main problem with this way of eating is that it imposes a set of arbitrary and unnecessarily strict eating rules, which, for some people, can be a slippery slope to rigid and obsessive behaviour around food. Taken to the extreme, clean eating can lead to orthorexia, an eating disorder in which sufferers become fixated on eating healthily and experience anxiety around certain foods. It differs from anorexia nervosa in that the goal isn't necessarily thinness but a desire to be pure, clean and healthy. This can become psychologically and socially inhibiting.

Studies have shown that having a more flexible approach to eating is more likely to result in successful weight control in the long run than sticking to rigid rules. Another major problem is with the language used and the casting of moral judgement over food. The term 'clean eating' implies that some foods are dirty and those who eat them less worthy, which is unhelpful. All foods can contribute to a balanced diet, if eaten in moderation. No food should be off-limits – even cakes, biscuits and crisps are perfectly fine every once in a while. Aim to eat a wide variety of foods in appropriate amounts and, above all, don't obsess over or feel guilty around food.

FAT

For so long it has been ingrained in us to cut down on fat. Research has now shown that, while high in calories (providing 9 cals per g, compared with 4 cals for protein and carbohydrate), not all fats are the enemy. It is important to remember that there are good and bad fats. Some are essential to our health and completely avoiding them is not a good idea (see p. 24). The unsaturated fats, which include monounsaturated and polyunsaturated fats, are vital for our body's physical and mental health. Researchers advise eating more of these types and less saturated fats. Monounsaturated fats, found in avocados, olive oil, nuts and seeds, help reduce the amount of LDL (bad) cholesterol and our overall risk of heart disease, high blood pressure and stroke. Focus on omega-3-rich foods – oily fish, walnuts and flax, chia, hemp and pumpkin seeds. These fats support brain performance and memory, and also influence behaviour and mood.

Fat is not inherently more fattening than other macronutrients. What makes people fat is being in caloric surplus, meaning you're eating more calories than you need, not any particular nutrient or food. What's more, cutting out fat can leave you hungry because fat is satiating, which means it gives the body the feeling of being full.

LOW-CARBOHYDRATE HIGH-FAT DIETS (LCHF)

Sometimes people find that cutting back on carbohydrate results in weight loss, not because there's anything magical about LCHF diets but because they have created a calorie deficit (consuming fewer calories than the body needs). Long-term studies show that LCHF diets produce no greater weight loss than other diets. Furthermore, those who follow LCHF diets often have low intakes of fibre, which can have a negative effect on their gut health (see p. 23). An analysis of 32 studies that compared diets of equal calorie content but differing in carbohydrate and fat content found that both regimes produced very similar body fat losses, with lower-fat diets having the slight edge. In other words, people lost weight when they cut down

on calories, whether they came from carbohydrate or fat. The key to successful long-term weight loss is to follow a diet that is sustainable for you, one which comprises foods you enjoy and mostly minimally processed foods.

GLUTEN

A gluten-free diet is often perceived as healthier but, for those who aren't coeliac, there is no scientific evidence to support this. Around 1 in 100 people have coeliac disease[1] – an autoimmune disease where gluten causes damage to the intestine's lining – and for these people a gluten-free diet is essential. The main problem with eliminating gluten if you don't have to is that you may miss out on important nutrients found in whole grains. What's more, there's no performance advantage of cutting gluten. In one study, non-coeliac cyclists who cut gluten for seven days fared no better in a time trial than those who consumed gluten. However, some people suffer from non-coeliac gluten sensitivity, experiencing symptoms such as bloating and wind. In these cases, a diet low in wind-causing carbohydrates, called FODMAPS (which stands for fermentable oligosaccharides, disaccharides, monosaccharides and polyols) can lead to an improvement of symptoms. It has also been shown to be helpful in reducing symptoms of irritable bowel syndrome (IBS). However, it is a very restrictive diet designed only for short-term use, so should only be followed under the guidance of a registered dietitian or nutritionist.

TIME-RESTRICTED EATING

Time-restricted eating (TRE) has recently become popular as a way of improving health as well as weight control. It is a type of intermittent fasting, that involves restricting your food intake to a fixed eating window, (e.g. between 8 a.m. and 6 p.m.) each day and then fasting for the remaining hours. The idea is that aligning our eating to our body clock will help our bodies work more efficiently, resulting in improved health and potentially help you lose some fat. People have reported improved better energy levels, better sleep and weight loss.

While it is not a weight-loss diet, studies have shown that restricting the time period in which you eat automatically makes you eat less. A 2018 study found that people who delayed their usual breakfast time by 90 minutes, and brought their usual dinner time forward by 90 minutes for 10 weeks lost more body fat than those who ate to whatever schedule they liked.[2] TRE is more aligned to our body clock, so may have other health benefits, such as a lower risk of type 2 diabetes and cardiovascular disease. If it suits your lifestyle and helps you eat less in the long term, then it may be a good option but it is not a miracle diet. Remember, you need to be in a calorie deficit, i.e. consume fewer calories than your body needs, if you want to lose weight. It is not suitable for pregnant women or anyone with a history of eating disorders.

SOYA

Claims that soya products cause breast cancer and other cancers are unfounded. They stem from soya's high content of phytoestrogens or plant oestrogens, which have a similar structure to the body's own oestrogen. However, they behave differently in the body so have much weaker effects. There is no evidence they promote cancer. Reassuringly, a number of large studies have concluded that diets high in soya are, in fact, *protective* against breast cancer and also may prevent breast cancer recurrence and increase survival rate.[3] To a limited extent, phytoestrogens may help relieve hot flushes during the menopause but are not a substitute for hormone replacement therapy (HRT). They may also help cut the risk of heart disease and lower blood cholesterol. Apart from tofu and soya milk and yogurt alternatives, phytoestrogens are also found in fruit, vegetables, grains, beans and lentils.

SMOOTHIES

On the plus side, smoothies can be a convenient way to eat more fruit, vegetables, milk, seeds and nuts. Instead of cutting and chopping, you just put everything in a blender. It's also a convenient way to add ingredients you wouldn't normally eat, like spinach or flax seeds, to your diet. In the UK it is recommended we eat a minimum of 400 g (14 oz), or five portions, of fruit and vegetables a day. A high fruit and vegetable consumption is linked to a lower risk of heart disease, cancer,

Roasted vegetables with tofu and walnuts, page 92.

stroke and type 2 diabetes. A study in 2017 suggested that eating up to 800 g (28 oz), or 10 portions a day, may have greater health benefits.[4] But there's nothing to suggest that smoothies offer greater health benefits than eating the same food in its whole form. We know that bullet blenders break food down into smaller particles compared to chewing, but no studies have shown the body actually absorbs more nutrients from smoothies. What's more, smoothies made from fruit have a high concentration of 'free' sugars, so it is easy to exceed your daily sugar requirement (see p. 22).

There is research to show that if you consume the same food as a drink instead of its whole-food form, then you may eat more.[5] That's because liquid calories don't satisfy the appetite as well as whole food. This is advantageous for those who struggle to eat enough or want to gain weight, but if you want to lose weight or avoid gaining weight, go easy on quantities and opt for recipes that contain more vegetables than fruit to increase the satiating fibre content.

DAIRY

Contrary to popular belief, milk, cheese and yogurt are associated with a reduced risk of heart disease, stroke and type 2 diabetes and some types of cancer. Although they contain saturated fat, they do not raise total and LDL-blood cholesterol levels. This is thought to be due – at least in part – to their high calcium content, which binds some of the saturated fat, stopping it from being absorbed. In other words, the potential harm of consuming saturated fat is effectively cancelled out when they are consumed as part of complex food matrices such as those in dairy products. What's more, there's no difference between full-fat or reduced-fat versions in terms of blood cholesterol or heart disease risk, according to a 2016 review of studies.[6]

ORGANIC FOODS

The idea that organic foods are healthier is certainly compelling. However, there is little evidence to support this, with some studies finding higher levels of certain nutrients in certain produce, and others finding no difference. A review of 237 studies found that while organic produce contained fewer pesticide residues than conventional, on balance, there are no clear nutritional advantages to be gained from choosing organic produce.[7]

What about health benefits? Interestingly, despite the fearmongering headlines that you may see, there is no evidence that eating organic food reduces your risk of cancer. A 2018 study at the University of Paris suggested that people who eat organic foods are 25 per cent less likely to get cancer.[8] But this figure is very misleading as it relates to relative risk (the risk of those consuming the most organic food compared with those consuming the least) not absolute risk (the risk of high organic consumers compared with the general population). In fact, the absolute risk in this study was miniscule, just 0.6 per cent. In other words, this study did not prove that pesticide residues cause cancer! It was an observational study based on a dietary questionnaire that asked people what they ate. Researchers did not measure people's pesticide residue intake. Association does not prove causation! People who eat organic food tend to be wealthier and lead healthier lifestyles so this can skew survey results. Furthermore, a bigger study in 2014 showed no decrease in cancer risk associated with eating organic food.[9]

It is worth knowing that pesticide residue levels in non-organic produce are regulated by strict laws in the UK. If you are worried about pesticide residues, then a thorough rinse under running tap water will dramatically reduce levels, as will peeling your fruit and veg.

What we do know is that organic farming has huge environmental benefits, helping reduce pollution and combating climate change through the use of sustainable systems such as crop rotation and animal and plant manures. It also creates more biodiversity and wildlife, and animals are kept in more natural, free-living conditions. However, organic foods are invariably more expensive than non-organic – a reflection of the higher costs of production – so, whether you decide to buy organic or not is a personal choice.

PART 2
RECIPES

CHAPTER 9

BEFORE YOU BEGIN COOKING

The recipes in this section will help you put all the information from the first part of this book into practice. It features more than 100 meals and snacks that you can make every day of the week. They are simple, delicious, nutritious and perfect for busy, active people like you and me. Crucially, they can be prepared in 30 minutes or less – the same time it takes to order and pick up a takeaway or heat up a ready meal in the oven. As no cookbook would be complete without a delicious (but healthy) cheesecake or two, I've squeezed in a few extra recipes that take a little longer to prepare (they're worth it!), denoted by the clock symbol.

My aim with these recipes is to make cooking a pleasure for you, not a chore. The key is to be organised and assemble all the ingredients and equipment that you'll need for the recipe before you start. I know it sounds obvious, but it's a simple step that most people (including me!) often skip in their haste to get cooking. The result is you'll invariably waste time going back and forth to your cupboards or discover halfway through cooking that you don't have a crucial ingredient!

So, before you cook any of these dishes, read through the recipe to work out what equipment you'll need and set everything out so that it's at hand. I find it really helpful to keep utensils such as wooden spoons and spatulas in a pot by the stove so they're easy to grab when cooking. You don't need fancy gadgets, but it is worth investing in a decent set of sharp knives (or at least a chopping and a paring knife), an easy-to-clean, durable chopping board, a heavy-based cooking pan or lidded wok and a hand blender (for soups). Using clear Kilner jars to keep store-cupboard ingredients like rice, lentils, herbs and spices makes it easy to find what you need straight away, and you don't have to worry about resealing packets afterwards. Clear a work space before you start cooking, place a large bowl or plate next to your chopping board for all the peelings, and clear up as you go. These tips sound simple but they'll save you lots of time and make cooking easier and more enjoyable.

NOTES

○ All the recipes are vegetarian, but always check all ingredients (e.g. cheese and condiments) are suitable for vegetarians.

○ The vast majority of hard cheeses are vegetarian but a few varieties, such as Parmesan, aren't, so you'll need to check the label that it's suitable for vegetarians.

○ All eggs in the recipes are medium unless otherwise stated.

VG This indicates the recipe is vegan or can easily be adapted to make it vegan by substituting non-dairy alternatives for milk, yogurt, cheese and butter or spreads, or egg substitutes (I have indicated how to do this at the end of each recipe).

 This is a bonus recipe, which takes longer than 30 minutes to prepare and cook.

I've divided the recipes in this book into breakfasts, salads, burgers and falafels, soups, curries and stews, weekend dinners, desserts, and sweet and savoury snacks. I've also included 'master' recipes for popular dishes, such as porridge, energy bars, hummus and granola, with a number of different variations so you can adapt them according to your own taste. I also provide advice on how to adapt many of the recipes to make them vegan. Most of the main meal recipes serve four, but use the quantities as a guide. Simply adjust them if you want bigger or smaller portions or if you are cooking for a different number of people. Save time later by making a larger quantity than you need (batch cooking!), then freeze or keep portions in the fridge.

Health and nutrition are at the core of every recipe. I've provided the nutritional rationale behind each one along with a breakdown of the calories, protein, fat, saturated fat, carbohydrate, sugar and fibre. This is not to encourage you to count calories or track macronutrients, as I don't think this is necessary, but to help you become familiar with the nutritional content of everyday meals. Knowing how many calories or how much protein is in a recipe allows you to plan your meals and ensure you are adequately fuelling for your day.

ALTERNATIVE MILKS

If you can't tolerate or prefer not to have dairy milk, there are now plenty of non-dairy alternatives out there. These include drinks made from a range of ingredients, including soya, almond, coconut, hemp, oat, cashew, flax, hazelnut and rice, all with different flavours and uses.

Nutritionally speaking, milk alternatives (which, according to European Food Regulations, cannot be called 'milk') cannot compete with dairy milk, which is naturally high in protein, calcium and riboflavin. Most are made with very small amounts of nuts, cereal or seeds, typically less than 2 g per 100 ml, which means that the overall nutritional value of the drink is minimal. What you're getting is mainly water! However, they can be useful in a vegan diet and used in much the same way as dairy milk.

When choosing milk alternatives, opt for brands with added calcium and vitamins – they contain amounts similar to those found in dairy milk – and choose unsweetened versions where possible. Most pasteurised brands are fortified but organic brands in the UK won't be.

Milk alternatives are typically more expensive than dairy milk, so if you use them regularly, it's worth having a go at making your own (see my recipe for almond milk on p. 45).

TOP FIVE MILK ALTERNATIVES

SOYA

Made from pressed ground soya beans, this is easily the best non-dairy option for protein, which is similar to the protein content of milk. One 250 ml (9 fl oz) glass provides 8 g of soya protein, a third of the 25 g experts say reduces cholesterol. It's a good all-rounder for drinks, cooking and baking.

ALMOND

This contains only very small quantities of almonds (most brands contain 2 g almonds per 100 ml/3½ fl oz or less), the rest being mainly water, so it is very low in protein (0.5 g/100 ml versus 3.4 g/100 ml in dairy milk) and, unless fortified, it is a poor source of calcium and vitamins.

COCONUT

Most brands contain less than 1 g protein per 100 ml (3½ fl oz), which makes them poor sources of protein. They generally contain less than 2 g fat per 100 ml (3½ fl oz), which is similar to the fat content of semi-skimmed milk, but canned coconut milk contains much more, around 18 g/100 ml (3½ fl oz), as it is made with higher amounts of coconut cream. Canned coconut milk is best for curries.

HEMP

Hemp milk is low in protein, but, unlike other milk alternatives, contains high levels of omega-3 fats. One 250 ml (9 fl oz) glass contains half the recommended daily amount.

OAT

Made from soaked oats, which are then blended and strained, oat milk alternative contains beta-glucan, a type of soluble fibre. A 250 ml (9 fl oz) glass provides 1 g, a third of the suggested daily intake for lowering cholesterol. It has a higher calorie content than other milk alternatives but is similarly low in protein. The creamy texture makes it a good substitute for milk in baking, drinks and porridge.

ALMOND MILK

Homemade almond milk is a healthier bet than shop-bought varieties and far easier to make than you might imagine. This recipe is made with more nuts than manufactured milk, so it has a higher content of protein, vitamins and calcium. If you want a thicker consistency, use less water. You can also make 'milk' using other nuts, such as hazelnuts, cashews and macadamias. Nut milk bags are widely available to buy online, but you can use a good old-fashioned cheesecloth or muslin square.

150 g (5 oz) blanched almonds
900 ml (1½ pints) cold water, plus more for soaking
Vanilla extract (optional)
Sugar, maple syrup or honey to taste (optional)

Makes 900 ml (1½ pints)

Place the almonds in a bowl with just enough water to cover them. Leave to soak overnight or for at least 10–12 hours (they will swell as they absorb water). Drain, discard the soaking water, and rinse the almonds under cold running water.

Put the nuts in a blender or food processor and add 900 ml (1½ pints pints) fresh water. Process on high speed for 1–2 minutes or until smooth.

Place a cheesecloth or muslin nut bag inside a large jug and pour in the liquid. Pull up the sides of the cloth and twist the whole bundle until you have squeezed out all the almond milk. Taste the almond milk, and if you want a sweeter drink then add vanilla extract, sugar, maple syrup or honey to taste.

Almond milk can be kept in the fridge for up to three days. It's normal for it to separate – just give it a good shake before using.

HOW TO COOK WITHOUT EGGS

There are a number of vegan egg substitutes, which can be successfully used in many recipes that call for eggs.

FLAX 'EGGS'

Ground flaxseeds help to bind and hold ingredients together. However, they have a distinctive but subtle flavour so work best in strong-flavoured recipes, such as wholegrain cakes, muffins, banana bread, pancakes and chocolate brownies. To replace 1 egg: mix 1 tablespoon ground flaxseed with 3 tablespoons water.

CHIA 'EGGS'

When chia seeds are added to water, they become gel-like and thick. This makes them a good substitute for eggs in cakes, muffins, pancakes and cookies. To replace 1 egg: mix 1 tablespoon chia seeds with 3 tablespoons water and leave to rest for 5–10 minutes until the mixture becomes a gel.

PURÉED FRUIT AND VEGETABLES

Mashed banana, puréed dates, mashed sweet potato and apple purée can all be used as an egg substitute in recipes for 'squidgier' bakes, such as brownies, fruit loaves and cakes. They help to bind ingredients together as well as provide moisture, flavour and sweetness. However, don't use too much, as they can make your bake dense and heavy.

BICARBONATE OF SODA

When bicarbonate of soda and lemon juice or vinegar are mixed together, carbon dioxide is produced, which aerates a mixture and helps it rise. It can be used in cakes, muffins and non-yeast breads, such as banana bread. To replace 1 egg: mix 1 teaspoon bicarbonate of soda with 1 tablespoon white vinegar or lemon juice.

SILKEN TOFU

Silken tofu doesn't fluff up like eggs, but it has a neutral flavour and adds an egg-like texture to dishes such as cheesecakes, custards and quiche filling. To replace 1 egg: use 50 g (2 oz) tofu.

Chia seeds can be used as a substitute for eggs.

EXTRA-FIRM TOFU

Use extra-firm tofu to recreate scrambled eggs. Sauté onions, spring onions and/or garlic until soft, add any chopped veg you want (e.g. courgettes or cherry tomatoes), then crumble in tofu, a teaspoon of turmeric and paprika, seasoning, and a pinch of nutritional yeast flakes, and cook for a few minutes.

GRAM (CHICKPEA) FLOUR

Gram flour swells when mixed with liquid, so it makes a good egg substitute in savoury dishes such as burgers, fritters, pizza bases (see p. 150) and nut roasts.

AQUAFABA

Aquafaba is the liquid left over from cooked or canned chickpeas (or other beans). It has a protein structure similar to that of egg whites, which means it can be whipped into semi-stiff peaks. It can be used to make meringues, Yorkshire pudding and macaroons or added un-whipped to cookies and mayonnaise. To make meringues, simply whisk with 1 teaspoon cream of tartar or a drop of lemon juice using an electric whisk for five minutes. Then add an equal amount of sugar, spoon by spoon, whisking between each addition of sugar.

HEALTHY OILS

Oils have numerous nutritional benefits, thanks largely to their high content of unsaturated fats. Swapping some of the saturated fat in your diet for unsaturated fats – found in nuts, seeds, olives and avocado (and their oils) – can protect your heart because these healthy fats raise high-density lipoproteins (HDL) and lower low-density lipoproteins (LDL) cholesterol levels. They also improve the ratio of total cholesterol to 'good' HDL cholesterol, lowering the risk of heart disease. All oils contain the same calories and fat. However, different oils have different chemical make-ups and nutritional benefits and are best suited to different cooking modes (see below).

EXTRA VIRGIN OLIVE OIL

It's cold-pressed, which means it retains a truer olive taste and more of the natural antioxidants and vitamins found in olives.

Rich in monounsaturated fats – the type linked to improvements in HDL or 'good' cholesterol (which carries excess cholesterol from the arteries to the liver) – olive oil has anti-inflammatory compounds that contribute to healthy blood vessels. Extra virgin olive oil has a relatively low smoking point (see 'What is the smoking point?' p. 49). This means it shouldn't be heated to very high temperatures, such as those used for frying or roasting, but is perfect for drizzling over salads and finishing soups and pasta dishes.

LIGHT OLIVE OIL

Light olive oil has a neutral flavour and a high smoking point. This makes it a good choice for frying, roasting or baking, where you don't want an olive flavour. Despite its name, light olive oil

Quinoa, edamame and broccoli salad with hazelnuts, page 91.

has just as many calories and just as much fat as the other types. The word 'light' refers to the fact that it's lighter in flavour — you don't get as much of that olive taste. Because of the heat used in the extraction process, this type of olive oil contains fewer antioxidants than extra virgin but still offers the same amount of monounsaturated fats.

RAPESEED OIL

Rapeseed oil is made from the seeds of the oilseed rape crop and has a delicate, nutty flavour that makes it really versatile. It is naturally high in omega-3s, which makes it beneficial for health, plus it has a high smoking point, which makes it excellent for cooking at high temperatures, such as frying, roasting and stir-frying. Nutritionally, it is good as a substitute for extra virgin or light olive oil, being high in monounsaturated fats, plus it has higher levels of vitamin E. It also boasts a lower level of saturated fat than any other oil. There has been some fearmongering about rapeseed oil. This stems from the high levels of erucic acid found in certain varieties grown for industrial use, which is associated with an increased risk of heart disease. However, in the UK, rapeseed oil grown for culinary use has low levels of erucic acid and does not pose a risk to health.

COCONUT OIL

Coconut oil is a popular substitute for butter in vegan dishes as it is solid at room temperature and therefore has similar culinary and textural qualities. The main problem with coconut oil, and why you won't find it in any of the recipes in this book, however, relates to its effects on health. Although many people perceive it to be 'natural' and therefore assume it is healthy, there is little evidence to support this. It contains a very high concentration of saturated fat (90 per cent versus 64 per cent in butter) and, to date, the majority of studies have found that coconut oil is not protective against heart disease.[1,2] While it may raise levels of 'good' HDL cholesterol, it also raises levels of 'bad' LDL cholesterol.

Other health claims for coconut oil, such as promoting fat loss or boosting metabolism, point to its high content of medium-chain triglycerides (MCTs). These fats have a shorter chain length than other fats and are water soluble, which means they are absorbed and metabolised more quickly. Theoretically,

> ## WHAT IS THE SMOKING POINT?
>
> Different oils have different smoking points, which is the temperature at which oils begin to break down to form potentially harmful compounds, resulting in undesirable smoke and flavour. Both rapeseed and olive oil have higher smoking points than sunflower and corn oil, which makes them better for you and why you'll see them recommended in the recipes in this book.

they have less opportunity to be deposited in fat stores. But such claims are unfounded as they are based on studies using MCT oil, a manmade oil that contains a different blend of fatty acids, not coconut oil. In fact, coconut oil contains just 13–15 per cent MCTs. While the jury is out on the health effects of coconut oil, I recommend using it sparingly and opting for olive or rapeseed oil instead.

VEGETABLE OIL

In the UK, oils labelled 'vegetable oil' comprise 100 per cent rapeseed oil. It is extracted in a different way from 'cold-pressed' rapeseed oil, using more pressure and heat so the oil becomes milder in both colour and taste. This makes it useful for frying, roasting, baking and other cooking where you want a flavourless oil.

BREAKFASTS

○ Clockwise from top left: *Performance porridge, Peanut butter with bananas,*
High-protein banana pancakes, Avocado with sesame.

PERFORMANCE PORRIDGE (SIX WAYS)

Porridge is a winter staple in my house. It is such a simple, warming and delicious way to start the day. The combination of oats and milk provides sustained energy to fuel your body for several hours and stave off hunger. This base recipe requires just two ingredients – oats and milk – and can be jazzed up with any of the nutritious toppings suggested below.

Preparation time: 1 minute
Cooking time: 5 minutes

40 g (1½ oz) oats
250 ml (9 fl oz) milk (any type)

Serves 1

Mix the oats and milk in a saucepan. Bring to the boil, turn down the heat to a simmer and cook for 4–5 minutes, stirring frequently. Once you have the consistency you prefer, pour into a bowl and top with any of the toppings suggested below.

NUTRITION per serving:
• 249 cals • 13 g protein • 4 g fat (1 g saturates)
• 38 g carbs (12 g total sugars) • 3 g fibre

variations

Blueberry and Coconut: Cook the porridge with a handful of fresh or frozen blueberries. Serve topped with a little desiccated coconut, a few chopped walnuts and a drizzle of honey (if you like).

Apple Pie: Cook the porridge with 1 grated apple, 1 tablespoon ground flaxseed, a handful of raisins and ½ teaspoon cinnamon. Serve topped with chopped apple (raw or cooked) and a drizzle of honey.

Chocolate Orange: Add 1 teaspoon cocoa or cacao powder (see p. 168), the juice of ½ orange and ¼ teaspoon cinnamon to the oats. Serve topped with a square of dark chocolate and a few orange or clementine slices.

Carrot Cake: Cook the porridge with 1 grated carrot, a handful of raisins, ¼ teaspoon ginger and ¼ teaspoon cinnamon. Serve topped with a few chopped walnuts.

Raspberry and Almond: Cook the porridge with ¼ teaspoon cinnamon powder. Serve topped with a spoonful of Chia jam (see p. 75) or a handful of fresh or frozen raspberries and a swirl of almond butter.

Pear, Cinnamon and Walnut: Cook a sliced pear with 1 teaspoon butter (or oil) and ½ teaspoon cinnamon powder in a small pan for 5 minutes. Once cooked, arrange on top of the porridge with 1 tablespoon chopped walnuts.

YOGURT BOWL (FIVE WAYS)

This recipe is my speediest breakfast. It's high in protein, packed with vitamins and a brilliant way to get at least two of your five-a-day in at breakfast. The best thing about it is that it takes just two minutes to make so it's perfect for a busy weekday. You can also make it in a plastic pot or glass jar (try an empty honey pot) and take it with you to work, gym or school. Feeling creative? Arrange the toppings in rows or swirls, depending on your mood! I like to use fresh blackberries when they're in season but will often use frozen ones in the winter months – they're just as nutritious.

Preparation time: 2 minutes

1 banana

75 g (3 oz) blackberries, fresh or frozen

150 ml (5 fl oz) low-fat plain Greek yogurt

75 g (3 oz) raspberries, fresh or frozen

1 tbsp granola

4–5 walnut halves

Serves 1

Peel and mash half of the banana with the blackberries and yogurt. Spoon into a bowl and top with the remaining banana (sliced), raspberries, granola and walnuts.

NUTRITION per serving:
• 397 cals • 23 g protein • 14 g fat (2 g saturates)
• 40 g carbs (33 g total sugars) • 9 g fibre

Make it vegan

Use a non-dairy yogurt alternative.

variations

Blueberry and Almond: Substitute blueberries for the blackberries and raspberries, and top with a swirl of almond butter.

Strawberry Pecan: Use 125 g (4 oz) strawberries instead of the blackberries, top with extra strawberries and toasted pecans.

Raspberry and Coconut: Mix the yogurt with 2 tablespoons Chia jam (see p. 75) and top with 125 g (4 oz) raspberries and a few toasted coconut flakes.

High Protein: Mix in a spoonful of your favourite protein powder (whey or vegan) and top with fresh or frozen berries.

BERRY BIRCHER MUESLI

This easy recipe is ideal before a workout as it's full of high-energy ingredients to fuel your body. Equally, it makes a fantastic post-workout breakfast as it's high in protein to aid muscle repair. The high content of polyphenols and vitamin C in the berries promotes faster recovery and may reduce soreness. Prepare it the night before and pop it in the fridge, so you'll have a nutritious breakfast waiting for you in the morning.

Preparation time: 5 minutes

150 g (5 fl oz) low-fat plain Greek yogurt
50 ml (2 fl oz) milk (any type)
25 g (1 oz) jumbo oats
2 semi-dried apricots, chopped
½ apple, cored and coarsely grated
1 tbsp walnuts, roughly chopped
100 g (3½ oz) fresh berries, e.g. raspberries, blueberries or blackberries

Serves 1

In a small bowl or wide-necked glass jar, mix together all the ingredients except the fresh fruit. Cover and leave overnight in the fridge.

Top with the berries just before eating.

> **NUTRITION per serving:**
> • 396 cals • 25 g protein • 13 g fat (2 g saturates)
> • 41 g carbs (24 g total sugars) • 8 g fibre

Make it vegan

Use a non-dairy
yogurt alternative.

OVERNIGHT OATS (FOUR WAYS)

Overnight oats are wonderfully simple and a brilliant time-saver in the morning because everything has been done the night before. The oats absorb the liquid and soften overnight, turning into porridge by the morning so you have a nutritious breakfast waiting for you. You can make it in a bowl, a wide-necked glass jar, or plastic food container that you can grab from the fridge, pop in your kit bag and take with you to the gym or work in the morning! This is my favourite base recipe, with just four ingredients, which you can top with any of the suggestions below.

Preparation time: 5 minutes

40 g (1½ oz) rolled oats
75 ml (3 fl oz) milk (any type)
2 tbsp low-fat plain Greek yogurt
2 tsp honey or maple syrup

Serves 1

Simply mix all the ingredients together in a bowl. Transfer to a wide-necked container or jar. Close the top and give it shake. Place in the fridge overnight.

In the morning, add extra milk if you wish (the oats soak up quite a lot of liquid) and top with any of the toppings below.

NUTRITION per serving:
• 257 cals • 15 g protein • 4 g fat (1 g saturates)
• 40 g carbs (12 g total sugars) • 3 g fibre

Make it vegan

Use a non-dairy yogurt alternative.

variations

Banana and Cinnamon: Mix a sliced banana, a handful of raisins and a pinch of ground cinnamon into the oats, then leave overnight.

Mango and Banana: Blend ½ mango and 1 ripe banana, peeled and chopped, in a food processor, then pour over the oats in the morning. Scatter over a few toasted coconut flakes.

Fresh Berry: Stir 100 g (3½ oz) fresh blueberries, raspberries or strawberries into the oats. Leave overnight, then top with a handful of chopped walnuts.

Peanut Butter: Stir 1 tablespoon peanut butter (or any other nut butter) into the oats, leave overnight and then top with 1 tablespoon chopped nuts or seeds.

CINNAMON FRENCH TOAST WITH STRAWBERRIES, BLUEBERRIES AND COCONUT

Here's a seriously tasty start to your day, ideal before a long walk or cycle ride or for a refuelling brunch after an early-morning workout. The bread is soaked in egg and milk before frying, so it's a brilliant way of adding protein to your breakfast and makes a lovely change from eggs on toast. Fresh berries add vitamin C, which enhances the body's absorption of iron in the egg yolk and bread, as well as lots of polyphenols, which promote muscle recovery.

Preparation time: 5 minutes
Cooking time: 6 minutes

2 eggs
75 ml (3 fl oz) milk (any type)
½ tsp cinnamon
¼ tsp nutmeg
4 slices wholegrain or sourdough bread
2 tsp light olive oil or butter
1 banana, peeled and sliced
100 g (3½ oz) each of blueberries and strawberries
2 tbsp desiccated coconut

Serves 2

Whisk together the eggs, milk, cinnamon and nutmeg in a shallow dish or lipped plate. Dip the bread slices in the egg mixture for about 30 seconds on each side, ensuring they are soaked through.

Heat the oil or butter in a large non-stick frying pan over a medium heat. Add the bread and cook for about 2 minutes until golden, then flip the slices over and cook for 1 further minute on the other side.

Serve immediately, topped with banana slices, blueberries, strawberries and desiccated coconut.

> **NUTRITION per serving:**
> • 385 cals • 17 g protein • 15 g fat (6 g saturates)
> • 41 g carbs (12 g total sugars) • 10 g fibre

TOAST TOPPERS

Breakfast can be as simple as a slice of toast. Choose wholegrain, nutty, seeded or sourdough bread and load it up with tasty, nutrient-packed nut butter, avocado, hummus or fruit. Here are some of my favourite toppings.

variations

Peanut Butter with Bananas: (bottom left) Spread a slice of toast with peanut butter, top with banana slices and, if you like, a sprinkle of cacao nibs or chocolate chips (see p. 168).

Hummus, Avocado and Tomato: (bottom right) Spread a slice of toast with 2 tablespoons hummus, then top with ½ sliced avocado, a few cherry tomato halves and a sprinkle of chopped chives or chilli flakes.

Almond Butter and Raspberry: Spread a slice of toast thickly with almond butter and top with a generous dollop of Chia jam (see p. 75). You can substitute any other nut butter, including cashew, pecan and hazelnut.

Chocolate Spread with Berries: (top right) Spread a slice of toast with cocoa and hazelnut butter (or mix a little cocoa or cacao powder into almond butter) and top with fresh strawberry slices, raspberries or frozen Black Forest fruits.

Avocado with Sesame: (top left) Top a slice of toast with smashed avocado and scatter over black sesame seeds.

Berry Compôte: Top a slice of toast with a simple berry compôte made with 200 g (7 oz) fresh or frozen berries cooked over a medium heat with 1 tablespoon water and 1 tablespoon sugar for 5 minutes, or until mushy.

WHAT IS SOURDOUGH BREAD?

Sourdough bread is made using wild yeast and a bacterial culture (lactobacillus) to ferment the dough, whereas standard bread is made using baker's yeast. Wild yeast uses the lactobacillus bacteria to convert proteins (like gluten) into lactic acid that gives sourdough bread its characteristic flavour. It has a longer fermentation period, during which the gluten is broken down and other nutrients in the flour (e.g. zinc, iron, calcium and magnesium) are made more bioavailable to the body. As a result, sourdough bread has a lower content of gluten and fructans (a type of carbohydrate that some people find hard to digest), making it more digestible for people with IBS or non-coeliac gluten sensitivity. Sourdough is also a prebiotic (see p. 23), meaning it helps feed the 'good' microbes in the gut. For greatest nutritional value, opt for wholegrain or rye sourdough.

HIGH-PROTEIN BANANA PANCAKES

These easy pancakes are a delicious way to get your protein at breakfast – without using protein powder! Instead, I've used cottage cheese and eggs, which are naturally rich in protein along with B vitamins and calcium. You can substitute quark, a virtually fat-free soft cheese, for the cottage cheese. There's lots of research to suggest that the distribution of protein throughout the day is just as important as the total daily amount and that we should aim for 20–30 g per meal for optimum muscle repair and building (see pp. 18–20). You'll get 20 g from four pancakes. The carbohydrate sources (oats and bananas) are better options than white flour as they provide more fibre.

Preparation time: 5 minutes
Cooking time: 10 minutes

100 g (3½ oz) rolled oats
1 tsp baking powder
1 banana, peeled and mashed
150 g (5 oz) plain cottage cheese or quark
2 eggs
1 tsp cinnamon
A little light olive oil, rapeseed oil or butter, for frying

To serve:
Strawberries, raspberries, blueberries or blackberries and maple syrup or honey

Makes 8

Place the oats in a food processor or blender and blitz for 30 seconds. Add the remaining ingredients, except the oil or butter, and process for another 30 seconds or until you have a smooth batter.

Heat a non-stick pan on a medium heat, add a little oil or butter. Drop large spoonfuls of batter into the pan and cook without disturbing until bubbles form and the edges are cooked. Flip the pancakes over with a spatula and cook until the other side is golden brown.

Transfer pancakes to a plate or, if you don't want to serve as you go, preheat your oven to 120 °C/fan 100 °C/gas mark ½ and stack the pancakes as you cook them, using a strip of greaseproof paper in between each to stop them from sticking while you cook the rest of the batter. Serve the pancakes with the berries, drizzled with maple syrup or honey.

NUTRITION per pancake:
• 97 cals • 5 g protein • 3 g fat (1 g saturates)
• 11 g carbs (3 g total sugars) • 1 g fibre

PEANUT BUTTER PANCAKES

If you're a peanut butter fan, then you'll fall in love with these super-tasty pancakes! They're
a brilliant way of combining all the goodness of nuts with oats, milk and eggs. The result is
a high-protein, high-fibre breakfast that'll fill you up nicely and keep you satiated for hours.
You can substitute almond or other nut butters for the peanut butter if you prefer.

Preparation time: 5 minutes
Cooking time: 10 minutes

2 eggs
150 ml (5 fl oz) milk (any type)
1½ tbsp smooth peanut butter
1 tbsp honey
75 g (3 oz) plain or wholemeal flour
25 g (1 oz) oats
1 tsp baking powder
A pinch of salt
Light olive or rapeseed oil, for frying

To serve:
Sliced banana, fresh berries
(e.g. blueberries or blackberries)
and honey or maple syrup

Makes 8

Whisk the eggs, milk, peanut butter and honey together in a bowl. In a
separate bowl, combine the flour, oats, baking powder and salt. Pour the
wet mixture into the flour mixture and mix until smooth (you can do this
with a hand blender if you prefer).

Heat a non-stick frying pan over a medium heat and add a little oil. Add
large spoonfuls of batter to the pan for each pancake, leaving enough
space between them so they don't touch, and cook until bubbles form
and the edges are cooked, about 2 minutes. Flip the pancakes over with a
spatula. Cook for another minute on the other side, then transfer to a plate.
If you don't want to serve as you go, preheat your oven to 120 °C/fan
100 °C/gas mark ½ and stack the pancakes as you cook them, using a strip
of greaseproof paper in between each to stop them from sticking. Repeat
with the remaining batter.

Serve the pancakes topped with sliced banana, fresh berries and a little
honey or maple syrup.

> NUTRITION per pancake:
> • 104 cals • 5 g protein • 4 g fat (1 g saturates)
> • 11 g carbs (3 g total sugars) • 2 g fibre

OMELETTE WRAPS

Early-morning workout? These wraps are brilliant to take with you, as they can be wrapped in foil and are delicious cold. They make a tasty change from flour tortilla wraps and, being higher in protein (thanks to the eggs), are ideal after a strength workout. I love them with feta and sliced avocado, which are loaded with heart-healthy monounsaturated fats and vitamin E, but you can fill them with baby spinach, tomatoes or hummus, or whatever takes your fancy.

Preparation time: 5 minutes
Cooking time: 5 minutes

1 tbsp olive oil
2 eggs, beaten
1 tbsp fresh parsley, or 1 tsp dried herbs
1 avocado, sliced
A handful of rocket
50 g (2 oz) feta, crumbled
Salt and freshly ground black pepper

Serves 2

Heat half the oil in a small frying pan over a medium-high heat, then add half the beaten eggs and tip the pan around to make sure you cover the whole base in a thin, even layer. Sprinkle over half the parsley or dried herbs. Cook for 1–2 minutes until just set, then flip the omelette and cook for another 30 seconds on the other side. Slide out on to a plate and repeat to make the other wrap.

Once you have both your wraps, put half the avocado, rocket and feta in each one, season with salt and black pepper, then roll them up. Eat straight away or wrap in foil for a portable breakfast.

NUTRITION per wrap:
• 345 cals • 14 g protein • 31 g fat (9 g saturates)
• 2 g carbs (1 g total sugars) • 4 g fibre

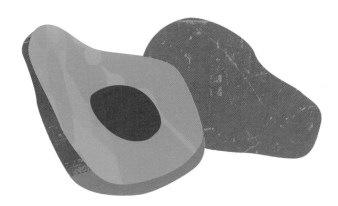

PECAN, ALMOND AND COCONUT GRANOLA

Crammed with toasted nuts, seeds and coconut, this granola has the perfect balance of sweetness from the raisins and honey. The benefit of making your own is that you can vary the nuts, seeds, dried fruit and the cereal flakes each time. You'll also be getting more protein, vitamins and minerals than manufactured granolas, which can contain high levels of added sugar. Pecans are especially beneficial for active people as they're packed with zinc and manganese (both of which promote post-exercise recovery and healing from sports injuries), while almonds supply high levels of vitamin E and calcium. The granola can be stored in an airtight container for up to a month.

Preparation time: 5 minutes
Cooking time: 40 minutes

250 g (9 oz) jumbo oats
100 g (3½ oz) flaked almonds
100 g (3½ oz) pecans, roughly chopped
50 g (2 oz) coconut flakes
125 g (4 oz) mixture of pumpkin, sunflower and chia seeds
3 tbsp runny honey or maple syrup
3 tbsp light olive or rapeseed oil
4 tbsp water
1 tsp vanilla extract
1 tsp ground cinnamon
100 g (3½ oz) raisins

To serve:
Milk or plain yogurt (any type) and fresh fruit

Makes 15 x 45 g servings

Preheat the oven to 150 °C/fan 130 °C/gas mark 2.

Mix together the oats, nuts and seeds in a bowl.

In a separate bowl, combine the honey or maple syrup, oil, water, vanilla and cinnamon. Add to the oat mixture and mix well.

Line a baking tray with parchment paper. Use a palette knife to spread out the granola mixture on the tray and bake in the oven for 30–40 minutes, stirring occasionally until evenly browned. Cool before breaking it into pieces and then mix in the raisins.

NUTRITION per serving:
• 275 cals • 7 g protein • 18 g fat (4 g saturates)
• 20 g carbs (7 g total sugars) • 3 g fibre

variations

Maple Walnut Granola: Substitute walnuts for the pecans and use maple syrup. Omit the coconut.

Cherry and Brazil: Substitute Brazil nuts for the pecans and use dried cherries or cranberries instead of the raisins. Add 1 teaspoon ground ginger instead of the cinnamon.

Hazelnut and Date: Substitute hazelnuts for the pecans and use chopped soft dates instead of raisins.

MUSHROOMS AND VITAMIN D

Exposing mushrooms to sunlight by popping them on a sunny window ledge, with their gills facing up, for a couple of hours greatly increases their content of vitamin D. This can be a useful source for vegetarians as there are not many other vegetarian dietary sources (see p. 33). Although the form of vitamin D produced in mushrooms (vitamin D2), is not the same as the form found in other foods (vitamin D3), it has been shown to be just as potent in the body.

MUSHROOM, TOMATO AND GOATS' CHEESE FRITTATA (FOUR WAYS)

Frittatas make an ideal post-workout breakfast or weekend brunch, as they're filling, delicious and packed with protein. They are endlessly customisable – as long as you have eggs and a few veg, you can make a frittata. I've used tomatoes in this recipe, which are rich in beta-carotene, vitamins C and E, and mushrooms, which are a fantastic source of vitamin D if you expose them to sunlight on a window sill (see p. 68). Alternatively, add sliced courgettes, broccoli, red peppers or spinach, and bingo, a quick high-protein breakfast that'll aid your muscle recovery!

Preparation time: 10 minutes

Cooking time: 10 minutes

2 tsp light olive or rapeseed oil
½ small onion, diced
50 g (2 oz) mushrooms, sliced
6 cherry tomatoes
2 eggs
½ tsp dried thyme
25 g (1 oz) soft goats' cheese, crumbled
Salt and freshly ground black pepper
A small handful of rocket

Serves 1

Preheat the grill to medium.

Heat the oil in a non-stick ovenproof frying pan over a medium-low heat and add the onion. Cook for about 3 minutes until softened, then add the mushrooms and tomatoes and cook for a further 2 minutes.

Beat the eggs with the seasoning and thyme in a bowl or jug. Pour over the vegetables, gently tilting the pan to ensure the egg is evenly distributed. Cook for a further 2 minutes over a low-medium heat until the base and edges begin to set, but the centre is still liquid. Dot the goats' cheese over the top.

Place the pan under the grill for 1–2 minutes until the top begins to puff up and is golden. Slide onto a plate and scatter over rocket.

> **NUTRITION per serving:**
> • 315 cals • 21 g protein • 22 g fat (8 g saturates)
> • 7 g carbs (6 g total sugars) • 3 g fibre

variations

Spinach and Feta: Add a handful of baby spinach and 25 g (1 oz) crumbled vegetarian feta and omit the tomatoes and mushrooms.

Red pepper and Courgette: Add sliced red or yellow peppers and courgettes in place of the tomatoes and mushrooms.

Pea and Courgette: Replace the mushrooms and tomatoes with 1 courgette (grated) and 125 g (4 oz) peas.

BREAKFAST BURRITO

A burrito is a great grab and go breakfast, which you can make the night before, wrap in foil and take with you to the gym or work. This tasty Mexican-inspired recipe is packed with protein, thanks to the scrambled eggs. They are paired with fresh tomatoes, which provide vitamin C to boost iron absorption, as well as avocado, which adds healthy monounsaturated fats. If you're short on time, simply chop the tomatoes instead of making a salsa, or add them to the pan with the eggs. Chopped red peppers and baby spinach also work well.

Preparation time: 5 minutes
Cooking time: 3 minutes

2 eggs
Dash of light olive or rapeseed oil
2 wholewheat tortilla wraps
½ avocado, peeled, pitted and sliced

For the salsa:
2 large tomatoes, finely diced
A handful of fresh coriander leaves, chopped
½ red onion, finely chopped
1 tbsp lemon or lime juice
Chilli flakes, to taste
Salt and freshly ground black pepper

Makes 2

Start by making the salsa. In a bowl, mix together the tomatoes, coriander, onion, lemon or lime juice and chilli flakes with salt and pepper.

Break the eggs into a bowl and beat with a fork. Heat the oil in a non-stick pan over a medium-low heat. Pour in the eggs and cook, stirring, until just beginning to set, then remove from the heat.

Lay the wraps on plates. Spoon the eggs in a horizontal line at one end, add a spoonful of salsa and top with slices of avocado. Fold the sides of each wrap inwards, then roll up.

NUTRITION per burrito:
• 349 cals • 13 g protein • 16 g fat (4 g saturates)
• 34 g carbs (7 g total sugars) • 8 g fibre

Make it vegan

Fill with canned black or red kidney beans instead of the scrambled eggs.

ENERGISING GREEN SMOOTHIE

This smoothie is an easy way to get three portions of fruit and veg into your morning. Bananas provide carbohydrate, while flax and chia seeds give your daily requirement for omega-3s, which help reduce inflammation after intense exercise. By incorporating spinach, you'll provide your body with iron and folate and, when combined with sweet-tasting pineapple and banana, the spinach is virtually tasteless.

Preparation time: 2 minutes

250 ml (9 fl oz) almond milk or coconut water
2 handfuls of baby spinach
75 g (3 oz) pineapple
1 banana, peeled and chopped
1 tbsp ground flaxseed or chia seeds
A few ice cubes

Serves 1

Blitz all the ingredients in a blender or food processor until smooth, then pour into a tall glass.

NUTRITION per serving:
- 233 cals • 7 g protein
- 9 g fat (1 g saturates)
- 27 g carbs (25 g total sugars)
- 8 g fibre

LEFT: Banana and oat breakfast smoothie (p. 73).
CENTRE: Energising green smoothie.
RIGHT: Pre-workout mocha smoothie (p. 73).

PRE-WORKOUT MOCHA SMOOTHIE

When you need a pick-me-up before working out, this smoothie is the perfect drink. It's made with coffee to give you a bit of an energy boost. Caffeine increases stamina and alertness, and reduces the perception of effort, making exercise feel a little easier! The cacao powder provides that rich dark chocolate taste and some bonus antioxidants (see p. 168).

Preparation time: 2 minutes

50 ml (2 fl oz) milk (any type)
125 ml (4 fl oz) plain yogurt
1 shot espresso
2 tsp cacao or cocoa powder
1 banana, peeled and chopped
Pinch of cinnamon
A few ice cubes

Serves 1

Blitz all the ingredients in a blender or food processor until smooth, then pour into a tall glass.

> **NUTRITION per serving:**
> • 189 cals • 10 g protein • 2 g fat (1 g saturates)
> • 31 g carbs (29 g total sugars) • 2 g fibre

BANANA AND OAT BREAKFAST SMOOTHIE

Perfect for breakfast on the go, this creamy smoothie also makes a great post-workout drink. It's high in protein, carbohydrate, vitamins, minerals and fibre. Adding oats and nut butter to smoothies helps slow down the absorption of sugar from the fruit into your bloodstream, which gives you longer-lasting energy. I like to use frozen blueberries but feel free to use any other berries you like.

Preparation time: 2 minutes

175 ml (6 fl oz) milk (any type)
1 banana, peeled and chopped
1 tbsp oats
½ tsp cinnamon
1 tbsp almond butter (or any other nut butter)
75 g (3 oz) blueberries (fresh or frozen)

Serves 1

Blitz all the ingredients in a blender or food processor until smooth, then pour into a tall glass.

> **NUTRITION per serving:**
> • 337 cals • 13 g protein • 10 g fat (1 g saturates)
> • 45 g carbs (32 g total sugars) • 6 g fibre

MIXED FRUIT COMPÔTE

This easy compôte takes only a few minutes to make and is lovely on porridge, pancakes, granola or stirred into plain yogurt. As the cooking time is kept to a minimum, most of the vitamins will be retained. You can substitute other fruit, such as raspberries and blueberries, for the fruit in this recipe.

Preparation time: 2 minutes
Cooking time: 5 minutes

1 apple, cored and sliced
2 plums, stones removed and cut into wedges
1 tsp ground cinnamon
2 tbsp water
½ tsp vanilla paste or a dash of vanilla extract
175 g (6 oz) strawberries
3 tbsp maple syrup

Makes 200 g (8 tbsp)

Place the apple, plums and cinnamon in a small pan with the water and cook for 2 minutes. Add the vanilla, strawberries and maple syrup and simmer over a very gentle heat for 2–3 minutes, until the fruit has softened but not turned mushy. It will keep in the fridge for up to two days.

NUTRITION per 1 tbsp (25 g) serving:
• 35 cals • 0 g protein • 0 g fat (0 g saturates)
• 7 g carbs (7 g total sugars) • 1 g fibre

CHIA JAM

This cheat's 'jam' is packed with polyphenols, fibre and omega-3s. Fresh fruit is simply cooked with chia seeds, which absorb the liquid and swell to form a delicious jam without having to add loads of sugar. Any berries – strawberries, blueberries or blackberries – will work with this recipe. Chia jam is a little softer than traditional jam but you can still spread it on toast, scones or stir it into porridge or yogurt. If you want a thicker consistency, stir in more chia seeds. Adjust the amount of honey or sugar to suit your taste.

Preparation time: 1 minute
Cooking time: 10 minutes

250 g (9 oz) berries, e.g. strawberries, raspberries, blueberries or blackberries (fresh or frozen)
1–2 tbsp lemon juice
1–2 tbsp honey or sugar, to taste
2 tbsp chia seeds

Makes 1 x 300 g jar

Place the berries in a saucepan with the lemon juice and honey or sugar. Bring to the boil and cook on a low heat for 5–10 minutes. Mash with the back of a spatula or spoon, then add the chia seeds.

Remove from the heat and leave it to cool (the jam will thicken as it cools). Once cooled, transfer to a sterilised jar or other storage container*. Seal, then store in the fridge for up to two weeks.

* The quickest way to sterilise jars (although not Kilner-style jars or those with metal lids) is just to wash your jar in hot soapy water, rinse, then place the wet jar in the microwave on full power for about 45 seconds (or until bone dry), and fill whilst the jar is still hot. Alternatively, wash your jar in the dishwasher at a high temperature setting and use as soon as the cycle has finished.

NUTRITION per tablespoon (25 g):
• 21 cals • 1 g protein • 1 g fat (0 g saturates)
• 2 g carbs (2 g total sugars) • 2 g fibre

CHAPTER 11

SALADS

○○

○ Clockwise from top left: *Crunchy vegetable gado gado salad, Puy lentil and butternut squash salad, Roasted vegetables with tofu and walnuts, Quinoa, edamame and broccoli salad with hazelnuts.*

ROASTED CARROTS, CHICKPEAS AND GRAINS WITH PECANS

This gorgeous salad of contrasting colours and textures is packed with nutrients for muscle recovery as well as being super-easy to make. It's a fabulous way of getting lots of beta-carotene, vitamin C and phytonutrients, as well as the protein you need for muscle repair and growth. Use a packet of cooked quinoa if you're pressed for time – it's just as nutritious and tasty. Pecans are an excellent source of vitamin E, a powerful antioxidant that helps protect cells from damage and aids muscle repair after exercise, as well as omega-3 fats that promote healthy blood vessels.

Preparation time: 10 minutes

Cooking time: 20 minutes

250 g (9 oz) carrots, cut into batons

1 red and 1 yellow pepper, deseeded and cut into 2-cm strips

1 red onion, cut into 8 wedges

2 tbsp light olive or rapeseed oil

1 tsp za'atar (Middle Eastern herbs available from most supermarkets) or dried thyme

125 g (4 oz) quinoa and bulgur (cracked) wheat mixture or 250-g (8-oz) packet cooked quinoa

400 g (14 oz) can chickpeas, rinsed and drained

50 g (2 oz) pecans, toasted
(see 'How to toast nuts and seeds' below)

A small handful of fresh coriander or parsley, chopped, plus extra to serve

Juice of ½ lemon

Salt and freshly ground black pepper

100 g (3½ oz) soft goats' cheese, crumbled (optional)

Serves 4

Preheat the oven to 200 °C/fan 180 °C/gas mark 6.

Toss the carrots, peppers and onion, oil, za'atar and seasoning in a roasting tin. Make sure the tin is large enough so the vegetables are in a single layer. Roast in the oven for about 20 minutes until the vegetables are slightly charred on the outside and tender in the middle.

Meanwhile, cook the quinoa and bulgur wheat according to the packet instructions.

Toss the roasted vegetables into the warm grains. Fold in the chickpeas, pecans, coriander or parsley and lemon juice, then season to taste. Mound onto a plate, top with a little extra coriander or parsley and crumbled goats' cheese, if using.

NUTRITION per serving (including goats' cheese):
• 460 cals • 17 g protein • 25 g fat (6 g saturates)
• 38 g carbs (12 g total sugars) • 11 g fibre

Make it vegan

Omit the goats' cheese.

HOW TO TOAST NUTS AND SEEDS

Oven: Spread them in an even layer on a baking tray and place in a preheated oven at 180 °C/fan 160 °C/gas mark 4 for 8–12 minutes, depending on size. Check them often and stir halfway through the cooking time to ensure all the nuts are toasting evenly. They are ready when golden brown and fragrant.

Frying Pan: Spread them in an even layer in a heavy-bottomed frying pan and toast over a medium-high heat, stirring or shaking frequently, for 3–5 minutes until golden brown and fragrant.

CRUNCHY VEGETABLE GADO GADO SALAD

This protein-rich salad of vegetables, boiled eggs and crispy tofu with a delicious peanut sauce drizzled over is ideal for kick-starting muscle recovery after exercise. It's based on a popular Indonesian dish – gado gado means medley, which refers to the different seasonal vegetables and ingredients that are used. The recipe is endlessly customisable so you can easily substitute any other vegetables you have in the fridge, such as avocado, broccoli or pak choi (Chinese cabbage). If you like a spicier sauce, add extra chilli; otherwise, leave it out. You can make a larger quantity for drizzling on tofu, vegetables, noodles or rice.

Preparation time: 10 minutes
Cooking time: 20 minutes

400 g (14 oz) new potatoes, halved
150 g (5 oz) green beans, ends trimmed, halved
4 eggs
250 g (9 oz) firm tofu
1 tbsp light olive or rapeseed oil
½ cucumber, thinly sliced
2 tomatoes, cut into wedges
A bunch of radishes, trimmed and halved
2 medium carrots, peeled, halved and cut into thin matchsticks
¼ red cabbage, shredded
A generous handful of beansprouts

For the gado gado sauce:
Juice of 1 lime
1 garlic clove, crushed
200 ml (7 fl oz) canned light coconut milk
65 g (2½ oz) peanut butter (smooth or crunchy)
2 tsp soy sauce
½–1 red chilli, deseeded and finely chopped (optional)
Salt and freshly ground black pepper

Serves 4

For the vegetable salad, cook the potatoes in boiling water for 15 minutes, adding the green beans for the final 2–3 minutes, until the beans and potatoes are tender. Drain.

Meanwhile, boil the eggs in a saucepan of water for 7 minutes or longer if you prefer them more cooked. Plunge them into cold water, peel, then cut into wedges.

Cut the tofu into 2-cm cubes. Heat the oil in a large frying pan over a medium heat and fry the tofu for 2–3 minutes on each side, until lightly golden.

For the gado gado sauce, place all the sauce ingredients in a blender or food processor and blitz until smooth. Adjust the seasoning. Warm gently in the microwave on a medium setting if you have time.

To serve, divide the cucumber, tomatoes, vegetables, tofu and eggs between four bowls. Drizzle the sauce over the salad or serve it separately on the side. Scatter over the beansprouts and serve.

NUTRITION per serving:
• 387 cals • 22 g protein • 20 g fat (5 g saturates)
• 26 g carbs (10 g total sugars) • 8 g fibre

Make it vegan
Simply leave out the hard-boiled eggs.

PUY LENTIL AND BUTTERNUT SQUASH SALAD

This glorious salad is full of amazing flavours and is a super-easy way of getting four of your five-a-day. The vibrant colour of roasted butternut squash contrasts wonderfully with the dark lentils and is an excellent source of beta-carotene and vitamin E. Lentils provide lots of protein, which promotes muscle repair after exercise, as well as prebiotic fibre to promote healthy gut microbes (see p. 23). I use ready-cooked puy lentils for speed, but dry lentils cooked for 30 minutes may also be used. I like to add red peppers for their high vitamin C content, which boosts the body's absorption of iron from the lentils; and avocado for heart-healthy monounsaturated fats.

Preparation time: 10 minutes

Cooking time: 20 minutes

½ butternut squash (approx. 500 g/1 lb 2 oz), peeled and cut into 1-cm (½-in) cubes (see p. 101)

2 red onions, cut into wedges

2 garlic cloves, crushed

A few sprigs of rosemary

2 tbsp light olive or rapeseed oil

2 courgettes, trimmed and thickly sliced

100 g (3½ oz) cherry tomatoes, halved

1 avocado, peeled, pitted and cut into 1-cm (½-in) cubes

2 x 250 g (9 oz) packets ready-cooked puy lentils

Juice of ½ lemon

A handful of fresh coriander or parsley, chopped

50 g (2 oz) walnuts

50 g (2 oz) vegetarian feta, crumbled (optional)

Sea salt flakes and freshly ground black pepper

To serve:
Warm flatbreads

Serves 4

Preheat the oven to 200 °C/fan 180 °C/gas mark 6.

Place the butternut squash and onions in a large roasting tin. Scatter over the garlic, rosemary, salt and black pepper. Drizzle over the oil and toss lightly so that the vegetables are well coated in oil. Roast in the oven for about 10 minutes, then add the courgettes and roast for a further 10 minutes until the vegetables are slightly charred on the outside and tender in the middle.

Mix together the roasted vegetables, tomatoes, avocado, lentils, lemon juice, coriander or parsley, walnuts and feta (if using) in a large serving bowl.

Serve with warm flatbreads.

> **NUTRITION per serving:**
> • 521 cals • 21 g protein • 27 g fat (5 g saturates)
> • 41 g carbs (13 g total sugars) • 16 g fibre

Make it vegan

Simply omit the feta.

FREEKEH, CHICKPEAS AND ROASTED VEGETABLES WITH PISTACHIOS

This is such a brilliant combination of ingredients for promoting muscle recovery and supporting your immune system. Freekeh, chickpeas and pistachios provide lots of amino acids that combine to build new proteins. They are also loaded with phytonutrients – plant nutrients that benefit your health and help speed recovery. Freekeh has a rich, nutty, smoky flavour, and is high in protein, magnesium, potassium, calcium and iron (see 'What is freekeh?' below). It also has prebiotic properties that promote a healthy gut microbiota.

Preparation time: 10 minutes

Cooking time: 20 minutes

½ butternut squash (approx. 500 g/1 lb 2 oz), peeled and cut into 2.5-cm (1-in) cubes (see p. 101)

1 red onion, cut into wedges

A few sprigs of rosemary

2 tbsp light olive or rapeseed oil

1 small aubergine, sliced

125 g (4 oz) cracked freekeh or 250 g (9 oz) packet cooked freekeh

2 x 400 g (14 oz) cans chickpeas

50 g (2 oz) pistachio nuts

A small handful of parsley, finely chopped

2 tbsp chopped chives

Juice of ½ lemon

Salt and freshly ground black pepper

Serves 4

Preheat the oven to 200 °C/fan 180 °C/gas mark 6.

Place the butternut squash and onion in a large roasting tin. Scatter over the rosemary, salt and black pepper. Drizzle over the oil and toss lightly. Roast in the oven for about 10 minutes, then add the aubergine and roast for a further 10 minutes until the vegetables are slightly charred on the outside and tender in the middle.

If you're using raw freekeh, cook it according to the instructions on the packet. In general, it will need to cook for 15–20 minutes depending how finely cracked it is.

In a large bowl, toss the cooked freekeh with the roasted vegetables, chickpeas, pistachios, chopped herbs and lemon juice until they are well mixed together, then season to taste.

> **NUTRITION per serving:**
> • 485 cals • 20 g protein • 18 g fat (2 g saturates)
> • 54 g carbs (10 g total sugars) • 16 g fibre

WHAT IS FREEKEH?

Freekeh is essentially wheat that has been harvested early while the grains are still tender and green. The kernels are roasted to give it a distinctive smoky flavour. It's widely available in supermarkets and works beautifully in lots of dishes – it's delicious in salads or used in the same way as rice for stir-fries or pilafs.

NOODLES WITH EDAMAME BEANS, LIME AND GINGER

If you thought noodles were only useful for stir-fries, then think again! They also make a nutritious base for delicious salads, which can be eaten straight away or packed in plastic boxes for lunch on the go. This recipe combines a tasty Asian-inspired sauce with soba noodles, which are made from buckwheat – a type of seed that's rich in manganese, magnesium and zinc, which are all important for the immune system, as well as lots of protein and fibre. Its slightly nutty flavour goes beautifully with edamame beans (see 'What are edamame beans?' below) and I've added pumpkin seeds for their high content of omega-3 fatty acids.

Preparation time: 10 minutes
Cooking time: 5 minutes

200 g (7 oz) soba or wholewheat noodles
250 g (9 oz) frozen edamame beans
1 tsp chilli flakes
2 tbsp tamari or soy sauce
2 tbsp extra virgin olive oil
1 tbsp honey or maple syrup
Juice of 1 lime
1 cm fresh ginger, peeled and finely grated
50 g (2 oz) pumpkin seeds, toasted (see p. 79)
6 spring onions, chopped
2 carrots, grated
1 red pepper, deseeded and thinly sliced
250 g (9 oz) sugar snap peas
A handful of fresh coriander, chopped

Serves 4

Cook the noodles in a large saucepan of boiling water according to the directions on the packet. Add the frozen edamame beans to the pan for the last 30 seconds of cooking, then refresh the noodles and beans under cold water, drain in a colander and set aside.

Make the sauce by whisking together the chilli flakes, tamari or soy sauce, oil, honey or maple syrup, lime juice and grated ginger in a large bowl.

Add the noodles, edamame beans, pumpkin seeds, vegetables and coriander and toss well to combine.

NUTRITION per serving:
• 451 cals • 22 g protein • 17 g fat (3 g saturates)
• 48 g carbs (12 g total sugars) • 10 g fibre

WHAT ARE EDAMAME BEANS?

Edamame beans are young soya beans and are an excellent source of protein and fibre, as well as phytochemicals that may help lower blood cholesterol levels. They contain all eight essential amino acids, which makes them particularly useful for vegetarians (see p. 18).

ROASTED SWEET POTATO, ASPARAGUS AND BLACK BEAN SALAD

This gorgeous marriage of sweet potatoes and black beans makes a super-easy recovery meal. Loaded with protein and carbohydrate, it also provides plenty of fibre and iron, along with beta-carotene. It's such a rainbow dish too, with its vibrant colours and textures, so it's a great salad to serve to guests. You can add other vegetables such as radishes and baby sweetcorn, and use any leftovers as a tasty filling for omelettes and wraps.

Preparation time: 10 minutes

Cooking time: 20 minutes

2 large sweet potatoes, peeled and cut into 1-cm cubes

2 carrots, cut into batons

2 tbsp light olive or rapeseed oil

1 tsp za'atar (Middle Eastern herbs available from most supermarkets) or dried thyme

100 g (3½ oz) asparagus, cut into 3-cm (1½-in) pieces

2 x 400 g (14 oz) cans black beans, drained and rinsed

6 spring onions, sliced

150 g cherry tomatoes, halved

A small handful of fresh coriander or parsley, chopped, plus extra to serve

Juice of 1 lemon

100 g (3½ oz) rocket

125 g (4 oz) soft goats' cheese, crumbled (optional)

Sea salt flakes and freshly ground black pepper

Serves 4

Preheat the oven to 200 °C/fan 180 °C/gas mark 6.

Arrange the sweet potatoes and carrots in a roasting tin. Add the oil, za'atar and seasoning and toss so that the vegetables are coated. Roast in the oven for about 20 minutes until the vegetables are tender and starting to brown on the outside.

Meanwhile, steam the asparagus for 3–4 minutes until tender-crisp.

In a large bowl, combine the roasted vegetables and asparagus with the beans, spring onions, tomatoes, coriander or parsley and lemon juice. Divide the rocket between four plates, pile on the beans and vegetables, then top with a little extra coriander or parsley and crumbled goats' cheese.

NUTRITION per serving:
- 444 cals • 20 g protein • 16 g fat (7 g saturates)
- 48 g carbs (11 g total sugars) • 15 g fibre

Make it vegan

Substitute cashews for the goats' cheese.

WARM BARLEY SALAD WITH PINE NUTS AND POMEGRANATE

VG

This salad is substantial and tasty and has a great combination of colours and flavours. Barley is a bit of an unsung hero among grains: it's rich in B vitamins, iron and magnesium and is chewy and nutty when cooked (see 'What is pot barley?' below). It also contains a type of fibre called beta-glucan (also found in oats), which is beneficial for gut health. The fresh herbs and pomegranate seeds provide vitamin C, an important nutrient for recovery. You can substitute the red kidney beans for chickpeas or crispy fried tofu (see p. 117). Any leftovers make a perfect packed lunch the next day.

Preparation time: 5 minutes
Cooking time: 60 minutes

175 g (6 oz) pearl barley
1 l (1¾ pints) vegetable stock or water
1 bunch of spring onions, sliced
A handful of flat-leaf parsley, finely chopped
A small bunch of chives, finely chopped
400 g (14 oz) can red kidney beans
100 g (3½ oz) pomegranate seeds
150 g bag mixed salad leaves
100 g (3½ oz) feta, crumbled (optional)
50 g (2 oz) toasted pine nuts, roughly chopped (see p. 79)

For the dressing:
Juice of 1 lemon
2 tsp honey or maple syrup
2 tbsp extra virgin olive oil
Salt and freshly ground black pepper

Serves 4

Make it vegan

Simply omit the feta.

Rinse the barley under running water then place in a large saucepan with the stock or water. Bring to the boil, then simmer for 45 minutes to 1 hour or until cooked and tender. Rinse in cold water, then drain.

To make the dressing, place all the ingredients in a screw-top jar and shake well.

Tip the barley into a mixing bowl, add the dressing and toss to combine. Mix in the spring onions, herbs, red kidney beans and pomegranate seeds.

Divide the salad leaves between four plates and top with the pearl barley mixture. Crumble over the feta (if using) and top with the pine nuts.

NUTRITION per serving (including feta):
• 470 cals • 15 g protein • 21 g fat (5 g saturates)
• 52 g carbs (7 g total sugars) • 7 g fibre

WHAT IS POT BARLEY?

Pot barley is the wholegrain form of barley and is rich in B vitamins, vitamin E, iron, magnesium and fibre, specifically beta-glucan, which can help maintain normal cholesterol levels. Pearl barley is the most common variety you'll find in supermarkets. It contains fewer nutrients and less fibre than pot barley because the outer husk and bran layers have been removed. It takes around 45–60 minutes to cook, but precooked (or quick-cook) barley takes just 10–12 minutes. Look out too for mixtures of barley, split peas and lentils, which are higher in fibre and protein, and are excellent in soups and casseroles.

SUMMER VEGETABLES WITH CHICKPEAS AND TAHINI DRESSING

VG

If you're looking for an easy, delicious summer salad then this is what you need. I make this often during the summer months as a way of using up surplus homegrown courgettes, but it also works well with other veg, such as aubergines or butternut squash. I've included three different protein sources – chickpeas, walnuts and tahini (sesame seed paste) – to ensure a full complement of amino acids to support muscle growth. Walnuts also supply plant-based omega-3s, which are essential for healthy cell membranes and brain function. It's a tasty way to gets lots of colourful veg into your meal and the leftovers make a perfect lunch the next day.

Preparation time: 10 minutes
Cooking time: 20 minutes

4 courgettes, sliced lengthways into thick ribbons
1 red pepper, deseeded and chopped into 2.5-cm (1-in) pieces
2 tbsp light olive or rapeseed oil
1 tsp za'atar (Middle Eastern herbs available from most supermarkets) or dried thyme
50 g (2 oz) walnuts
400 g (14 oz) can chickpeas, rinsed and drained
100 g (3½ oz) mixed salad leaves
Salt and freshly ground black pepper

For the dressing:
2 tbsp tahini (sesame seed paste)
1 garlic clove, very finely chopped
Juice of 1 lemon
1 tbsp olive oil
1–2 tbsp water

Serves 4

Preheat the oven to 200 °C/fan 180 °C/gas mark 6.

Toss the courgettes and red pepper with the oil, za'atar and seasoning in a large roasting tin. Roast for 15–20 minutes or until the vegetables are tender and a little charred around the edges.

Spread the walnuts out on a baking tray and roast in the oven for about 5 minutes until fragrant.

For the dressing, mix together all the ingredients in a bowl. If the consistency is a bit too thick, thin out with a little water.

In a large bowl, mix together the roasted vegetables with the chickpeas, dressing and salad leaves. Divide between four bowls and scatter over the roasted walnuts.

> **NUTRITION per serving:**
> • 466 cals • 21 g protein • 25 g fat (3 g saturates)
> • 36 g carbs (7 g total sugars) • 5 g fibre

QUINOA, EDAMAME AND BROCCOLI SALAD WITH HAZELNUTS

One of my favourite simple salads, this is so quick and easy to put together and a great post-workout option during the week. It includes three protein sources – quinoa, edamame beans and hazelnuts – which provide an excellent combination of amino acids. The red peppers and broccoli add lots of vitamin C, which helps increase the amount of iron that can be absorbed from the quinoa and nuts. I love the contrasting colours and the mix of flavours. With a zesty kick from the lemon juice, it's a delicious way of speeding your muscle recovery.

Preparation time: 10 minutes

Cooking time: 20 minutes

150 g (5 oz) quinoa
200 g (7 oz) tenderstem broccoli
250 g (9 oz) frozen edamame beans
2 red peppers, deseeded
and cut into 3-cm (1½-in) strips
1 red onion, cut into 8 wedges
2 tbsp light olive or rapeseed oil
50 g (2 oz) hazelnuts
Salt and freshly ground black pepper

For the dressing:
2 tbsp olive oil
2 tbsp lemon juice
1 tsp honey or maple syrup

Serves 4

Preheat the oven to 200 °C/fan 180 °C/gas mark 6.

Cook the quinoa in a large saucepan of boiling water according to the directions on the packet. Add the broccoli to the pan for the last 5 minutes and the frozen edamame beans for the last 30 seconds of cooking. Refresh under cold water, drain in a colander and set aside.

Arrange the peppers and onion in a roasting tin. Drizzle with oil and sprinkle with a pinch of salt and pepper. Roast in the oven for about 15 minutes until the vegetables are slightly charred on the outside and tender in the middle.

Place the hazelnuts in another baking tray and roast for 8–10 minutes, until golden and fragrant. Meanwhile, make the dressing. Put the olive oil, lemon juice and honey or maple syrup in a bottle or screw-top jar and shake until combined.

Mix the roasted vegetables into the warm quinoa mixture. Add the dressing, mix together, then season to taste. Place in a serving bowl and sprinkle with the toasted hazelnuts.

NUTRITION per serving:
• 449 cals • 18 g protein • 26 g fat (3 g saturates)
• 32g carbs (8 g total sugars) • 10 g fibre

ROASTED VEGETABLES WITH TOFU AND WALNUTS

This is a brilliant salad for athletes as it combines three different protein sources: tofu, walnuts and peas. These combine to give you all the essential amino acids needed for muscle building and repair, so this recipe is ideal after any strength workout. It's also packed with phytonutrients, fibre and vitamin C. You can substitute sugar snap peas or edamame beans for the peas. I like to make big batches of this and eat the leftovers for lunch the next day.

Preparation time: 10 minutes
Cooking time: 20 minutes

2 red peppers, deseeded and cut into 3-cm (1½-in) strips
1 red onion, cut into 8 wedges
2 courgettes, sliced
3 tbsp light olive or rapeseed oil
1 tsp Italian seasoning (see Cook's tip)
250 g (9 oz) fresh or frozen peas
400 g (14 oz) firm tofu, cubed
50 g (2 oz) walnuts, toasted
(see 'How to toast nuts and seeds', p. 79)
Large handful of fresh coriander, chopped
Salt and freshly ground black pepper

For the dressing:
2 tbsp olive oil
Juice of ½–1 lemon
1 tsp honey or maple syrup

Serves 4

Preheat the oven to 200 °C/fan 180 °C/gas mark 6.

Arrange the peppers, onion and courgettes in a roasting tin. Drizzle with half the oil, sprinkle with the herbs and a little salt and pepper. Roast in the oven for about 15 minutes until the vegetables are slightly charred on the outside and tender in the middle.

Meanwhile, boil the peas in a little water for 3 minutes; drain.

Fry the tofu in the remaining oil until crispy on the outside (about 10 minutes). Meanwhile, make the dressing. Put the olive oil, lemon juice and honey or maple syrup in a bottle or screw-top jar and shake until combined.

Mix the roasted vegetables with the tofu and peas. Add the dressing and mix together. Transfer to a serving bowl and sprinkle with toasted walnuts and coriander.

> **NUTRITION per serving:**
> • 357 cals • 19 g protein • 23 g fat (3 g saturates)
> • 15 g carbs (11 g total sugars) • 8 g fibre

COOK'S TIP

Italian seasoning is a mixture of marjoram, onion, rosemary, thyme, basil, oregano, garlic powder and paprika. It's widely available in supermarkets but you can use dried thyme or oregano instead for this dish.

NEW POTATO AND BUTTER BEAN SALAD WITH PUMPKIN SEEDS

Creamy new potatoes and butter beans make one of the simplest salads ever! Here, I've combined them with colourful yellow peppers and green beans, both of which are rich in vitamin C, but feel free to swap them for asparagus, courgettes or tenderstem broccoli. I've included boiled eggs to increase the protein value of the dish, but you can substitute slices of grilled halloumi, if you prefer.

Preparation time: 10 minutes
Cooking time: 15 minutes

500 g (1 lb 2 oz) new potatoes
250 g (9 oz) green beans, trimmed and sliced
4 eggs
400 g (14 oz) can butter beans, rinsed and drained
1 bunch of spring onions, sliced
1 yellow pepper, deseeded and chopped into 2.5-cm (1-in) pieces
A handful of rocket
50 g (2 oz) pumpkin seeds, toasted (see 'How to toast nuts and seeds', p. 79)
Salt and freshly ground black pepper

For the dressing:
2 tbsp olive oil
1 garlic clove, very finely chopped
Juice of 1 lemon

Serves 4

Preheat the oven to 200 °C/fan 180 °C/gas mark 6.

Cook the new potatoes in a steamer or in boiling water for 15 minutes until just tender. Meanwhile, boil or steam the green beans in a separate pan for 5 minutes until tender-crisp. Drain.

At the same time, boil the eggs in a saucepan of water for 7 minutes (longer, if you prefer them more cooked). Plunge them into cold water, peel, then cut into wedges.

To make the dressing, place all the ingredients in a screw-top jar and shake well.

In a large bowl, mix together the potatoes, green beans, eggs, butter beans, spring onions and yellow pepper with the dressing and rocket. Season to taste. Scatter over the pumpkin seeds.

NUTRITION per serving:
• 328 cals • 17 g protein • 17 g fat (3 g saturates)
• 23 g carbs (5 g total sugars) • 9 g fibre

HARISSA ROASTED AUBERGINE WITH TABBOULEH

Aubergine halves are roasted with harissa, a traditional North African chilli and herb paste, and served on a bed of tabbouleh, a healthy Lebanese salad made with bulgur (cracked) wheat and fresh herbs. It's super-easy to make and a fantastic source of fibre, iron, zinc and vitamin C – all important nutrients for recovery after exercise.

Preparation time: 5 minutes
Cooking time: 25 minutes

2 aubergines
2 tbsp olive oil
1 tbsp runny honey
2 tsp harissa paste
1 garlic clove, crushed
1 tbsp water
150 g (5 oz) feta
Salt and freshly ground black pepper

For the tabbouleh:
225 g (8 oz) bulgur (cracked) wheat or
2 x 250 g (9 oz) pouches ready-to-eat bulgur wheat
A small bunch of spring onions, finely chopped
A large handful of flat-leaf parsley, chopped
A large handful of mint, chopped
225 g (8 oz) cherry tomatoes, halved
2 tbsp extra virgin olive oil
Juice of 1 lemon
Salt and freshly ground black pepper

Serves 4

Preheat the oven to 200 °C/ fan 180 °C/ gas mark 6.

Trim and slice the aubergines in half lengthways. Using a sharp knife, score the flesh side 1 cm (½ in) deep in a criss-cross diagonal pattern. Place, cut side up, in a roasting tin.

In a small bowl, mix together the olive oil, honey, harissa paste, garlic and seasoning and the water. Spoon half the glaze over the cut side of the aubergines and roast in the oven for 15 minutes. Spoon the remaining glaze over the aubergines and return to the oven for a further 8–10 minutes or until the aubergine is soft and the glaze sticky.

Meanwhile, make the tabbouleh. Cook the bulgur (cracked) wheat according to the packet instructions. Drain, fluff up with a fork and mix with the spring onions, herbs and tomatoes. Pour the olive oil and lemon juice into a bottle or screw-top jar and shake until combined. Mix into the tabbouleh and season with salt and freshly ground black pepper.

Divide the tabbouleh among four bowls, top with the aubergine and crumble the feta over the top to serve.

> **NUTRITION per serving:**
> • 471 cals • 15 g protein • 21 g fat (7 g saturates)
> • 51 g carbs (10 g total sugars) • 10 g fibre

Make it vegan

Swap the feta for toasted walnuts or pine nuts (see p. 79), and substitute maple syrup for honey.

CHAPTER 12

BURGERS AND FALAFELS

○ Clockwise from top left: *Chickpea and carrot burgers with lemon tahini dressing,
Bean and mushroom veggie balls, Falafel with tahini dressing,
Sweetcorn and black bean fritters with tomato salsa.*

CHICKPEA AND CARROT BURGERS WITH LEMON TAHINI DRESSING

These burgers were one of the most popular recipes from *The Vegetarian Athlete's Cookbook* (Bloomsbury, 2017). Here, I've made a few tweaks and added courgette for a slightly different flavour. Simple, delicious, crispy on the outside and soft on the inside, these burgers don't fall apart when cooked. They are high in protein, iron and fibre, thanks to the chickpeas and sunflower seeds, which make them an ideal recovery meal for promoting muscle repair after your workout.

Preparation time: 10 minutes

Cooking time: 20 minutes

1 small onion, roughly chopped
1 carrot, roughly chopped
1 small courgette, roughly chopped
400 g (14 oz) can chickpeas, drained
50 g (2 oz) oats
½ tsp each of: ground cumin, ground coriander and paprika
Small handful of chopped fresh coriander
1 tbsp lemon juice
1 egg
2 tbsp sunflower seeds
Olive oil, for brushing
Salt and freshly ground black pepper

For the dressing:
4 tbsp tahini (sesame seed paste)
4 tbsp hot water
1 garlic clove, minced
Juice of 1 lemon
Salt and freshly ground black pepper, to taste

To serve:
Sweet potato wedges (see p. 157) and a leafy salad

Makes 8

Preheat the oven to 190 °C/fan 170 °C/gas mark 5.

Place all the ingredients except the egg and sunflower seeds in a food processor and process for about 30 seconds until thoroughly combined (you may need to stop to scrape down the bowl during the process). Add the egg, salt and pepper and process for a further 10–15 seconds. Transfer to a bowl and stir in the sunflower seeds.

Shape the mixture into 8 balls and place on an oiled baking tray. Flatten lightly with your palm, then brush the burgers with a little olive oil. Bake in the oven for 20 minutes until crisp and light golden on the outside.

For the dressing, place all the ingredients in a small bowl and mix together.

Arrange the burgers on plates and serve with Sweet potato wedges (see p. 157) and a leafy salad with dressing on the side.

> **NUTRITION per burger:**
> • 107 cals • 5 g protein • 4 g fat (1 g saturates)
> • 12g carbs (2 g total sugars) • 3 g fibre

Make it vegan

Substitute the egg for a chia or flax egg (see p. 46).

BLACK BEAN AND BUTTERNUT SQUASH BURGERS

Although vegetarian burgers are widely available in supermarkets nowadays, they tend to be either very salty or lacking in flavour, so it really is worth making your own. These easy-to-make burgers, based on black beans, are full of flavour and vibrant colour, and packed with protein, fibre and iron. They are also a brilliant way of using up leftover roasted butternut squash, but feel free to substitute other veg, such as cooked sweet potatoes or red peppers. Make your own breadcrumbs by whizzing day-old bread for a few seconds in a food processor. Alternatively, substitute leftover cooked quinoa or rice.

Preparation time: 10 minutes

Cooking time: 20 minutes

1 tbsp light olive or rapeseed oil

1 small onion, finely chopped

1 garlic clove, crushed

400 g (14 oz) can black beans, rinsed and drained

225 g (8 oz) roasted butternut squash (see Cook's tip)

75 g (3 oz) wholemeal breadcrumbs

40 g (1½ oz) chopped walnuts

½ tsp each of ground cumin, smoked paprika and mild chilli powder

Small handful of chopped fresh coriander or parsley

Salt and freshly ground black pepper

1 egg

Olive oil, for brushing

To serve:

Wholemeal pitta breads, baby spinach, avocado slices, toasted pine nuts and tahini (sesame seed paste)

Makes 8

Preheat the oven to 190 °C/fan 170 °C/gas mark 5.

Heat the oil in a non-stick frying pan over a medium heat. Add the onion and fry for 3 minutes until translucent. Add the garlic and continue cooking for a further minute.

Put the onion, half the black beans and the remaining ingredients in a food processor and process for 30 seconds until combined (you may need to stop to scrape down the bowl a couple of times). Turn out into a large bowl and mix in the remaining beans. Alternatively, mix the ingredients together with a potato masher or fork.

Shape the mixture into 8 patties and place on an oiled baking tray. Flatten lightly with your palm, then brush the burgers with a little olive oil. Bake in the oven for 20 minutes until they are lightly crisp on the outside.

Serve in toasted wholemeal pitta breads with baby spinach, avocado slices, pine nuts and drizzled with tahini.

> **NUTRITION per burger:**
> • 126 cals • 6 g protein • 5 g fat (1 g saturates)
> • 13 g carbs (3 g total sugars) • 4 g fibre

HOW TO PEEL A BUTTERNUT SQUASH

Place the butternut squash on a chopping board and slice about 1 cm (½ in) off the ends with a chef's knife (a large sharp knife). Holding the squash in one hand, peel off the outer layer with a vegetable peeler. Cut the squash in half at the neck. To cut the neck end, cut the squash into rings the desired width of your squash pieces, then lay them flat on the chopping board. Cut them into long rectangles, then crosswise to make cubes. To cut the body, cut the squash in half and scrape out the seeds using a metal spoon. Lay the halves cut side down, slice lengthways and then crosswise to make cubes.

COOK'S TIP

I recommend making a big batch of roasted butternut squash and keeping it in the fridge for up to three days for use in salads, curries and burgers, or adding to lunchboxes. Place the butternut squash cubes in a large roasting tin. Season with salt and black pepper, drizzle over a little olive oil and toss lightly to coat. Roast in a preheated oven at 200 °C/fan 180 °C/gas mark 6 for about 25 minutes until slightly charred on the outside and tender in the middle.

Make it vegan

Substitute the egg for a chia or flax egg (see p. 46).

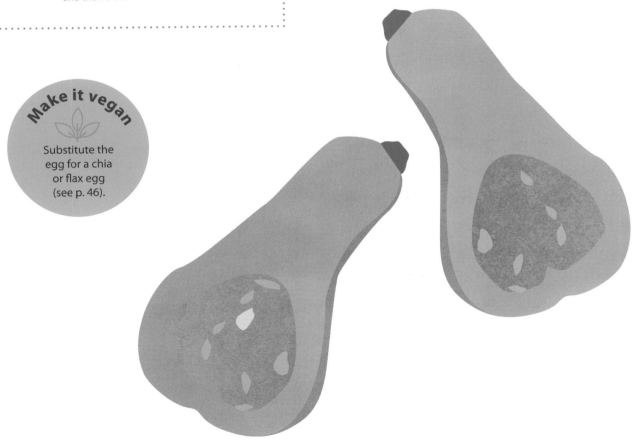

BEAN AND MUSHROOM VEGGIE BALLS

This tasty veggie alternative to meatballs is made with red kidney beans and mushrooms. They're super-easy to make, packed with protein, fibre and loads of vitamins. You can swap the red kidney beans for black beans or borlotti beans. I prefer baking them instead of frying (which, of course, you can) as it's less messy, but just as tasty! Should you have any leftover balls, wrap them in foil and keep in the fridge for up to three days or in the freezer for up to one month.

Preparation time: 10 minutes
Cooking time: 20 minutes

1 onion, finely chopped
2 carrots, grated
225 g (8 oz) mushrooms, sliced
1 garlic clove, crushed
400 g (14 oz) can red kidney beans, drained and rinsed
½ tsp cayenne pepper or chilli powder (optional)
1 tsp dried oregano
50 g (2 oz) wholemeal bread, torn into pieces
A handful of parsley, chopped
1 tbsp lemon juice
1 egg
Olive oil for brushing
Salt and freshly ground black pepper

To serve:
Spaghetti and fresh tomato sauce

Makes 20

Preheat the oven to 190 °C/fan 170 °C/gas mark 5.

Place the onion, carrots, mushrooms, garlic, kidney beans, cayenne or chilli powder (if using), oregano and bread in a food processor and blitz until well combined. Add the parsley, lemon juice and egg and season with salt and freshly ground black pepper. Pulse until combined. Alternatively, place in a large mixing bowl and mash together with a potato masher until well combined.

Form the mixture into 20 balls. Place on an oiled baking tray, brush with a little oil and bake in the oven for 15–18 minutes until golden. Serve with spaghetti and fresh tomato sauce.

> **NUTRITION per ball:**
> • 31 cals • 2 g protein • 0 g fat (0 g saturates)
> • 4 g carbs (1 g total sugars) • 2 g fibre

Make it vegan

Substitute the egg for a chia or flax egg (see p. 46).

SWEETCORN AND BLACK BEAN FRITTERS WITH TOMATO SALSA

VG

These Mexican-inspired fritters are super-quick to make and perfect for brunch after your workout or as a main dish with a leafy salad. Black beans are a brilliant source of protein and fibre and also supply significant amounts of iron, which is important for making haemoglobin in your red blood cells. These fritters can be made using fresh or canned sweetcorn, or sweetcorn thawed from frozen. If you want to make them from fresh sweetcorn, you'll need three cobs of fresh corn. Remove the husks, then cut the kernels off the cob (see 'Cook's tip' below).

Preparation time: 10 minutes
Cooking time: 10 minutes

400 g (14 oz) can black beans, drained and rinsed
340 g (13 oz) can sweetcorn (or 2 x 198 g cans)
2 garlic cloves, crushed
1 tsp ground cumin
½ tsp smoked paprika
½–1 red or green chilli, deseeded and finely chopped (or 1 tsp chilli powder)
175 g (6 oz) cornmeal (or plain flour)
100 ml (3½ fl oz) water
1 egg
A handful of parsley or coriander leaves, finely chopped
2 tbsp light olive oil
Salt and freshly ground black pepper

Mix together the salsa ingredients in a medium bowl. Season with salt and pepper to taste.

In a large bowl, roughly mash the beans with a fork, add the remaining fritter ingredients, except the oil, and stir to combine.

Heat the oil in a large frying pan over a medium heat and fry tablespoons of the fritter mixture, pressing lightly with a spatula to flatten. Cook for about 2–3 minutes each side until golden brown and cooked through. Serve with the salsa and a leafy salad.

NUTRITION per fritter:
- 175 cals • 6 g protein
- 5 g fat (1 g saturates)
- 25 g carbs (2 g total sugars)
- 4 g fibre

Make it vegan

Substitute the egg for a chia or flax egg (see p. 46).

For the salsa:
2 large tomatoes, finely diced
A handful of fresh coriander, chopped
½ green chilli, deseeded and finely chopped (optional)
1 tsp olive oil
½ red onion, finely chopped
1 tbsp lemon or lime juice
Salt and freshly ground black pepper

To serve:
A leafy salad

Makes 8

COOK'S TIP

To remove the corn from the cob, place the cob flat on a chopping board. Using a sharp knife, cut down the side of the cob to remove all the kernels, then rotate the cob so the cut end is on the board. Continue cutting and rotating until all the kernels are removed.

FALAFEL WITH TAHINI DRESSING

The recipe for Baked falafel in *The Vegetarian Athlete's Cookbook* (Bloomsbury, 2017) uses tinned chickpeas, but since then, I've discovered that using raw chickpeas and frying them instead of baking produces an even tastier falafel that's wonderfully crispy on the outside and soft and moist on the inside. Chickpeas are a brilliant source of plant protein, fibre, iron and magnesium. This recipe takes no more time to make (apart from remembering to soak the chickpeas the night before!) and the falafels hold together well when you cook them. It's important to heat the oil to a high temperature before cooking the falafels to ensure they don't absorb too much oil.

Preparation time:
10 minutes (plus soaking)
Cooking time: 10 minutes

125 g (4 oz) raw chickpeas
1 small onion, roughly chopped
A small bunch of fresh coriander, roughly chopped
2 garlic cloves, crushed
2 tsp ground cumin
½ tsp ground coriander
½ tsp paprika
Juice of ½ lemon
½ tsp salt
1 tbsp gram flour (or plain flour)
½ tsp baking powder
2 tbsp tahini (sesame seed paste)
4 tbsp light olive or rapeseed oil, for frying

For the dressing:
3 tbsp tahini (sesame seed paste)
3 tbsp hot water
1 garlic clove, crushed
Juice of ½ lemon
Dash of Tabasco
Salt and freshly ground black pepper

To serve:
Warmed wholemeal pittas, hummus,
shredded lettuce and sliced tomatoes

Makes 16

The day before you make the falafel, place the chickpeas in a large bowl and cover with plenty of cold water. Leave overnight – they will double in size as they soak.

The following day, drain and rinse the chickpeas. Put them in a food processor along with the remaining falafel ingredients. Pulse until combined (you may need to stop and scrape the bottom and sides of the food processor a couple of times). The mixture should hold together, be fairly smooth but still with a bit of texture.

Take spoonfuls of the mixture and form into walnut-sized balls using wet hands. You can make them larger or smaller, if you prefer. They will be fairly crumbly, but don't worry – they will miraculously stick together when you cook them.

Heat the oil in a non-stick frying pan over a medium-high heat and lower the falafel into the oil using a spoon (you may need to do this in two batches). After browning on one side, about 2 minutes, flip them over gently, and brown on the other side. Remove with a slotted spoon.

For the tahini dressing, simply stir all the ingredients together until smooth. Taste and adjust the seasoning, if necessary. Serve with the falafels alongside warmed pittas, hummus, shredded lettuce and sliced tomatoes.

NUTRITION per falafel:
• 79 cals • 3 g protein • 5 g fat (1 g saturates)
• 5 g carbs (1 g total sugars) • 2 g fibre

BAKED SWEET POTATO FALAFELS WITH YOGURT DRESSING

In this recipe, I've combined cooked sweet potatoes with ground chickpeas for a softer texture and a more interesting flavour. The addition of the sweet potato makes the falafel moist, so, unlike most baked falafel, they won't become dry or turn crumbly during baking. They are high in protein and beta-carotene, which is an antioxidant that helps support the immune system. You can substitute a 400 g (14 oz) can of chickpeas for the raw chickpeas to save time.

Preparation time: 10 minutes
(plus overnight soaking)
Cooking time: 55 minutes

1 large sweet potato, peeled and cubed
1 tbsp olive oil
100 g (3½ oz) raw chickpeas, soaked overnight
1 garlic clove, crushed
1 tsp ground cumin
1 tsp ground coriander
½ tsp ground cinnamon
2 tbsp fresh coriander
Sesame seeds, to coat
Salt and freshly ground black pepper

For the dressing:
½ cucumber, peeled, deseeded and diced
200 g (7 oz) plain Greek yogurt
1 tbsp chopped coriander
1 tbsp chopped fresh mint
Salt and freshly ground black pepper

Makes 12

Preheat the oven to 180 °C/fan 160 °C/gas mark 4.

Place the sweet potato on a baking tray, drizzle with the oil, season with salt and pepper, then roast in the oven for 30 minutes.

Rinse the chickpeas and put them in a food processor. Process until they resemble couscous. Add the roasted sweet potato, garlic, spices and fresh coriander and pulse until just combined. Alternatively, use a fork to mash together.

Form the mixture into 12 balls. Roll them in the sesame seeds, then arrange on a baking sheet lined with greaseproof paper. If you have time, place the mixture in the fridge for a couple of hours to firm up as this makes it easier to shape the falafels. Turn the oven up to 200 °C/fan 180 °C/gas mark 6, then bake for 20–25 minutes until crisp and golden.

For the dressing, mix the diced cucumber, yogurt and herbs in a bowl and season with salt and pepper.

NUTRITION per falafel:
• 53 cals • 2 g protein • 1 g fat (0 g saturates)
• 7 g carbs (1 g total sugars) • 2 g fibre

Make it vegan

Substitute soya yogurt for the Greek yogurt.

SPINACH AND BUTTER BEAN BURGERS

Butter beans add a creaminess to these burgers while spinach provides vibrant colour, making them a brilliant way of getting lots of protein, iron, folate and fibre. The garlic, cumin and paprika give a fantastic flavour. If you want more heat, add a small chopped red chilli or a sprinkling of cayenne pepper. They are perfect for making ahead – keep them in the freezer and pop under the grill whenever you need a quick meal.

Preparation time: 10 minutes
Cooking time: 20 minutes

1 small onion, roughly chopped
1–2 garlic cloves, crushed
400 g (14 oz) can butter beans, rinsed and drained
50 g (2 oz) oats
1 tsp ground cumin
1 tsp sweet paprika
Juice of ½ lemon
Generous pinch of salt
Freshly ground black pepper
100 g (3½ oz) baby spinach
1 egg
2 tbsp mixed seeds
Olive oil, for brushing

To serve:
Wholemeal buns, rocket, tomato and avocado slices, salsa

Makes 8

Preheat the oven to 190 °C/fan 170 °C/gas mark 5.

Place the onion, garlic, butter beans, oats, spices, lemon juice and seasoning in a food processor and process until roughly combined. Add a handful of spinach, pulse and then repeat until all the spinach is incorporated. Add the egg and process for a few more seconds. Stir in the mixed seeds. Taste and adjust the seasoning if necessary.

Shape the mixture into 8 balls and place on an oiled baking tray. Flatten lightly with your palm, then brush the burgers with a little olive oil. Bake in the oven for 20 minutes until lightly crisp on the outside.

Place burgers in toasted wholemeal buns with rocket, tomato and avocado slices and salsa.

NUTRITION per burger:
- 91 cals • 5 g protein • 3 g fat (1 g saturates)
- 9 g carbs (1 g total sugars) • 3 g fibre

Make it vegan

Substitute the egg for a chia or flax egg (see p. 46).

SOUPS

○ Clockwise from top left: *Spinach and broccoli soup with cannellini beans, Ramen noodle soup with crispy tofu, Thai curry soup, Butternut squash soup with chickpeas.*

SPINACH AND BROCCOLI SOUP WITH CANNELLINI BEANS

This is such an easy way of getting your daily vitamin C in one dish. Broccoli and spinach are loaded with it, along with lots of iron, which is so important for regular exercisers. The addition of the cannellini beans is a brilliant way to increase your protein and fibre and makes the soup filling and satiating. You can substitute other types of beans, such as butter beans or chickpeas, for the cannellini beans. Make a large batch and it will keep in the fridge for up to three days or in the freezer for up to three months (see 'How to freeze soup', below).

Preparation time: 10 minutes
Cooking time: 20 minutes

2 tbsp light olive oil or rapeseed oil
1 onion, finely chopped
1 garlic clove, crushed
1 celery stick, chopped
1 carrot, peeled and sliced
300 g (10 oz) broccoli
1 small potato, chopped
2 tsp vegetable bouillon (stock) powder dissolved in 900 ml (1½ pints) hot water
150 g (5 oz) baby spinach
400 g (14 oz) can cannellini beans, rinsed and drained
Freshly ground black pepper

To serve:
Grated Cheddar cheese and wholegrain bread

Serves 4

Heat the oil in a large saucepan over a medium heat. Add the onion and fry for 2–3 minutes until translucent. Add the garlic and celery and continue cooking for another minute. Add the carrot, broccoli, potato and vegetable stock. Bring to the boil, then reduce to a simmer for 15 minutes or until the vegetables are cooked through (add a little more stock or water if you think it needs it). Stir in the spinach, then turn off the heat.

Liquidise the soup using a hand blender or conventional blender. Stir in the cannellini beans and heat through. Season with freshly ground black pepper and serve sprinkled with grated Cheddar and with wholegrain bread on the side.

NUTRITION per serving:
- 198 cals • 10 g protein • 7 g fat (1 g saturates)
- 20 g carbs (5 g total sugars) • 10 g fibre

Make it vegan

Serve with toasted pumpkin seeds instead of cheese (see 'How to toast nuts and seeds', p. 79).

HOW TO FREEZE SOUP

Allow the soup to cool, then ladle individual portions into zip-lock freezer bags (remember to label and date them first). Let out any excess air and seal. Soup will expand in the freezer, so don't over-fill the bags. Place in rigid plastic containers or simply lay in a single layer in the freezer. Once frozen, remove the containers and your soups will be frozen into easily storable shapes.

PEA AND COURGETTE SOUP

This healthy soup is full of green goodness and a brilliant way of getting lots of phytonutrients (plant nutrients that are beneficial to health). The peas add a lovely, vibrant colour to the soup, as well as protein, vitamin C and fibre. It is also a great way to use up any vegetables you have in the fridge. You can swap the cabbage for other green veg, such as spinach, kale or Baby Gem lettuce. This soup will keep in the fridge for up to three days or in the freezer for up to three months (see 'How to freeze soup', p. 113).

Preparation time: 10 minutes
Cooking time: 15 minutes

2 tbsp light olive or rapeseed oil
1 onion, finely chopped
2 garlic cloves, crushed
125 g (4 oz) green cabbage, shredded
2 medium courgettes, sliced
1 l (1¾ pints) vegetable stock
(or 2–3 tsp vegetable bouillon (stock) powder dissolved in 1 l/1¾ pints hot water)
200 g (7 oz) frozen peas
A squeeze of lemon juice
Salt and freshly ground black pepper

To serve:
4 tbsp plain Greek yogurt
Wholegrain bread

Serves 4

Heat the oil in a large saucepan over a low heat and cook the onion for 5 minutes. Add the garlic and continue cooking for 1 minute before adding the cabbage, courgettes and vegetable stock. Bring to the boil, cover and simmer for 4 minutes. Add the peas and cook for a further 3 minutes.

Add the lemon juice, then liquidise the soup using a hand blender or conventional blender. Season to taste before ladling into bowls. Serve swirled with the Greek yogurt and some wholegrain bread on the side.

> **NUTRITION per serving (including yogurt):**
> • 153 cals • 10 g protein • 6 g fat (1 g saturates)
> • 12 g carbs (9 g total sugars) • 5 g fibre

Make it vegan

Serve with a non-dairy yogurt alternative instead of Greek yogurt.

RED LENTIL AND CARROT SOUP

This warming soup is simple and easy to make, and can be made in advance and kept in the fridge for up to three days, or in the freezer for up to three months (see 'How to freeze soup', p. 113). Red lentils are filling and highly nutritious, packed with protein, iron and B vitamins. They provide a sustained energy release, making this a perfect pre- or post-workout meal.

Preparation time: 5 minutes
Cooking time: 25 minutes

2 tbsp light olive or rapeseed oil
1 onion, finely chopped
2 garlic cloves, crushed
2 carrots, peeled and sliced
150 g (5 oz) red lentils
1 l (1¾ pints) vegetable stock
(or 2–3 tsp vegetable bouillon (stock)
powder dissolved in 1 l/1¾ pints water)
A handful of fresh coriander, chopped
Salt and freshly ground black pepper, to taste

To serve:
Plain Greek yogurt and toasted
wholewheat pitta breads

Serves 4

Heat the oil in a large saucepan over a medium heat and fry the onion for 5 minutes until translucent. Add the garlic and cook for 1 minute, stirring continuously. Add the carrots, lentils and stock. Bring to the boil, then reduce the heat and simmer for about 20–25 minutes until the lentils are very soft.

Add the coriander, liquidise the soup with a hand blender or in a conventional blender (or leave chunky, if you prefer). Add a little more water or stock if you want a thinner consistency. Season to taste, ladle into bowls, swirl some yogurt on top and serve with toasted pitta bread.

> **NUTRITION per serving (without yogurt):**
> • 207 cals • 10 g protein • 6 g fat (1 g saturates)
> • 26 g carbs (6 g total sugars) • 5 g fibre

Make it vegan

Serve with a non-dairy yogurt alternative instead of Greek yogurt.

THAI CURRY SOUP

If you like Thai food, then you'll love the subtle curry flavours of this simple soup, which makes an ideal recovery meal. I use red curry paste for speed, but if you prefer more heat, then you can add extra fresh or dried chilli. This recipe is rich in protein, thanks to the tofu, and packed with lots of vitamins and phytonutrients. You can add any other vegetables you've got to hand, such as red peppers, pak choi (Chinese cabbage) or broccoli.

Preparation time: 10 minutes
Cooking time: 20 minutes

1 tbsp sesame or light olive oil
1–2 tbsp red curry paste, or to taste
200 ml (7 fl oz) light coconut milk
1 l (1¾ pints) vegetable stock
(or 2–3 tsp vegetable bouillon (stock) powder dissolved in 1 l/1¾ pints hot water)
1 tbsp tamari or soy sauce
175 g (6 oz) thin rice noodles
250 g (9 oz) firm tofu, cut into 1–2cm (½–1in) cubes
125 g (4 oz) sugar snap peas, halved
175 g (6 oz) baby corn
100 g (3½ oz) shiitake mushrooms, sliced

To serve:
25 g (1 oz) peanuts, toasted
A small handful of basil leaves, torn

Serves 4

Heat the oil in a large pan or wok over a medium heat. Add the curry paste and cook for 30 seconds until aromatic. Gradually add the coconut milk and stir until blended. Add the vegetable stock and tamari or soy sauce.

Add the noodles, tofu and vegetables to the pan. Simmer for 3 minutes, or until the vegetables are crisp-tender.

Take the pan off the heat. Ladle the soup into four bowls, scatter the peanuts and basil leaves on top and serve.

NUTRITION per serving:
• 318 cals • 14 g protein • 11 g fat (4 g saturates)
• 39 g carbs (4 g total sugars) • 4 g fibre

WHAT IS TOFU?

Tofu is basically soya milk that is coagulated and pressed. There are several ways manufacturers coagulate the tofu and that's what makes all the difference. Tofu made with nigari (a powder produced from seawater that's rich in magnesium chloride) has a smoother texture than tofu made with calcium sulphate, which has a less cohesive structure. However, this type of tofu is rich in calcium. Silken tofu is made with gluconolactone (derived from cornflour) and calcium sulphate, which produces a smooth jelly-like texture.

The difference between soft, medium and firm tofu is in how much water is pressed out of the tofu. Soft tofu has the least amount of water pressed out, while extra-firm has a low moisture content and a dense texture, as well as a higher protein content. Firm tofu absorbs flavours well and is best used for stir-frying or crumbling for tofu scramble (see p. 46). Extra-firm tofu holds its shape well and can be cut into cubes or slices for frying, grilling or baking. Silken tofu is unpressed and has a more gelatinous texture, so is best suited to smoothies, desserts, sauces and dips.

BUTTERNUT SQUASH SOUP WITH CHICKPEAS

This comforting soup is a staple in my house during the autumn and winter months. It's such an easy way to get lots of vitamins, minerals, fibre and protein all in one dish. Butternut squash is packed with carotenoids, which support the immune system and protect cells from damaging free radicals. Adding chickpeas is a great way of bumping up the protein as well as giving the soup interesting texture. It will keep in the fridge for up to three days or in the freezer for up to three months (see 'How to freeze soup', p. 113).

Preparation time: 10 minutes
Cooking time: 20 minutes

2 tbsp light olive oil or rapeseed oil
1 onion, finely chopped
½ medium butternut squash (about 500 g/1 lb 2 oz), peeled and cut into 2cm (1in) cubes
1 carrot, peeled and sliced
1 garlic clove, crushed
1 tsp fresh ginger, peeled and grated
Pinch of nutmeg, freshly grated (optional)
1 l (1¾ pints) vegetable stock
(or 2–3 tsp vegetable bouillon (stock) powder dissolved in 1 l/1¾ pints hot water)
400 g (14 oz) can chickpeas, drained and rinsed
Salt and freshly ground black pepper

To serve:
4 tbsp low-fat plain Greek yogurt
Rye bread

Serves 4

Heat the oil in a large saucepan over a medium heat. Add the onion and fry for about 5 minutes until translucent. Add the butternut squash, carrot, garlic, ginger and nutmeg, if using. Stir and continue cooking for a few minutes.

Add the vegetable stock, bring to the boil, then lower the heat, cover and simmer for about 20 minutes until the vegetables are tender. Remove from the heat and liquidise with a hand blender or in a conventional blender until smooth.

Return to the saucepan, add the chickpeas and heat through again. Season with salt and freshly ground black pepper. Serve topped with a swirl of Greek yogurt and rye bread on the side.

> **NUTRITION per serving (including yogurt):**
> • 233 cals • 12 g protein • 8 g fat (1 g saturates)
> • 26 g carbs (11 g total sugars) • 8 g fibre

Make it vegan

Serve with a non-dairy yogurt alternative instead of Greek yogurt.

RAMEN NOODLE SOUP WITH CRISPY TOFU

This quick ramen soup is packed with lots of fresh flavours. The delicious combination of noodles and tofu gives you sustained energy, making this an ideal pre-workout meal. You'll also be getting plenty of vitamins and phytonutrients that support the immune system. Intense exercise can sometimes depress the immune system for several hours, so consuming a nutrient-rich meal beforehand can help mitigate the effects. I like to add crispy tofu, but you can substitute halved hard-boiled eggs if you prefer – allow one egg per portion.

Preparation time: 10 minutes
Cooking time: 10 minutes

2 tbsp sesame or light olive oil
1–2 garlic cloves, crushed
2.5 cm (1 in) fresh ginger, peeled and grated
2 tbsp brown miso paste
1 l (1¾ pints) vegetable stock
(or 2–3 tsp vegetable bouillon (stock) powder dissolved in hot water)
200 g (7 oz) soba or wheat noodles
4 heads pak choi (Chinese cabbage), trimmed and sliced
150 g (5 oz) mixed mushrooms, sliced
2 carrots, cut into thin strips
2 tbsp light soy sauce
250 g (9 oz) firm tofu, cut into triangular pieces

To serve:
6 spring onions, sliced on the diagonal
Sriracha sauce or chilli oil, to taste (optional)

Serves 4

Heat half the oil in a large pan over medium-low heat. Add the garlic and ginger; stir-fry for 1–2 minutes or until soft and fragrant. Add the miso paste, vegetable stock and noodles. Bring to the boil, then reduce to a simmer and cook for 3 minutes. Add the pak choi, mushrooms, carrots and soy sauce and cook for a further 2–3 minutes.

Meanwhile, heat the remaining oil in a non-stick frying pan or wok over a high heat. Add the tofu and fry for 10 minutes, stirring frequently, until golden and crispy on the outside.

Divide the soup between four bowls and top with the spring onions, crispy tofu and sriracha sauce or chilli oil to taste.

NUTRITION per serving:
- 329 cals • 18 g protein • 11 g fat (2 g saturates)
- 38 g carbs (6 g total sugars) • 6 g fibre

CURRIES, STEWS AND MORE

○ Clockwise from top left: *Lentil, chickpea and spinach dahl, Vegetarian shepherd's pie with sweet potato mash, Yellow rice and black beans with broccoli, Quick vegetarian chilli.*

BLACK BEAN AND
SWEET POTATO CURRY

Black beans and sweet potatoes provide a fantastic combination of carbohydrate and protein to replenish your muscles after a workout. They are also packed with fibre, which feeds the trillions of good microbes that live in your gut, as well as iron that you need for making haemoglobin in your red blood cells (see 'The health benefits of beans' below). I like to add spinach to this curry for extra vitamin C, which helps the body absorb iron from the beans and also makes a lovely colour contrast.

Preparation time: 5 minutes
Cooking time: 25 minutes

2 sweet potatoes, scrubbed and cubed
½ butternut squash (approx. 500 g/1 lb 2 oz), peeled and cut into 1 cm (½ in) cubes (see p. 101)
1½ tsp each: ground cumin, ground coriander, turmeric, sweet paprika and garam masala
2 tbsp light olive or rapeseed oil
1 onion, finely chopped
2–3 garlic cloves, crushed
1 tsp grated fresh ginger
400 g (14 oz) can chopped tomatoes
1 tbsp tomato purée
250 ml (9 fl oz) hot water
2 x 400 g (14 oz) cans black beans, drained and rinsed
200 g (7 oz) baby spinach, or pak choi (Chinese cabbage), roughly chopped
A handful of fresh coriander, chopped
Juice of ½ lemon
50 g (2 oz) cashews
Salt and freshly ground black pepper

To serve:
Plain Greek yogurt

Serves 4

Make it vegan

Serve with a non-dairy yogurt alternative.

Preheat the oven to 200 °C/fan 180 °C/gas mark 6. Place the prepared sweet potatoes and butternut squash on a baking tray, sprinkle over a little salt and ½ teaspoon each of cumin and paprika. Add 1 tablespoon of the oil and toss so all vegetables are well coated. Roast in the oven for 20–25 minutes.

Meanwhile, heat the remaining oil in a large pan over a low to moderate heat. Add the onion and fry for 3–4 minutes until softened. Add the garlic, ginger and remaining spices. Continue cooking for 1 minute. Add the canned tomatoes, tomato purée, hot water and beans. Bring to the boil then reduce the heat and simmer for 10 minutes.

Add the roasted vegetables and baby spinach or pak choi and turn off the heat (the spinach will wilt down). Stir in the coriander (reserve a little to serve), lemon juice and cashews and season to taste. Serve with the yogurt and scatter over the remaining coriander.

NUTRITION per serving:
• 462 cals • 18 g protein • 13 g fat (2 g saturates)
• 57 g carbs (17 g total sugars) • 16 g fibre

THE HEALTH BENEFITS OF BEANS

All beans are rich in protein, iron, magnesium and B vitamins, as well being an excellent source of fibre, which feeds the healthy microbes in your gut (see p. 23). The recommended daily fibre intake is 30 g, but the average person consumes only 18 g. Eating beans regularly will promote a healthy and diverse gut microbiome, which can affect your exercise performance through improved immunity, faster recovery and lowered inflammation. A healthy gut microbiome also improves the body's ability to gain energy and nutrients from the food we eat.

ROASTED CAULIFLOWER AND LENTIL CURRY

A bowl of this tasty curry with brown rice is perfect when it's cold outside and you want to fill your stomach with warming goodness. Lentils are a fantastic source of plant-based protein as well as fibre, iron and zinc, making this an ideal post-workout meal. I use pre-cooked puy lentils, which provide a nice colour contrast with the cauliflower, but any lentils will work for this recipe. Roasting the cauliflower this way brings out extra depth of flavour and sweetness, and saves time as it cooks while you're making the sauce.

Preparation time: 5 minutes
Cooking time: 25 minutes

1 medium cauliflower, broken into bite-sized florets
1 tsp each: cumin, sweet paprika
2 tbsp olive oil
1 onion, finely chopped
2 garlic cloves
1 cm (½ in) fresh ginger, peeled and grated
4 cardamom pods, crushed
1 tsp each: coriander, turmeric and garam masala
100 g (3½ oz) mangetout (or green beans)
200 g (7 oz) canned chopped tomatoes
200 ml (7 fl oz) water
250 g (9 oz) packet cooked Puy lentils
1 tbsp lemon juice
1 tbsp toasted pine nuts
A handful of chopped flat-leaf parsley
½ fresh red chilli, deseeded and finely sliced (optional)
Salt and freshly ground black pepper

To serve:
Cooked wholegrain rice and plain yogurt

Serves 4

Make it vegan
Simply serve with a non-dairy yogurt alternative.

Preheat the oven to 200 °C/fan 180 °C/gas mark 6.

Place the cauliflower on a baking tray, sprinkle over a little salt and ½ teaspoon each of cumin and paprika. Add 1 tablespoon oil and toss so the cauliflower is well coated. Roast in the oven for 20–25 minutes until tender.

Meanwhile, heat the remaining oil in a large pan over a low to moderate heat. Add the onion and fry for 3–4 minutes until softened. Add the garlic, ginger and remaining spices. Continue cooking for 1 minute. Add the mangetout (or green beans), tomatoes and water, bring to the boil then reduce the heat and simmer for 10 minutes.

Add the lentils, roasted cauliflower and lemon juice, season and stir through. Remove from the heat and scatter over the pine nuts, chopped parsley and chilli slices (if using). Serve with the rice and yogurt.

NUTRITION per serving:
• 243 cals • 12 g protein • 10 g fat (1 g saturates)
• 22 g carbs (9 g total sugars) • 9 g fibre

THE HEALTH BENEFITS OF CAULIFLOWER

Cauliflower is a member of the cruciferous family of vegetables, and is a good source of beta-carotene, vitamin C and folic acid. It is also rich in a group of phytochemicals called glucosinolates, which break down in the body to isothiocyanates, which may have a protective effect against certain cancers. People who eat large amounts of cruciferous vegetables (which also include cabbage, Brussels sprouts, broccoli and kale) have been shown to have a lower risk of cancer.

THAI GREEN CURRY WITH TOFU

This Asian-inspired curry is full of colourful vegetables, so it's rich in phytochemicals, vitamins and fibre. I've added tofu for protein and pak choi (Chinese cabbage) for its high vitamin C content and distinctive Thai flavour. You can substitute other vegetables, such as green cabbage, asparagus, broccoli, green peppers or carrots, for the ones in this recipe. I recommend frying the tofu before adding to the other ingredients as it imparts a lovely crispiness to an otherwise bland ingredient, yet absorbs surprisingly little oil.

Preparation time: 10 minutes
Cooking time: 15 minutes

3 tbsp light olive or rapeseed oil
400 g (14 oz) firm tofu, cut into 2.5-cm (1-in) cubes
1 onion, diced
2 tbsp Thai green curry paste (bought or homemade, see Cook's note)
400 ml (14 fl oz) light coconut milk
125 g (4 oz) baby corn
100 g (3½ oz) mushrooms, sliced
125 g (4 oz) mangetout
250 g (9 oz) pak choi (Chinese cabbage), cut into large pieces
1 tbsp lime juice
A handful of fresh coriander, chopped
50 g (2 oz) cashews, toasted
Salt and freshly ground black pepper

To serve:
Cooked brown rice

Serves 4

Heat 2 tablespoons of the oil in a wok or large non-stick pan. Add the tofu cubes and fry until golden brown, about 5 minutes. Transfer to a plate.

Heat the remaining oil in the wok, add the onion and fry for 3 minutes. Add the curry paste, continue cooking for 1 minute, then add the coconut milk. Add the baby corn, mushrooms and mangetout. Bring to the boil, reduce the heat, cover and simmer for 4–5 minutes, then add the pak choi.

Continue cooking for 1 minute, then add the tofu and lime juice. Season with salt and pepper and stir in the coriander, reserving a little for the garnish. Divide into bowls (add a layer of cooked brown rice first) and top with cashews and the remaining coriander.

NUTRITION per serving:
- 384 cals • 19 g protein • 28 g fat (10 g saturates)
- 11 g carbs (7 g total sugars) • 5 g fibre

COOK'S NOTE

Here's how to make your own Green Thai Curry Paste:
1 cm (½ in) fresh ginger, unpeeled
4 garlic cloves
A bunch of fresh coriander, roughly chopped
1 small green chilli, deseeded and roughly chopped
Place all the ingredients in a food processor and blitz for a few seconds until you have a coarse paste.

LENTIL, CHICKPEA AND SPINACH DAHL

This warming dahl includes three different protein sources – lentils, chickpeas and cashews – which makes it an excellent recovery meal after a workout. Lentils and chickpeas both supply lots of iron, important for making haemoglobin in red blood cells, which carry oxygen from the lungs to the rest of the body. It is estimated that 30 per cent of female athletes, although not anaemic, have iron deficiency. I've added mangetout and spinach, which are both rich in vitamin C and increase iron uptake by the body. Courgettes, tomatoes, squash or other vegetables can be added as well.

Preparation time: 5 minutes
Cooking time: 25 minutes

2 tbsp light olive or rapeseed oil
1 large onion, finely chopped
3 cardamon pods, crushed
2 garlic cloves, crushed
2.5 cm (1 in) fresh ginger, peeled and grated
1 green chilli, deseeded and finely sliced, or to taste
1 tsp each: ground cumin and ground coriander
2 tsp turmeric
½ tsp garam masala
200 g (7 oz) red lentils
600 ml (1 pint) hot water
250 g (9 oz) mangetout
400 g (14 oz) can chickpeas, rinsed and drained
100 g (3½ oz) baby spinach
50 g (2 oz) cashew nuts
Juice of 1 lemon
A small bunch of fresh coriander, chopped
Salt and freshly ground black pepper

To serve:
Plain yogurt

Serves 4

Heat the oil in a heavy-based pan over a medium heat. Add the onion and cardamom pods and fry for 4–5 minutes until the onion is translucent. Add the garlic, ginger, chilli and spices and continue cooking for a further minute, stirring continuously.

Add the lentils and hot water, then bring to the boil. Cover and simmer for about 20 minutes, adding the mangetout and chickpeas for the final 5 minutes of cooking. Turn off the heat and stir in the spinach (it will wilt down and cook in the heat of the pan).

Stir in the cashew nuts and lemon juice and season with salt and freshly ground black pepper. Finally, stir in the fresh coriander. Serve with a swirl of plain yogurt.

> **NUTRITION per serving (without yogurt):**
> • 415 cals • 22 g protein • 14 g fat (2 g saturates)
> • 44 g carbs (6 g total sugars) • 10 g fibre

Make it vegan

Simply serve with a non-dairy yogurt alternative.

QUICK VEGETARIAN CHILLI

This recipe is made almost entirely from store-cupboard ingredients, so it's perfect for those evenings when you are tempted to order a takeaway! Beans and sweetcorn are fantastic sources of fibre and the tomato chilli sauce adds wonderful spicy flavour. I've included spinach for extra iron and vitamin C, but you can omit it, if you prefer.

Preparation time: 10 minutes
Cooking time: 15 minutes

1 tbsp light olive or rapeseed oil
1 large onion, finely chopped
2–3 garlic cloves, crushed
1 tsp chilli powder, or to taste
1 tbsp sweet paprika
½ tsp dried oregano
1 tsp ground cumin
400 g (14 oz) can chopped tomatoes
1 tbsp tomato purée
2 x 400 g (14 oz) cans red kidney beans, drained and rinsed
200 g (7 oz) can sweetcorn, drained
100 g (3½ oz) fresh or frozen spinach
A handful of fresh parsley, chopped (optional)
Salt and freshly ground pepper

To serve:
Cooked brown rice or pitta breads and grated cheese

Serves 4

Heat the oil in a large non-stick pan over a medium heat. Add the onion and fry for 3–4 minutes until translucent. Add the garlic, chilli powder, paprika, oregano and cumin and cook for a further minute. Add the tomatoes, tomato purée, kidney beans and sweetcorn and bring to the boil. Reduce the heat and simmer for 10 minutes until the sauce has thickened.

Season with salt and freshly ground pepper, then stir in the spinach and parsley, if using. Turn off the heat – the spinach will wilt down in the heat of the pan. Serve with rice or pitta bread and a sprinkling of grated cheese.

NUTRITION per serving:
• 237 cals • 12 g protein • 4 g fat (1 g saturates)
• 31 g carbs (10 g total sugars) • 14 g fibre

Make it vegan

Substitute a non-dairy yogurt alternative for the grated cheese.

VEGETARIAN SHEPHERD'S PIE WITH SWEET POTATO MASH

This recipe is a firm favourite with my family and I often make it on chilly winter evenings as it's so warming and comforting. It combines nutritious root vegetables with beans and paprika for a rich, spicy flavour. It's then topped off with a layer of creamy sweet-potato mash. Sweet potatoes have a similar calorie and carbohydrate content to ordinary potatoes but are richer in beta-carotene. They also supply lots of fibre, B vitamins and vitamin C. Although it doesn't qualify as a 30-minute recipe, I wanted to include it as it is perfect if you want to meal prep and freezes brilliantly (for up to three months). So make extra and save the rest for when you don't feel like cooking.

Preparation time: 10 minutes
Cooking time: 40 minutes

350 g (12 oz) sweet potatoes
350 g (12 oz) butternut squash, peeled and cut into 3-cm (1½-in) pieces (see p. 101)
2 tbsp milk (any type)
1 tbsp olive oil
1 large onion, finely chopped
2 garlic cloves, crushed
1 tsp sweet paprika
1 red pepper, deseeded and finely chopped
2 carrots, sliced
150 g (5 oz) button mushrooms
2 celery stalks, chopped
400 g (14 oz) can black beans, drained and rinsed
400 g (14 oz) can red kidney beans, drained and rinsed
400 g (14 oz) can chopped tomatoes
3 tbsp tomato purée
2 tsp dried thyme
Splash of water or stock
A handful of fresh parsley, roughly chopped
Salt and freshly ground black pepper

To serve: Broccoli and green beans

Serves 4

Preheat the oven to 200 °C/fan 180 °C/gas mark 6.

Boil the sweet potatoes and butternut squash for about 15 minutes until tender. Drain, then mash with the milk, and salt and pepper to taste.

Meanwhile, heat the olive oil in a large non-stick pan over a medium heat and fry the onion for 3 minutes until translucent. Add the garlic and paprika and cook for 1 minute before adding the pepper, carrots, mushrooms and celery. Stir, and cook for a further 5 minutes.

Add the beans, canned tomatoes, tomato purée, thyme and a splash of water or stock. Mix then bring to the boil. Lower the heat and simmer for 10 minutes until slightly thickened and reduced. Stir in the parsley.

Spoon the bean mixture into an ovenproof dish, top with the mash and then bake in the oven until the mashed potato starts to crisp and brown at the edges, about 20 minutes. Serve with broccoli and green beans.

NUTRITION per serving:
• 373 cals • 15 g protein • 5 g fat (1 g saturates)
• 58 g carbs (21 g total sugars) • 19 g fibre

COOK'S TIP
You can substitute other types of beans or canned green or puy lentils for the beans in this recipe.

SPICY BEANS WITH QUINOA

This is one of my go-to midweek speedy meals when I am pressed for time. The secret ingredient is cooked quinoa, which is widely available in packets and pouches in supermarkets, but cooked rice or other grain mixtures will also work well. Quinoa has one and a half times more protein than pasta, rice and other grains, and is rich in anti-inflammatory nutrients, which makes it ideal after a workout. I've used black beans in this recipe because they provide an attractive colour contrast with the quinoa, but you can substitute red kidney or flageolet beans. The red peppers in this recipe are rich in vitamin C, which helps increase the absorption of iron from the beans and quinoa.

Preparation time: 5 minutes
Cooking time: 15 minutes

2 tbsp light olive or rapeseed oil
1 onion, finely chopped
1–2 garlic cloves, crushed
1 red pepper, deseeded and finely chopped
1 celery stick, finely chopped
400 g (14 oz) can black beans (or other beans)
400 g (14 oz) can chopped tomatoes
1 tsp ground cumin
1 tsp oregano
½ tsp chilli powder, or to taste
250 g (9 oz) packet cooked quinoa
A handful of fresh coriander or parsley, chopped
Salt and freshly ground black pepper

To serve:
Plain Greek yogurt

Serves 4

Heat the oil over a moderate heat in a non-stick frying pan then add the onion and fry for 3 minutes until translucent. Add the garlic and cook for a further 30 seconds. Add the red pepper and celery and continue cooking for 5 minutes.

Add the beans, tomatoes, cumin, oregano and chilli powder and cook for 5 minutes. Stir in the quinoa, most of the coriander or parsley, warm through, and season with salt and pepper. Spoon into bowls, garnish with remaining coriander or parsley and serve with plain yogurt.

> **NUTRITION per serving:**
> • 290 cals • 11 g protein • 9 g fat (1 g saturates)
> • 37 g carbs (9 g total sugars) • 9 g fibre

Make it vegan

Simply serve with a non-dairy yogurt alternative.

VEGETARIAN GOULASH

This recipe comes courtesy of my Hungarian mother, who made it regularly during my childhood (evoking much curiosity from our Hungarian relatives, who had never tasted a goulash without meat!). Here, I've replaced the meat in the traditional version with butter beans, although you can use borlotti or black beans. The secret ingredient in any goulash is sweet paprika, which lends a distinctive, rich flavour to the stew. This dish provides plenty of protein, vitamin C, fibre and phytonutrients, making it an ideal recovery meal.

Preparation time: 10 minutes

Cooking time: 20 minutes

1 tbsp light olive or rapeseed oil

1 large onion, finely chopped

3 garlic cloves, crushed

1 carrot, sliced

2 peppers (any colour), deseeded and sliced

400 g (14 oz) can chopped tomatoes

1 courgette, sliced

150 g mushrooms, halved or quartered

2 large potatoes, sliced

400 g (14 oz) can butter or borlotti beans, drained and rinsed

500 ml (17 fl oz) vegetable stock (or 2 tsp vegetable bouillon/stock powder dissolved in hot water)

2 tbsp Hungarian (sweet) paprika

2 tbsp tomato purée

2 bay leaves

Salt and freshly ground black pepper

To serve:

4 tbsp plain Greek yogurt

Serves 4

Heat the oil in a large non-stick pan over a medium heat. Add the onion and fry for 3 minutes until translucent, then add the garlic and continue cooking for 1 minute. Add the remaining vegetables and cook for a further 2–3 minutes.

Add the remaining ingredients, apart from the yogurt. Season, stir and bring to the boil, then simmer for 10 minutes until the vegetables are tender, the flavours have infused nicely and the sauce has reduced a little. Serve with a spoonful of yogurt.

NUTRITION per serving (including yogurt):
- 277 cals • 15 g protein • 4 g fat (1 g saturates)
- 41 g carbs (15 g total sugars) • 11 g fibre

Make it vegan

Simply serve with a non-dairy yogurt alternative.

YELLOW RICE AND BLACK BEANS WITH BROCCOLI

This classic combination of rice and beans provides plenty of protein and carbohydrate, so is ideal before or after a workout. Here, I've given it a modern twist with miso (see 'The health benefits of miso', p. 148) and spices, and added broccoli for a vibrant colour contrast and additional phytonutrients. These play a role in muscle adaptation as well as having cancer preventative properties.

Preparation time: 10 minutes
Cooking time: 15 minutes

2 tbsp light olive or rapeseed oil
1 onion, finely chopped
2 garlic cloves, crushed
1 tsp grated fresh ginger
2 tsp white miso paste
½ tsp turmeric
½ tsp ground coriander
½ tsp ground cumin
Pinch of cayenne pepper
225 g (8 oz) basmati rice
600 ml (20 fl oz) vegetable stock or water
1 head (approx. 350 g/12 oz) of broccoli, broken into small florets
150 g (5 oz) green beans, trimmed and cut into 3-cm (1½-in) lengths
400 g (14 oz) can black beans, rinsed and drained

Serves 4

Heat the oil in a large non-stick pan over a medium heat. Add the onion and fry for 3 minutes until translucent, then add the garlic and ginger and cook for 1 minute. Stir in the miso paste, turmeric, coriander, cumin, cayenne and rice.

Add the stock or water and bring to the boil. Lower the heat, cover and cook for 10–12 minutes, stirring occasionally, until the rice is tender. Make sure it does not boil dry; add extra stock or water if necessary.

Stir in the broccoli and green beans 5 minutes before the end of cooking time. Stir in the black beans and serve hot.

NUTRITION per serving:
• 418 cals • 16 g protein • 8 g fat (1 g saturates)
• 65 g carbs (7 g total sugars) • 11 g fibre

PUY LENTIL BOLOGNESE

This speedy dish combines puy lentils and vegetables in a tasty tomato sauce. Lentils are brilliant for athletes as they digest slowly and produce a gradual, sustained rise in blood sugar levels, making them an ideal pre-workout food. I've added lots of colourful vegetables to this recipe, so it's full of vitamins, phytonutrients and iron to support your immunity. You can also make it with uncooked puy lentils: add them with the canned tomatoes, then cook for 30 minutes.

Preparation time: 10 minutes
Cooking time: 20 minutes

2 tbsp light olive or rapeseed oil
1 onion, finely chopped
2 garlic cloves, crushed
2 sticks of celery, finely chopped
100 g (3½ oz) mushrooms, chopped
1 carrot, finely chopped
1 red pepper, deseeded and finely diced
1 courgette, diced
400 g (14 oz) can chopped tomatoes
1 tsp vegetable bouillon (stock) powder
1 tsp dried thyme
2 bay leaves
2 tbsp tomato purée
2 x 250 g (9 oz) packets cooked puy or beluga lentils (or 2 x 400 g/14 oz cans lentils, drained)
100 g (3½ oz) baby spinach
Salt and freshly ground black pepper, to season

To serve:
Wholemeal pasta and plain Greek yogurt

Serves 4

Heat the oil in a large pan over a medium heat. Add the onion and fry for 3 minutes until translucent. Add the garlic, celery, mushrooms, carrot, pepper and courgette. Cook for a further 2 minutes then add the canned tomatoes, vegetable bouillon, herbs, tomato purée and lentils. Bring to the boil, reduce the heat, half-cover the pan and simmer for 15 minutes until the vegetables are tender. Add a little water or stock if the mixture starts to stick to the pan.

Add the spinach, mix, cover and cook for a further minute to wilt the leaves. Season with salt and freshly ground black pepper and serve with pasta and yogurt.

NUTRITION per serving (without yogurt):
• 299 cals • 17 g protein • 8 g fat (1 g saturates)
• 33 g carbs (10 g total sugars) • 13 g fibre

Make it vegan
Simply serve with a non-dairy yogurt alternative.

MOUSSAKA BOWLS

I love the sweet, charred flavours of moussaka, but rarely have the time to make the oven-baked version. This speedy recipe contains all the ingredients and flavours of a slow-cooked moussaka but without the wait. It's high in protein, thanks to the lentils and yogurt, so is perfect for aiding muscle recovery after a workout.

Preparation time: 10 minutes
Cooking time: 20 minutes

2 tbsp light olive or rapeseed oil
1 onion, finely chopped
2 courgettes, trimmed and sliced
1 red or yellow pepper, deseeded and chopped into 1-cm (½-in) pieces
2 garlic cloves, crushed
½ tsp ground cinnamon
1 tbsp fresh oregano or 1 tsp dried oregano
400 g (14 oz) can chopped tomatoes
2 tbsp tomato purée
400 g (14 oz) can green lentils, drained and rinsed
1 tsp vegetable bouillon (stock) powder
2 aubergines, sliced into 1-cm (½-in) rounds
4 large tomatoes, sliced
400 g (14 oz) low-fat plain Greek yogurt or non-dairy yogurt alternative
Pinch of freshly grated nutmeg
4 tbsp vegetarian Parmesan (optional)

To serve:
A handful of fresh flat-leaf parsley, roughly torn

Serves 4

Make it vegan
Use a non-dairy yogurt alternative and omit the cheese.

Preheat the grill to high.

Heat half the oil in a large non-stick pan over a medium-high heat and fry the onion for 2–3 minutes until translucent. Add the courgettes and pepper and cook, stirring, until softened, about 5 minutes. Add the garlic, cinnamon and oregano, and cook for 1 minute more.

Stir in the chopped tomatoes, tomato purée, lentils and vegetable bouillon (stock) powder, and simmer for 10 minutes. If the sauce gets too dry, just add a splash of water.

Meanwhile, place the aubergine slices on a baking tray, brush with the remaining olive oil and grill for about 2–3 minutes on each side or until golden brown and softened. Alternatively, you can cook them on a griddle pan over a high heat until charred and tender.

Assemble your bowls with the lentils, tomato and aubergine slices. Spoon over the yogurt and sprinkle with grated nutmeg and cheese (if using). Grill the moussaka until the cheese is golden and bubbling, about 5 minutes, then scatter over the parsley to serve.

> **NUTRITION per serving:**
> • 305 cals • 22 g protein • 9 g fat (2 g saturates)
> • 29 g carbs (18 g total sugars) • 12 g fibre

VEGETARIAN PARMESAN

You can get Parmesan-like Italian-style cheeses, and variations of others which are suitable for vegetarians. Vegetarian cheese is made with non-animal rennet derived from microbial sources, rather than animal sources. In cheese making, rennet is used to separate the milk into curds and whey. Traditionally, rennet was sourced from calves' stomachs, but it is only used for a few cheeses nowadays. These include Parmesan Reggiano, Grana Padano, Pecorino Romano, Manchego, Gruyere and Gorgonzola.

TURKISH-STYLE CHICKPEA PILAF

This simple one-pot dish made with brown rice and chickpeas is an ideal pre-workout meal.
The combination of brown basmati rice and chickpeas will give you sustained energy and stop
you feeling hungry for hours. Chickpeas are great for athletes as they're high in protein, carbs,
B vitamins and fibre, while dried apricots add iron and beta-carotene. I like to add a green
vegetable such as cavolo nero (a dark-leaved variety of kale) or spinach for extra iron.
If you don't have allspice, use 2 teaspoons curry powder instead.

Preparation time: 10 minutes
Cooking time: 20 minutes

200 g (7 oz) basmati rice
(or 2 x 250 g/9 oz packets cooked basmati rice)
150 g (5 oz) cavolo nero (shredded) or kale
2 tbsp light olive or rapeseed oil
1 onion, finely chopped
1–2 garlic cloves, crushed
½–1 green chilli, deseeded and finely chopped
½–1 tsp ground allspice
400 g (14 oz) can chickpeas, rinsed and drained
50 g (2 oz) dried apricots, chopped
A handful of fresh parsley, chopped
50 g (2 oz) pistachios
Salt and freshly ground black pepper

To serve:
4 tbsp plain Greek yogurt and a leafy salad

Serves 4

If using dried rice, bring 500 ml (17 fl oz) water or vegetable stock to the boil in a large pan. Add the rice and cook for 10–12 minutes or until the rice is tender and the water has been absorbed. Make sure it does not boil dry; add extra water, if necessary. Add the cavolo nero for the last 5 minutes of cooking.

Meanwhile, heat the oil in a large non-stick pan and fry the onion for 3 minutes. Add the garlic, chilli and allspice, and cook a further 1 minute.

Drain the rice of any excess water (or open the packets of cooked rice, if using). Add to the frying pan with the drained chickpeas and apricots and heat through over a gentle heat for a further 3 minutes. Stir in the parsley and pistachios, season and serve with a spoonful of plain Greek yogurt and salad.

NUTRITION per serving (including yogurt):
• 473 cals • 19 g protein • 17 g fat (2 g saturates)
• 57 g carbs (10 g total sugars) • 9 g fibre

Make it vegan

Simply use a
non-dairy yogurt
alternative.

WEEKEND DINNERS

○ Clockwise from top left: *Black bean and avocado quesadillas, Halloumi, vegetable and sesame skewers, Bean enchiladas, Udon noodles and crunchy vegetables with crisp tofu.*

BEAN ENCHILADAS

This recipe is a long-standing favourite in my house, and one I have been making for more than 25 years! Made mostly from store-cupboard ingredients, it's rich in fibre and packed with lots of protein, thanks to the beans and cheese, and vitamin C from the colourful peppers. You can substitute other kinds of beans, such as borlotti, black-eyed beans or chickpeas, or add other vegetables, such as chopped broccoli or spinach. For a spicier flavour, use a jar of enchilada or tomato and chilli pasta sauce instead of the passata.

Preparation time: 10 minutes

Cooking time: 20 minutes

2 tbsp light olive or rapeseed oil
1 onion, finely chopped
1 red pepper, deseeded and diced
1 yellow pepper, deseeded and diced
1 tbsp taco seasoning mix (or mix together
1 tsp cumin, 1 tsp cayenne pepper and ¼ tsp salt)
400 g (14 oz) can red kidney beans,
drained and rinsed
200 g (7 oz) can sweetcorn, drained and rinsed
200 g (7 oz) can chopped tomatoes
300 ml (10 fl oz) passata
4 soft wheat tortillas
125 g (4 oz) Cheddar, grated

To serve:
Leafy salad

Serves 4

Preheat the oven to 180 °C/fan 160 °C/gas mark 4.

Heat the oil in a non-stick ovenproof frying pan over a medium-low heat and add the onion. Fry for about 3 minutes until softened, then add the peppers and cook for a further 2 minutes. Mix in the taco seasoning (or spices), followed by the beans, sweetcorn and chopped tomatoes. Cook for a further 2 minutes.

Place 1–2 tablespoons of the passata in an ovenproof dish and spread out evenly along the base (this prevents the enchiladas from sticking to the bottom). Spoon a quarter of mixture into the centre of each tortilla and a little cheese (save some for the topping), then roll up. Place the tortillas folded side down side by side in the dish. Pour the remaining passata over the tortillas and scatter over the rest of the cheese.

Bake in the oven for 15 minutes or until golden on top, then serve with salad.

> **NUTRITION per serving:**
> • 497 cals • 21 g protein • 17 g fat (8 g saturates)
> • 58 g carbs (18 g total sugars) • 15 g fibre

HALLOUMI, VEGETABLE AND SESAME SKEWERS

These kebabs are perfect for barbecues and outdoor cooking, although I also cook them under the grill during winter. I'm a big fan of halloumi – it's lower in fat than most hard cheeses but equally rich in protein and calcium – and this is my favourite way to eat it. Its chewy texture and salty taste go beautifully with the crispiness of the vegetables in this recipe. As the vegetables are cooked only briefly and over a high heat, they retain most of their nutrients. I've included colourful peppers here (see 'The health benefits of peppers' below) but you can use other vegetables too, such as cherry tomatoes, aubergines or pieces of corn on the cob.

Preparation time: 10 minutes

Cooking time: 10 minutes

250 g (9 oz) halloumi, cut into 2.5-cm (1-in) cubes

2 red onions, quartered

2 red or yellow peppers, deseeded and cut into 2.5-cm (1-in) pieces

3 courgettes, cut into 2.5-cm (1-in) pieces

16 button mushrooms

For the dressing:

2 tbsp extra virgin olive oil

Juice of 1 lemon

A small handful of chopped fresh herbs, such as thyme, rosemary, mint or parsley

2 tbsp sesame seeds

Salt and freshly ground black pepper

To serve:

Warm flatbreads, rocket and watercress

Makes 8 skewers

Make it vegan

Substitute cubes of firm tofu for the halloumi.

Soak 8 bamboo skewers in a bowl of water for a few minutes (this stops them burning). Thread the halloumi cubes and vegetables onto the skewers. In a bowl, mix together the ingredients for the dressing and brush the skewers with half the dressing.

Place a griddle pan or barbecue on a medium heat. Add the skewers and cook for 5 minutes before turning over and cooking on the other side for 5 minutes until lightly charred. Drizzle with the remaining dressing before serving with warm flatbreads, rocket and watercress.

NUTRITION per skewer:
• 181 cals • 10 g protein • 13 g fat (6 g saturates)
• 6 g carbs (5 g total sugars) • 3 g fibre

THE HEALTH BENEFITS OF PEPPERS

Peppers are loaded with vitamin C – half a pepper provides your daily requirement – as well as fibre, beta-carotene and polyphenols. The brighter the colour, the more phytonutrients peppers contain. Red peppers can contain up to five times more polyphenols as the green varieties. Grilling (and roasting) them further improves the polyphenol content, as the nutrients become more concentrated in the cooking process.

MISO AUBERGINES WITH TOFU, SESAME AND CHILLI

Aubergines are rich in antioxidant phytochemicals, specifically nasunin, which gives the skin its purple hue and protects cell membranes from damage by free radicals. In this recipe, it pairs beautifully with the salty and sweet Japanese flavours in the miso glaze (see 'The health benefits of miso' below). Chilli adds a punchy kick to liven up both the aubergines and the crispy tofu.

Preparation time: 5 minutes
Cooking time: 25 minutes

2 aubergines
250 g (9 oz) firm tofu, cut into 1.5-cm (¾-in) slices
2 tbsp white miso paste
1 tbsp honey or maple syrup
2 tbsp tamari or soy sauce
2 tbsp sesame or olive oil
1 red chilli, deseeded and finely chopped
2.5 cm (1 in) fresh ginger, peeled and grated
2 garlic cloves, crushed
2 tbsp sesame seeds
4 spring onions, thinly sliced

To serve:
Wholewheat couscous, stir-fried pak choi (Chinese cabbage) or spring greens

Serves 4

Preheat the oven to 200 °C/fan 180 °C/gas mark 6.

Slice the aubergines in half lengthways then score the cut sides in a criss-cross pattern, cutting almost all the way down through the flesh but without piercing the skin. Transfer to a baking tray, cut sides up, along with the tofu.

Mix the miso paste, honey or maple syrup, tamari or soy sauce, oil, chilli, ginger and garlic with 2–3 tablespoons water in a bowl. Spread half the dressing over the aubergine flesh. Roast the aubergines in the oven for 20 minutes until the flesh is soft. Brush with the remaining glaze and return to the oven for a further 5 minutes until the top is bubbling and golden brown.

Arrange on a plate and scatter with the sesame seeds and spring onion slices. Serve with wholewheat couscous and stir-fried pak choi (Chinese cabbage) or spring greens.

> **NUTRITION per serving:**
> • 236 cals • 12 g protein • 15 g fat (2 g saturates)
> • 11 g carbs (8 g total sugars) • 7 g fibre

THE HEALTH BENEFITS OF MISO

This protein-rich ingredient is made from fermented soy beans and contains millions of probiotic bacteria. As a fermented food, miso provides the gut with beneficial bacteria that help us to stay healthy, ward off illnesses and absorb nutrients.

BUTTERNUT SQUASH AND FETA 'SAUSAGE ROLLS'

Butternut squash is such a healthy ingredient for athletes and its naturally sweet flavour pairs beautifully with salty feta, which also binds the filling together (see 'How to peel a butternut squash', p. 101). It's rich in beta-carotene and vitamins C and E, as well as the phytonutrients, zeaxanthin and lutein, which promote eye health and may help prevent age-related macular degeneration. I'll often make the filling with leftover roasted butternut squash (I recommend making a big batch as it's so versatile for salads and lunches on the go). Alternatively, follow the roasting instructions below, which will take you over the 30-minute recipe allocation but save time later if you make enough for leftovers. These rolls are equally delicious filled with cooked spinach or grated courgettes and feta.

Preparation time: 15 minutes
Cooking time: 15–40 minutes

1 onion, roughly chopped
½ medium (500 g/1 lb 2 oz) butternut squash, peeled and cut into 5 mm (¼ in) cubes
1 tbsp light olive oil
A few sprigs of rosemary (alternatively, 1 tsp dried thyme)
200 g (7 oz) feta cheese, roughly crumbled
50 g (2 oz) pine nuts, toasted
4 sheets filo pastry (each approx. 380 x 300 mm/15 x 12 in)
4 tbsp extra virgin olive oil for brushing
Salt and freshly ground black pepper

To serve:
A leafy salad and a baked sweet potato

Serves 4

Preheat the oven to 200 °C/fan 180 °C/gas mark 6.

Arrange the onion and squash in a roasting tin. Drizzle with olive oil and sprinkle with rosemary (or thyme), then season. Toss lightly so that the vegetables are coated in oil, then roast in the oven for 25 minutes or until the squash is tender.

Crumble the feta into a large bowl, then add the cooked squash and mash roughly with a fork. Mix in the pine nuts.

Unfold the filo sheets. Brush each one lightly with olive oil. Fold in half lengthways so they are half the length (i.e. 380 x 150 mm/15 x 6 in), then brush again with oil. Place a quarter of the butternut and feta mixture on the end of each piece, fold a little pastry over the filling, then fold in the edges. Roll up to form a neat roll.

Place on an oiled baking sheet, seam side down. Brush with olive oil, then bake for 15 minutes until lightly golden and crisp.

NUTRITION per serving:
• 475 cals • 14 g protein • 33 g fat (10 g saturates)
• 28 g carbs (9 g total sugars) • 5 g fibre

WHAT IS SOCCA

Socca is a type of pancake originating from Nice that also doubles as a flatbread or pizza base. It's made with chickpea (gram) flour, which is produced simply from ground chickpeas and is widely available from supermarkets. Use in place of flour to make pancakes, flatbreads and pizza bases. It has a wonderful nutty flavour reminiscent of falafel that lends itself to the contrasting crisp textures of fresh Mediterranean vegetables.

SOCCA FLATBREAD WITH ROASTED MEDITERRANEAN VEGETABLES

This easy flatbread is made with chickpea (gram) flour, which is a brilliant alternative to standard wheat flour as it's high in protein, rich in fibre and has all the nutritional benefits of chickpeas (see 'What is socca?', opposite). It requires no kneading – you simply add water to it and leave for 30 minutes or so. It magically transforms into a thick batter that you fry in much the same way as making pancakes. In this recipe, I've used it to make a thick pancake or flatbread, which I've layered with fresh tomatoes, roasted peppers, courgettes and olives, but you can substitute other vegetables.

Preparation time: 10 minutes
Cooking time: 20 minutes

250 g (9 oz) chickpea (gram) flour
A pinch of salt
300 ml (14 fl oz) water
Pinch of bicarbonate of soda (or baking powder)
1 red onion, cut into wedges
1 red or yellow pepper, deseeded and sliced
1 courgette, sliced on the diagonal
2 tbsp olive oil, plus extra for cooking
2 garlic cloves, crushed
2 tbsp pesto (optional)
2–3 large tomatoes, thinly sliced
A handful of black olives
100 g (3½ oz) mozzarella, sliced (optional)

To serve: A leafy salad

Makes 8

Place the chickpea flour and salt in a bowl. Gradually whisk in the water (use a handheld or electric whisk or blender) until you have a smooth, thick batter. Leave to stand for 30 minutes to allow the chickpea flour to absorb the water, then stir in the bicarbonate of soda or baking powder.

Preheat the oven to 200 °C/fan 180 °C/gas mark 6.

Toss the onion, pepper, courgette slices and garlic with the olive oil in a large roasting tin so they are well-coated. Roast in the oven for 10 minutes.

To make the flatbreads, heat a little olive oil in a non-stick frying pan over a medium–high heat. When the pan is hot, pour in a ladleful of the batter. Swirl around the pan to coat. Cook for 2 minutes, flip and then cook the other side for 1–2 minutes. Slide onto an oiled baking tray. Repeat the process with the remaining batter.

Spread the pesto (if using) over the socca base, then arrange the tomato slices and roasted vegetables on top. Scatter over the olives and cheese (if using). Return to the oven for 5–7 minutes until the cheese has melted and the socca is crisp at the edges. Serve with a leafy salad.

> **NUTRITION per flatbread (including mozzarella):**
> • 212 cals • 10 g protein • 9 g fat (3 g saturates)
> • 20 g carbs (4 g total sugars) • 5 g fibre

Make it vegan

Omit the mozzarella and scatter over pine nuts instead before returning to the oven.

BLACK BEAN AND AVOCADO QUESADILLAS

Quesadillas are a fun take on wraps – they're essentially fried tortilla sandwiches filled with Mexican-inspired ingredients, such as beans and cheese. They're more substantial than sandwiches and look infinitely more impressive – I've even served them to lunchtime guests to much awe and praise! This recipe with black beans takes minutes to make and is a fantastic way of adding lots of fibre, protein, vitamin E and iron to your diet. Make it in advance then wrap in foil for a tasty post-workout meal on the go.

Preparation time: 5 minutes
Cooking time: 10 minutes

2 tbsp olive oil
1 red onion, sliced
1 red pepper, deseeded and diced
1 tbsp taco seasoning (see box), or to taste
400 g (14 oz) can black beans, drained and rinsed
Juice of 1 lime
4 flour tortillas
75 g (3 oz) Cheddar cheese, grated
2 handfuls baby spinach or rocket
A large handful of chopped fresh coriander
1 large avocado, peeled, pitted and chopped
Salt and freshly ground black pepper

To serve: Lime wedges

Makes 4

Heat half the oil in a non-stick frying pan over a medium heat and fry the onion and pepper for 2–3 minutes until softened. Add the taco seasoning and cook for 1 minute more. Add the beans, season with salt and pepper, then cook for about 2 minutes. Remove from the heat, stir in half the lime juice and crush lightly with a potato masher or fork.

Lay two of the tortillas on a clean work surface. Spread the bean mixture out using a spoon to completely cover the tortillas, then scatter over the cheese and a layer of baby spinach or rocket. Place the remaining tortillas on top, gently pressing down.

Heat the remaining oil in a non-stick frying pan over a medium heat and fry the quesadillas for about 2 minutes on each side or until the cheese has begun to melt and the tortillas are crisp.

Remove the quesadillas from the pan and slice each one into 6 wedges. Scatter over the chopped avocado and serve garnished with the coriander leaves and lime wedges.

Make it vegan

Simply omit the cheese.

NUTRITION per serving:
• 458 cals • 15 g protein • 25 g fat (8 g saturates)
• 39 g carbs (6 g total sugars) • 10 g fibre

HOW TO MAKE YOUR OWN TACO SEASONING

1 tbsp chilli powder
1 tsp paprika
½ tsp garlic powder
¼ tsp dried oregano
½ tsp ground cumin
1 tsp salt

Put all ingredients into a small airtight jar, close the lid and shake to combine.

GREEN SPANISH TORTILLA

This nutritious combination of eggs, potato and vegetables contains plenty of carbohydrates, protein and healthy fats, making it an ideal pre-workout meal. It provides sustained energy so will fuel the toughest of workouts and keep hunger at bay. Adding spinach and peas gives a vibrant twist as well as extra fibre and phytonutrients to fuel your good gut microbes. It's also rich in iron, which is needed for making haemoglobin, the oxygen-carrying protein component in your red blood cells.

Preparation time: 10 minutes
Cooking time: 20 minutes

300 g (10 oz) new potatoes, peeled and cut into medium slices
150 g (5 oz) green beans, halved
200 g (7 oz) frozen peas
200 g (7 oz) baby spinach
1 tbsp light olive or rapeseed oil
1 onion, finely chopped
2 garlic cloves, crushed
3 sprigs of thyme, leaves picked, or ½ tsp dried
2 handfuls of flat-leaf parsley, chopped
6 large eggs
Salt and freshly ground black pepper

To serve:
Crusty wholegrain bread and a tomato salad

Serves 4

Cook the potatoes in a large steamer or pan of boiling water for 6 minutes or until tender. Add the green beans, peas and spinach for the last 3 minutes. Remove from the heat and set aside.

Meanwhile, heat the oil in an ovenproof frying pan over a medium-low heat. Add the onion and fry for 3 minutes or until softened. Add the garlic, thyme, salt and pepper, mix well and cook for a further 1 minute. Add the potato-vegetable mixture plus the parsley.

Preheat the grill to medium.

In a large bowl, beat the eggs, then add to the pan. Swirl the pan and cook over a gentle heat for 4–5 minutes until the mixture starts to set. Transfer to the grill and cook for 2–3 minutes or until the top of the top of the tortilla is golden and the middle no longer runny. Slide onto a board and serve with crusty bread and a tomato salad.

NUTRITION per serving:
• 273 cals • 18 g protein • 12 g fat (3 g saturates)
• 21 g carbs (7 g total sugars) • 7 g fibre

BEAN AND SWEET POTATO TORTILLA

This simple tortilla provides an ideal combination of carbohydrate and protein for speeding muscle recovery after exercise. It's made with sweet potatoes, which are higher in beta-carotene than standard potatoes, and red kidney beans, which are a brilliant source of protein, iron, zinc and fibre that feeds the beneficial microbes in your gut (see p. 23). It's also delicious served cold – great for making ahead or using in lunchboxes.

Preparation time: 10 minutes
Cooking time: 20 minutes

2 medium (about 400 g/14 oz) sweet potatoes, scrubbed
6 large eggs
A handful of fresh coriander, chopped
2 tbsp olive oil
1 onion, finely chopped
1 garlic clove, crushed
400 g (14 oz) can red kidney beans, drained and rinsed
Salt and freshly ground black pepper

To serve:
A leafy salad

Serves 4

Cut the sweet potato into 5-mm (¼-in) thick slices. Cook in a steamer or small pan of boiling water for 5–6 minutes until just tender. Drain and set aside.

In a bowl, lightly whisk the eggs and stir in the seasoning and fresh coriander.

Preheat the grill to medium.

Heat the oil in an ovenproof frying pan and fry the onion over a medium heat for 5 minutes or until softened. Add the garlic, sweet potato and red kidney beans, and cook for a further 2–3 minutes.

Pour in the egg mixture and cook over a gentle heat for 4–5 minutes until the egg starts to set. Transfer to a hot grill and cook for 2–3 minutes or until the top is golden and the tortilla is cooked through.

Slide the tortilla onto a plate and serve cut into wedges with salad.

NUTRITION per serving:
• 346 cals • 17 g protein • 14 g fat (3 g saturates)
• 33 g carbs (8 g total sugars) • 9 g fibre

CHILLI AND SESAME TOFU WITH SWEET POTATO WEDGES

Tofu is a fantastic source of protein as it contains all the essential amino acids needed for muscle growth. It's also rich in isoflavones, which have strong antioxidant and anti-inflammatory effects, help keep blood vessels flexible and reduce cancer risk. Tofu can taste bland on its own, so I prefer cooking it with strong flavours, such as chilli, garlic and ginger. This is one of my favourite ways of cooking tofu, as 'steaks' with tamari and sesame seeds, which add extra crunch as well as iron, magnesium and calcium. Alternatively, you can cut the tofu into 2.5-cm (1-in) cubes, if you prefer.

Preparation time: 5 minutes

Cooking time: 25 minutes

275 g (9 ½ oz) block firm tofu

A little cornflour

1 tbsp light olive or rapeseed oil

4 spring onions, thinly sliced

3 garlic cloves, finely sliced

½–1 red chilli (or to taste), deseeded and finely chopped

5 cm (2 in) fresh ginger, peeled and finely chopped

4 tbsp tamari or soy sauce

2 tbsp sesame seeds

To serve: Stir-fried pak choi (Chinese cabbage) or baby spinach

For the sweet potato wedges:
2 large sweet potatoes, peeled and cut into long wedges

1 tbsp light olive or rapeseed oil

Salt and freshly ground black pepper

Serves 4

Preheat the oven to 220 °C/fan 200 °C/gas mark 7.

Place the sweet potato wedges on a baking tray and drizzle over the oil. Toss until lightly coated in oil then season with salt and freshly ground black pepper. Roast in the oven for 25–30 minutes, turning halfway through cooking, until tender and lightly browned.

Meanwhile, cut the block of tofu along its side then crosswise into 4 equal-sized slices, about 1 cm (½ in) thick. Use a sieve to dust with cornflour, shaking any excess off.

Heat half the oil in the pan. Add the spring onions, garlic, chilli and ginger and fry for 1–2 minutes or until fragrant. Remove from the pan and set aside.

Return the pan to the heat. Add the remaining oil and the tofu 'steaks'. Fry until they start to turn golden brown, about 2–3 minutes, then flip and cook for another 2–3 minutes on the other side. Return the spring onions, garlic, chilli and ginger mixture to the pan and stir to coat the tofu. Add the tamari or soy sauce and cook for another minute, turning the tofu in the tamari.

Remove the steaks from the pan, spoon over the sauce and scatter over the sesame seeds. Serve with the sweet potato wedges and stir-fried pak choi or baby spinach.

COOK'S TIP

After opening a package of tofu, place any leftovers in an airtight container, cover with water and refrigerate. Make sure you use it within two to three days.

NUTRITION per serving:
• 300 cals • 12 g protein • 14 g fat (2 g saturates)
• 29 g carbs (10 g total sugars) • 5 g fibre

UDON NOODLES AND CRUNCHY VEGETABLES WITH CRISP TOFU

Full of interesting textures and flavours, this delicious recipe of noodles and vegetables is packed with vitamins, fibre and phytonutrients, which all support your immune function. Tofu is rich in protein, making this an ideal pre- or post-workout meal. Udon is a thick noodle made from wheat and has a wonderful chewy, soft texture. You can substitute other vegetables such as mushrooms or spring onions for the ones I've used here.

Preparation time: 10 minutes

Cooking time: 10 minutes

200 g (7 oz) dried udon noodles or 2 x 150 g (5 oz) packets straight-to-wok udon noodles

2 tbsp light olive or rapeseed oil

1 onion, thinly sliced

1 yellow or red pepper, deseeded and sliced

100 g (3½ oz) sugar snap peas

150 g (5 oz) pak choi (Chinese cabbage), sliced

150 g (5 oz) shiitake mushrooms, thickly sliced

400 g (14 oz) extra-firm tofu (see 'What is tofu?' p.117), cut into 1 cm (½ in) thick slices

For the sauce:

2 tbsp sriracha chilli sauce, or to taste

2 tbsp soy sauce

2 tbsp rice wine vinegar

Juice of 1 lime

1 tbsp chopped coriander

2 tsp sesame oil

To serve: 2 tbsp toasted sesame seeds

Serves 4

Cook the udon noodles (if using dried) in a saucepan according to the packet instructions. Drain and place in a large bowl. Meanwhile, make the spicy udon sauce by combining the chilli sauce, soy sauce, rice wine vinegar, lime juice, coriander and sesame oil in a small bowl.

Heat half of the rapeseed oil in a wok over a medium-high heat until it is hot, add the onion and stir-fry for 2 minutes. Add the remaining vegetables and continue stir-frying for 4 minutes. Transfer to a separate bowl.

For the tofu, wipe out the wok with absorbent kitchen paper. Heat the remaining oil over a high heat, add the tofu and fry for about 2 minutes on each side until they are crisp and brown. Remove to a plate.

Add the vegetables and fried tofu to the noodles and toss with the sauce. Serve sprinkled with sesame seeds.

NUTRITION per serving:
• 446 cals • 22 g protein • 18 g fat (3 g saturates)
• 46 g carbs (10 g total sugars) • 6 g fibre

DESSERTS

○ Clockwise from top left: *Mango and coconut, Raspberry and yogurt and Piña colada lollies, Baked strawberry and vanilla cheeecake, Blackberry and apple crumble, Cherry and almond clafoutis.*

WHAT IS QUARK?

Quark is a soft cheese with a thick, creamy texture and mild flavour, neither sweet nor sour. It's made from milk, which is soured using lactic acid bacteria to make it separate. The solids (curds) are then separated from the whey to give you quark. Most quark sold in the UK is made from skimmed milk, which means it has a very low-fat content, typically less than 1 per cent. It also has a high protein content, around 12 g per 100 g, making it a brilliant ingredient for healthy cheesecakes.

BAKED STRAWBERRY AND VANILLA CHEESECAKE

If you're looking for a healthy summery dessert, this is the one! Admittedly the baking time takes it over the 30-minute allowance, but I had so many requests for more cheesecake recipes after the Blueberry New York-style cheesecake from *The Vegetarian Athlete's Cookbook* proved so popular! It's made with quark and Greek yogurt, and a delicious base of oats and almonds with fresh strawberries on the top. You can use other kinds of fruit – it's lovely with blackberries, blueberries and raspberries – or mix them into the cheesecake filling before baking.

Preparation time: 15 minutes
Cooking time: 60 minutes

500 g (1 lb 2 oz) quark, cottage cheese or ricotta
2 eggs
200 ml (7 fl oz) low-fat plain Greek yogurt
1 tbsp cornflour
75 g (3 oz) sugar
1 tsp vanilla bean paste
(or the seeds of 1 vanilla pod)

For the base:
25 g (1 oz) butter or olive spread
75 g (3 oz) rolled oats
50 g (2 oz) almonds
25 g (1 oz) brown sugar

To decorate:
400 g (14 oz) strawberries, hulled and halved
Icing sugar

Serves 8

Preheat oven to 180 °C/fan 160 °C/gas mark 4 and line an 18-cm (7-in) round cake tin with baking paper.

To make the base, melt the butter or olive spread in a small saucepan over a low heat. Put the oats, almonds and brown sugar in a food processor or blender and process for 1–2 minutes until coarse crumbs are formed. Add the melted butter or spread and pulse or mix on low speed until the mixture starts to clump together.

Transfer the mixture to the tin and press down firmly with the back of a large spoon. Bake for 15 minutes, then increase the heat to 190 °C/fan 170 °C/gas mark 5 and bake for 5 minutes more, or until the edges are golden brown. Remove from the oven to cool slightly, then reduce the heat to 160 °C/fan 140 °C/gas mark 3.

For the filling, place the quark, cottage cheese or ricotta, eggs, yogurt, cornflour, sugar and vanilla in a mixing bowl. Mix using a mixer, blender or a large wooden spoon until thoroughly combined.

Pour the mixture onto the base. Bake for 40–45 minutes until just set but slightly wobbly in the centre. Turn off the oven and leave the cheesecake to cool in the oven (to prevent it cracking).

Allow to cool completely before removing from the tin and refrigerate until you are ready to serve. Arrange the strawberries over the cheesecake then sprinkle with sifted icing sugar just before serving.

NUTRITION per serving
(including strawberries):
• 253 cals • 16 g protein • 8 g fat (2 g saturates)
• 27 g carbs (19 g total sugars) • 3 g fibre

---

variation

Blackberry Cheesecake: **Instead of strawberries, use 225 g (8 oz) fresh or frozen blackberries. You can arrange on the top after baking or purée (using a hand blender), then swirl into the mixture in the tin just before baking.**

CHOCOLATE ORANGE CHEESECAKE

Devising new cheesecake recipes has been my passion since childhood. Over the years, I've experimented with different types of cheese, sweeteners (sugar, honey, dates, maple syrup) and hundreds of flavours. This is my current love: dark chocolate and orange, an incredibly tasty – and healthy – marriage of two of my favourite flavours. Like the Baked strawberry and vanilla cheesecake (see p. 163), the baking time exceeds the 30-minute limit, but I have taken the liberty of including the recipe anyway (which you are free to ignore!). Again, the topping is made with quark and Greek yogurt, which means it's low in fat and high in protein, perfect for promoting muscle recovery.

 Preparation time: 15 minutes
Cooking time: 60 minutes

100 g (3½ oz) dark chocolate (min. 70 per cent cocoa solids)
500 g (1 lb 2 oz) quark, cottage cheese or ricotta
2 eggs
150 ml (5 fl oz) low-fat plain Greek yogurt
1 tbsp cornflour
75 g (3 oz) sugar, honey or maple syrup
Zest and juice of 1 large orange

For the base:
25 g (1 oz) butter or olive spread
75 g (3 oz) rolled oats
50 g (2 oz) hazelnuts
25 g (1 oz) brown sugar

Serves 8

Preheat the oven to 180 °C/fan 160 °C/gas mark 4 and line an 18-cm (7-in) round cake tin with baking paper.

To make the base, melt the butter or olive spread in a small saucepan over a low heat. Place the oats, hazelnuts and brown sugar in a food processor or blender and process for 1–2 minutes until coarse crumbs are formed. Add the melted butter or spread and pulse or mix on low speed until the mixture starts to clump together.

Transfer the mixture to the tin and press down firmly with the back of a large spoon. Bake for 15 minutes, then increase the heat to 190 °C/fan 170 °C/gas mark 5 and bake for 5 minutes more, or until the edges are golden brown. Remove from the oven to cool slightly, then reduce the heat to 160 °C/fan 140 °C/gas mark 3.

For the filling, break the chocolate into pieces, place in a Pyrex bowl over a pan of simmering water and leave to melt, stirring occasionally.

Place the quark, cottage cheese or ricotta, eggs, yogurt, cornflour, sugar (or honey or maple syrup) and orange zest and juice in a mixing bowl. Mix using a mixer, blender or a large wooden spoon until thoroughly combined.

Transfer one third of the mixture to a separate bowl and stir in the melted chocolate.

Place alternating spoonfuls of each mixture onto the base of the cheesecake. Swirl round a couple of times with a knife to create a marbled effect. Bake for 40–45 minutes until just set but slightly wobbly in the centre. Turn off the oven and leave the cheesecake to cool in the oven (to prevent it cracking).

Allow to cool completely before removing from the tin and refrigerate until you are ready to serve.

NUTRITION per serving:
• 298 cals • 16 g protein • 11 g fat (4 g saturates)
• 32 g carbs (24 g total sugars) • 2 g fibre

MANGO AND COCONUT LOLLIES

These irresistible ice lollies are a super-healthy alternative to the sugar-laden bought versions. The natural sugars in the mangoes provide more than enough sweetness for my palate, but if you like a sweeter lolly, add a ripe banana or a tablespoon of honey. Mangoes are also a fantastic source of beta-carotene, vitamin C and potassium.

Preparation time:
5 minutes (plus freezing)

2 ripe mangoes, stone removed and peeled
100 ml (3½ fl oz) canned coconut milk

Makes 6

Roughly dice the mango flesh then place in a blender with the coconut milk and blend until smooth. Pour into lolly or ice pop moulds. Freeze for about 30 minutes, then pop the lolly sticks in. Freeze for at least 4 hours or until solid.

To unmould, dip the moulds in hot water for 10–15 seconds and serve immediately.

NUTRITION per serving:
• 61 cals • 1 g protein • 3 g fat (3 g saturates)
• 7 g carbs (7 g total sugars) • 2 g fibre

HOW TO PREPARE A MANGO

Slice through the mango either side of the stone. Score the flesh in a criss-cross pattern, cutting through the flesh but not through the skin. Push the skin up from underneath, separating the cubes of flesh, then slice off the cubes and discard the skin. Cut the remaining flesh around the stone into cubes.

RASPBERRY AND YOGURT LOLLIES

With just three ingredients, these healthy lollies are so easy to make. You can substitute blueberries, blackberries or strawberries, or mix them all in! I find this quantity of honey is just the right amount to balance the tartness of the berries but if it's too sweet for your taste, then reduce the amount. Greek yogurt is thick and creamy, making the lollies deliciously ice cream-like.

Preparation time:
5 minutes (plus freezing)

300 ml (10 fl oz) plain Greek yogurt
1–2 tbsp runny honey
150 g (5 oz) raspberries
(fresh or frozen)

Make it vegan

Substitute coconut yogurt for the Greek yogurt, and sugar for the honey.

Makes 6

Place all the ingredients in a blender, blitz until smooth and then pour into lolly or ice pop moulds to just below the rim. Pop the lolly sticks in and freeze for at least 4 hours. Alternatively, mash the raspberries and honey with a fork and fold into the yogurt for a marbled effect.

To unmould, dip the moulds in hot water for 10–15 seconds and serve immediately.

NUTRITION per lolly:
• 52 cals • 5 g protein • 1 g fat (1 g saturates)
• 5 g carbs (5 g total sugars) • 1 g fibre

PIÑA COLADA LOLLIES

This lolly version of my favourite cocktail is incredibly easy to make and the perfect summer treat. Requiring just four ingredients, it's lower in sugar than conventional lollies and guaranteed to transport you to exotic beach holidays!

Preparation time:
5 minutes (plus freezing)

200 g (7 oz) fresh
pineapple chunks
200 ml (7 fl oz) coconut milk
50 ml (2 fl oz) Malibu
Finely grated zest of 1 lime

Makes 6

Blend the pineapple, coconut milk and Malibu together in a blender until smooth, then stir in the lime zest. Pour into the moulds and freeze for about 30 minutes, then pop the lolly sticks in. Freeze for at least 4 hours or until solid.

To unmould, dip the moulds in hot water for 10–15 seconds and serve immediately.

NUTRITION per serving:
• 94 cals • 1 g protein • 6 g fat (5 g saturates)
• 7 g carbs (6 g total sugars) • 1 g fibre

CHOCOLATE BANANA 'ICE CREAM'

This healthy 'ice cream' is made with only two ingredients and takes just minutes to make in a food processor. It tastes like soft-serve ice cream but has fewer calories and contains no added refined sugar. Both cacao and cocoa are rich in polyphenols, which help improve levels of nitric oxide in the body and increase oxygen delivery to muscles during endurance exercise (see 'Cacao versus cocoa: what's the difference?' below).

Preparation time:
5 minutes (plus freezing)

4 ripe bananas
2–3 tbsp cacao or cocoa powder
(according to taste)

To serve:
Raspberries or strawberries (optional)

Serves 4

Peel and slice the bananas into ½-cm (¼ in) thick slices. Lay them on a large plate or baking sheet that will fit into your freezer, then freeze, uncovered, for 2 hours (or overnight).

Remove from the freezer and pop the banana slices into a food processor, along with the cacao or cocoa powder. If the banana slices have been frozen longer than 2 hours, allow to stand for 20 minutes at room temperature to soften slightly – you want the banana to be about 80 per cent frozen so it will still blend easily. Process until smooth, about 2–3 minutes, and serve straight away with raspberries or strawberries, if liked.

NUTRITION per serving:
• 113 cals • 3 g protein • 2 g fat (1 g saturates)
• 20 g carbs (17 g total sugars) • 3 g fibre

CACAO VERSUS COCOA: WHAT'S THE DIFFERENCE?

Cacao and cocoa are both widely available from supermarkets nowadays and are often used interchangeably in recipes. The main difference relates to the method of production. Raw cacao is made by cold pressing unroasted cocoa beans, while cocoa powder is produced by roasting the beans at high temperatures. Cocoa powder tends to be darker, more mellow in flavour and contains slightly lower levels of polyphenols, magnesium, iron and potassium. However, it is still a rich source of these nutrients. Because it is less processed, cacao retains more of the natural cacao bean taste, which gives it a slightly bitter but intense chocolate taste.

BERRY 'ICE CREAM'

Like my Chocolate banana 'ice cream' (see p. 168), this gorgeous dessert is so easy to make and a healthier alternative to commercial ice cream. It's packed with potassium, vitamin C and polyphenols, so great for muscle recovery. You can use any fresh or frozen berries you like.

Preparation time:
5 minutes (plus freezing)

4 ripe bananas
400 g (14 oz) frozen berries, such as raspberries, blackberries, blueberries or mixed berries

To serve:
Banana slices, granola and fresh blueberries

Serves 4

Peel and cut the bananas into ½ cm- (¼ in) thick slices. Lay them on a large plate or baking sheet that will fit into your freezer, then freeze, uncovered, for 2 hours (or overnight).

Remove from the freezer and pop the slices into a food processor, along with the frozen berries. If the banana slices have been frozen longer than 2 hours, allow them to stand for 20 minutes at room temperature to soften slightly – you want the banana to be about 80 per cent frozen so it will still blend easily. Process until smooth, about 2–3 minutes, and serve straight away topped with banana slices, granola and fresh blueberries.

NUTRITION per serving:
• 118 cals • 3 g protein • 0 g fat (0 g saturates)
• 24 g carbs (22 g total sugars) • 5 g fibre

CHERRY AND ALMOND CLAFOUTIS

Clafoutis is a brilliant dessert for active people because it is rich in protein and low in sugar and saturated fat. It's like a thick fluffy pancake studded with cherries, which are a perfect post-workout food (see 'The health benefits of cherries'). You can swap the cherries for other fruit, such as raspberries, blackberries, plums, apricots, blueberries or apples.

Preparation time: 5 minutes
Cooking time: 25 minutes

Butter for greasing
300 g (10 oz) cherries, pitted and halved
2 eggs
40 g (1½ oz) plain flour
40 g (1½ oz) ground almonds
25 g (1 oz) caster sugar
1 tsp almond essence
250 ml (9 fl oz) milk (any type)

To serve:
Ice cream or plain Greek yogurt

Serves 4

Preheat the oven to 190 °C/fan 170 °C/gas mark 5. Butter a 23-cm (9-in) flan dish or tin (not loose-bottomed) and scatter the cherries over the base.

Place the remaining ingredients in a blender and blend until smooth. Pour the batter over the fruit and bake for 25–30 minutes until risen and golden brown. Serve warm with ice cream or Greek yogurt.

NUTRITION per serving (with semi-skimmed milk):
• 220 cals • 9 g protein • 9 g fat (2 g saturates)
• 24 g carbs (16 g total sugars) • 2 g fibre

THE HEALTH BENEFITS OF CHERRIES

Cherries may help reduce muscle soreness and inflammation after an intense workout, as well as speed up muscle recovery. This is thought to be due to their high concentration of anthocyanins, which have powerful antioxidant and anti-inflammatory properties. Although most of the studies were done with tart cherry juice, which has a higher level of anthocyanins, sweet cherries will have similar benefits.

RASPBERRY FRANGIPANE CAKE

Almond cakes are my favourite type of cake – they combine all the nostalgic flavours of Bakewell tart as well as the nutritional benefit of almonds. Ground almonds are loaded with vitamin E, protein and healthy unsaturated fats. Here, I've used a half and half mixture of butter and olive oil, which gives a lovely buttery flavour as well as a soft texture. Fresh raspberries are rich in polyphenols and vitamin C, both of which aid muscle adaptation after exercise. You can easily substitute other fruit, such as apricots, pears and apples, for the raspberries.

Preparation time: 10 minutes
Cooking time: 40 minutes

75 g (3 oz) butter
50 ml (2 fl oz) olive oil
100 g (3½ oz) sugar
125 g (4 oz) ground almonds
100 g (3½ oz) plain flour
2 tsp baking powder
2 eggs
100 ml (3½ fl oz) plain Greek yogurt
1 tsp natural almond extract
200 g (7 oz) raspberries
2 tbsp flaked almonds

To serve:
Plain Greek yogurt or vanilla ice cream

Serves 8

Preheat the oven to 180 °C/fan 160 °C/gas mark 4. Line a 20-cm (8-in) loose-bottomed cake tin with baking paper.

Mix together the butter, oil and sugar in a food mixer or mixing bowl. Add all the remaining ingredients except the raspberries and flaked almonds and mix. You should have a fairly soft mixture that falls easily from a spoon.

Reserve a few raspberries and gently fold the rest into the cake mixture. Spoon into the cake tin. Arrange the reserved raspberries on top, pressing down lightly. Scatter over the flaked almonds and bake for 40 minutes until golden and a skewer inserted in the centre comes out clean. Leave to cool in the tin for 10 minutes before transferring to a cooling tray. Serve with Greek yogurt or ice cream.

NUTRITION per serving:
• 363 cals • 10 g protein • 24 g fat (7 g saturates)
• 25 g carbs (15 g total sugars) • 3 g fibre

BLACKBERRY AND APPLE CRUMBLE

Fruit crumble is a staple pudding in my house all year round, and it's a delicious way to get at least one of your five-a-day portions for fruit and veg. This version has a tasty flapjack topping made with oats and almonds, so it's higher in fibre, protein and vitamin E than regular crumbles. Blackberries are rich in polyphenols, which help reduce muscle soreness after exercise. I often use frozen berries, particularly in the winter, when fresh are more expensive. In any case, frozen fruit is just as nutritious as fresh, as it is frozen within hours of picking with minimal loss of vitamins.

Preparation time: 10 minutes
Cooking time: 20 minutes

2 Bramley cooking apples, peeled, cored and thinly sliced
300 g (10 oz) blackberries (fresh or frozen)
1 tsp cinnamon
2 tbsp ground almonds

For the crumble:
50 g (2 oz) plain flour
40 g (1½ oz) brown sugar
75 g (3 oz) oats
50 g (2 oz) butter
50 g (2 oz) flaked almonds

To serve:
Custard or Greek yogurt

Serves 6

Preheat the oven to 190 °C/fan 170 °C/gas mark 5.

Place the apples in a saucepan with the blackberries and cinnamon and just enough water to cover the base of the pan by about 1 cm (½ in). Cover, bring to the boil and simmer for 5 minutes.

Meanwhile, prepare the crumble. Place the flour, brown sugar and oats in a mixing bowl. Add the butter and rub by hand or mixer into the mixture until it resembles breadcrumbs. Stir in the flaked almonds.

Tip the fruit into a baking dish and stir in the ground almonds. Scatter the topping over the top. Bake for 15–20 minutes until golden brown. Serve with custard or Greek yogurt.

NUTRITION per serving:
• 289 cals • 6 g protein • 16 g fat (5 g saturates)
• 28 g carbs (13 g total sugars) • 5 g fibre

Make it vegan

Use a non-dairy spread instead of butter and serve with non-dairy custard or coconut yogurt.

CHAPTER 17

SNACKS

○ Clockwise from top left: *Five-ingredient peanut butter cookies, Wholewheat banana bread, Rice cakes, Black bean brownies.*

FRUIT AND NUT ENERGY BARS (FIVE WAYS)

These no-bake bars are super-easy to make and a more nutritious option than manufactured energy bars. Dates provide three different types of sugar – glucose, fructose and sucrose – which are perfect for fuelling high-intensity activities longer than an hour. Nuts add extra fibre and unsaturated fats, which gives a mores sustained release of energy instead of a quick hit. The addition of almonds produces a bar with a softer texture.

Preparation time: 10 minutes (plus chilling)

100 g (3½ oz) ground almonds
125 g (4 oz) ready-to-eat soft or Medjool dates (or use standard dried dates soaked in boiling water for 10–15 minutes, then drained)
1 tbsp cacao or cocoa powder (see p. 168)
1 tsp vanilla extract

Makes 8 bars

NUTRITION per bar:
• 131 cals • 4 g protein • 7 g fat (1 g saturates)
• 11 g carbs (10 g total sugars) • 2 g fibre

Place the almonds, dates, cacao or cocoa powder and vanilla extract in a food processor or high-power blender and blend for about 1 minute until crumbly and evenly combined. You may need to stop the motor and scrape down the edges of the bowl once or twice. Add 2–3 tablespoons water if the dates are quite hard and don't break down readily. Continue processing for another 1–2 minutes until the ingredients clump together to form a ball.

Turn the sticky ball out of the processor and press or roll between two sheets of baking parchment or cling film to a 1 cm (½ in) thickness. Alternatively, press into an 18 x 18 cm (7 x 7 in) baking tin lined with cling film. Refrigerate for 1 hour or so until firm, then peel off the parchment and cut into bars, approximately 10 x 2 cm (4 x ¾ in). Wrap in cling film or foil. The bars will keep in the fridge for up to two weeks or in the freezer for up to three months.

variations

Try these combinations too, following the main method above.

Date and Cashew Bars: 100 g (3½ oz) cashew nuts, 125 g (4 oz) ready-to-eat soft or Medjool dates, a pinch of salt

Peanut Bars: 75 g (3 oz) peanuts, 125 g (4 oz) ready-to-eat soft or Medjool, 25 g (1 oz) smooth peanut butter

Cocoa Coconut Bars: 125 g (4 oz) ready-to-eat soft or Medjool dates, 50 g (2 oz) cashews, 40 g (1½ oz) raisins, 40 g (1½ oz) desiccated coconut, 1 tbsp cacao or cocoa powder

Pecan Pie Bars: 125 g (4 oz) ready-to-eat soft or Medjool dates, 50 g (2 oz) pecans, 50 g (2 oz) ground almonds

PROTEIN BALLS

If you're looking for a portable snack that's not made with dates and isn't super-sweet, this is what you need. These little balls have a chickpea base, which may sound a little unusual, but it gives them a perfect texture, similar to cookie dough. The addition of cacao powder and chocolate protein powder masks the 'beany' flavour, which means you cannot taste the chickpeas at all. Instead, you have a snack that's full of goodness and with just the right balance of sweetness.

Preparation time: 10 minutes
(plus chilling)

400 g (14 oz) canned chickpeas, drained and rinsed
60 g (2½ oz) almond or peanut butter
½ tsp vanilla extract
1 tbsp cacao powder
25 g (1 oz) chocolate protein powder
(whey or vegan)
3 tbsp honey or maple syrup
1–2 tbsp water
50 g (2 oz) dark chocolate chips
Desiccated coconut for rolling (optional)

Makes 16

Place all the ingredients, except the water, chocolate chips and coconut, in a food processor and pulse until the mixture begins to clump together. Add a tablespoon or two of water, then process for a further minute until the mixture resembles cookie dough. You may need to stop and scrape the mixture from the sides of the food processor a couple of times.

Transfer to a bowl, then fold in the chocolate chips. Form the dough into 16 balls. Sprinkle the desiccated coconut on a plate (if using), then roll each ball in coconut and arrange on a tray or in a bowl.

Chill for 1 hour or until firm. Transfer to an airtight container and store in the fridge for up to a week, or in the freezer for up to three months.

NUTRITION per ball:
• 63 cals • 3 g protein • 3 g fat (1 g saturates)
• 5 g carbs (3 g total sugars) • 1 g fibre

RICE CAKES

If you're tired of sweet sticky gels and energy bars, then these tasty rice cakes are a healthy alternative. I love them because they remind me of my favourite school pudding (rice pudding)! This recipe is high in carbohydrate but lower in sugar than manufactured sports snacks, making it ideal for long cycle rides, hikes or runs. The addition of soft cheese acts like glue, binding the mixture together and making it easy to cut into cakes, and adds some protein and fat, which reduces the sugar spike you get from rice alone. They can be varied by adding sultanas, dried apple, ground nuts, jam or maple syrup. I recommend using risotto or short-grain rice rather than standard white rice as it sticks together better. Make a big batch and keep in the fridge for up to three days or in the freezer for up to three months.

Preparation time: 5 minutes (plus chilling)
Cooking time: 25 minutes

250 g (9 oz) arborio (risotto) or short-grain (pudding) rice
500 ml (17 fl oz) water
1 tsp cinnamon
150 g (5 oz) soft cheese (full-fat or reduced fat)
1 tbsp brown sugar, honey, maple syrup or raisins

Makes 12

Place the rice and water in a non-stick pan, bring to the boil, then reduce the heat and simmer for 25 minutes, or according to the packet instructions (short-grain rice may take slighter longer). Alternatively, if using a rice cooker, follow the manufacturer's instructions. Once the rice is cooked and all the liquid absorbed, stir in the cinnamon, soft cheese and sugar, honey, maple syrup or raisins (see Cook's tip).

Line a 20-cm (8-in) square baking tin with cling film, leaving plenty of overhang. Turn the rice mixture into the tin, pressing down with the back of a wetted spoon or spatula. Fold the overhang of cling film over the rice to encase it.

Leave in the fridge for a few hours, preferably overnight. Cut into 12 pieces, then wrap individually in cling film, foil or baking paper.

NUTRITION per cake
(with reduced-fat soft cheese):
• 88 cals • 3 g protein • 1 g fat (0 g saturates)
• 18 g carbs (1 g total sugars) • 0 g fibre

NUTRITION per cake
(with full-fat soft cheese):
• 107 cals • 2 g protein • 3 g fat (2 g saturates)
• 17 g carbs (0 g total sugars) • 0 g fibre

COOK'S TIP

Add the sugar, honey or syrup or raisins after, not before, you cook the rice, otherwise it burns and sticks to the bottom of the pan.

variations

Raspberry: Spoon half the rice mixture into the tin, spread over a thin layer of raspberry jam, then spoon the remainder of the rice on top.

Almond and Banana: Mix 1 mashed banana and 2 tablespoons ground almonds into the cooked rice.

Coconut and Cherry: Mix 75 g (3 oz) desiccated coconut and 50 g (2 oz) dried cherries into the cooked rice.

Apple and Raisin: Mix 75 g (3 oz) raisins and 75 g (3 oz) dried apple pieces into the cooked rice.

COCONUT RICE BALLS

 VG

Like Rice cakes, these balls are an excellent alternative to manufactured gels and bars. They are easy to make, high in carbohydrate, virtually sugar-free, and can be popped in your pocket or rucksack when heading out on long walks, runs or cycle rides. Cooking the rice in coconut milk makes it stickier and helps the balls firm up, as well as adding coconut flavour.

Preparation time: 5 minutes (plus chilling)
Cooking time: 25 minutes

125 g (4 oz) arborio (risotto) or short-grain (pudding) rice
250 ml (9 fl oz) canned coconut milk

Makes 10

Place the rice and coconut milk in a pan, bring to the boil, then reduce the heat and simmer for 25 minutes until all the liquid is absorbed, or follow the packet instructions.

Place a tablespoon of the rice mixture on a square of cling film, then gather it up, squeezing tightly, to form a bite-sized ball. Twist the top to form a seal. Arrange the balls on a tray or plate and place in the fridge for a few hours, preferably overnight, to firm up. They will keep in the fridge for up to three days or in the freezer for up to three months.

> **NUTRITION per ball:**
> • 73 cals • 1 g protein • 4 g fat (3 g saturates)
> • 9 g carbs (0 g total sugars) • 0 g fibre

variations

Peanut Butter: **Stir a tablespoon of peanut butter into the cooked rice.**

Banana Walnut Rice Balls: **Mix 1 mashed banana, 1 teaspoon ground cinnamon, 1 tablespoon honey and 50 g (2 oz) crushed walnuts into the cooked rice.**

Feta and Tomato: **Mix 150 g (5 oz) crumbled vegetarian feta cheese and 6 chopped sundried tomatoes into the cooked rice.**

POWER BALLS (FIVE WAYS)

These bite-sized morsels provide a perfect blend of simple sugars, protein and healthy fats, and are a healthy alternative to manufactured energy gels and chews for fuelling your workouts and competitions (or just a tasty snack). The addition of nuts and oats slows the digestion of sugars, which means you'll get sustained energy instead of a short-lived burst. They also supply lots of other nutrients, including iron, B vitamins, zinc and magnesium. Wrap individually and pop in your jersey pocket when going on a long run, hike or bike ride.

Preparation time: 10 minutes
(plus chilling)

100 g (3½ oz) ready-to-eat soft or Medjool dates (or use standard dried dates soaked in boiling water for 10–15 minutes, then drained)
50 g (2 oz) ground almonds
25 g (1 oz) cacao or cocoa powder
50 g (2 oz) rolled oats
20 g (¾ oz) nut butter
(e.g. almond, peanut or cashew)
1 tbsp runny honey or maple syrup
1 tbsp water

To coat (optional):
Cacao or cocoa powder, sesame seeds, finely chopped pistachios, finely chopped mixed nuts, desiccated coconut or chocolate chips

Makes 16 balls

Place all the ingredients in a food processor. Pulse until well combined and until the mixture forms the consistency of stiff cookie dough.

Take a small amount of mixture and roll it in your hands to form small, bite-sized balls. Choose your coating, sprinkle it onto a large plate, then roll each ball around until nicely coated and arrange on a tray or plate.

Chill for 1 hour or until firm. Transfer to an airtight container and store in the fridge for up to a week, or in the freezer for up to three months.

> **NUTRITION per ball:**
> • 67 cals • 2 g protein • 3 g fat (0 g saturates)
> • 7 g carbs (5 g total sugars) •1 g fibre

variations

Hazelnut and Raisin: Use hazelnuts instead of almonds, substitute 50 g (2 oz) raisins for half the dates, omit the cocoa powder and add ½ teaspoon ground cinnamon

Peanut Butter: Use peanuts instead of almonds and omit the cocoa powder.

Coconut: Use desiccated coconut instead of the almonds.

Cashew and Apricot: Substitute cashew nuts for the ground almonds, omit the cocoa powder, add 50 g (2 oz) chopped dried apricots and 2 teaspoons chia seeds.

BLUEBERRY AND COCONUT MUFFINS

These healthy muffins are light and fluffy, and make a lovely post-workout treat. They're made with olive oil, so they're lower in saturated fat than traditional cakes, and contain less sugar. I've used yogurt, which gives them a deliciously light, moist texture. If you want to make them with wholewheat flour for an extra fibre boost, add an extra tablespoon of yogurt or milk.

Preparation time: 10 minutes

Cooking time: 20 minutes

75 g (3 oz) honey or sugar
75 ml (3 fl oz) olive oil
2 eggs
1 tsp vanilla extract
200 g (7 oz) self-raising flour
150 ml (¼ pint) low-fat plain yogurt
50 g (2 oz) desiccated coconut
125 g (4 oz) fresh or frozen blueberries

Makes 12 muffins

Preheat the oven to 200 °C/fan 180 °C/gas mark 6. Meanwhile, line a 12-hole muffin tin with paper cases.

Place all the ingredients except the blueberries in a large mixing bowl or food mixer. Mix together until well combined. Fold in the blueberries.

Divide the mixture among the muffin cases and bake for approximately 20 minutes until the muffins are risen and golden. Allow to cool. They will keep in an airtight container (lined with a paper towel) for two days.

NUTRITION per muffin:
- 188 cals • 4 g protein • 10 g fat (4 g saturates)
- 29 g carbs (7 g total sugars) • 2 g fibre

Make it vegan

Use flax or chia instead of eggs (see p. 46) and substitute a non-dairy yogurt alternative.

variations

Cherry and Coconut: **Substitute chopped glacé cherries for the blueberries.**

Blueberry and Almond: **Use ground almonds instead of the coconut.**

Blueberry and Walnut: **Use chopped walnuts instead of the coconut.**

DOUBLE CHOCOLATE MUFFINS

If, like me, you find coffee shop muffins too sweet for your palate, then here's a less sugary alternative. These delicious muffins are made with ground almonds, which makes them super-moist and adds extra protein, fibre and unsaturated fats.

Preparation time: 5 minutes
Cooking time: 20 minutes

50 g (2 oz) butter
50 ml (2 fl oz) light olive oil
65 g (2½ oz) soft brown sugar
2 eggs
1 tsp vanilla extract
100 g (3½ oz) ground almonds
75 g (3 oz) self-raising flour
1 tsp baking powder
25 g (1 oz) cacao or cocoa powder (see p. 168)
50 g (2 oz) dark chocolate chips
4–5 tbsp milk (any type)

Makes 12 muffins

Preheat the oven to 200 °C/fan 180 °C/gas mark 6. Line a 12-hole muffin tin with paper cases.

In a bowl (or use a mixer) mix all the ingredients except the chocolate chips and milk. Add the milk until you have a soft batter, then stir in the chocolate chips.

Divide the mixture among the muffin cases. Bake for 18–20 minutes until risen and firm. Leave to cool in the tin for a few minutes, then cool on a wire rack. They will keep in an airtight container (lined with a paper towel) for two days.

NUTRITION per muffin:
- 195 cals • 5 g protein • 14 g fat (4 g saturates)
- 13 g carbs (8 g total sugars) • 1 g fibre

variation

Chocolate and Walnut Muffins: **Substitute 75 g (3 oz) chopped walnuts and 50 g (2 oz) raisins for the chocolate chips.**

RASPBERRY, APPLE AND ALMOND MUFFINS

These irresistible muffins contain less fat and sugar than traditional muffins. I've used ground almonds in place of some of the flour to increase the nutritional value, as well as yogurt, which gives a light, moist texture. The raspberries add polyphenols and vitamin C as well as contrasting vibrant colour.

Preparation time: 5 minutes
Cooking time: 25 minutes

75 g (3 oz) butter
200 g (7 oz) self-raising flour
1 tsp baking powder
50 g (2 oz) ground almonds
75 g (3 oz) sugar
1 tsp natural almond extract
2 eggs
150 ml (5 fl oz) plain, low-fat yogurt
150 g (5 oz) fresh raspberries
1 eating apple, such as Granny Smith, peeled and grated

Makes 12 muffins

Preheat the oven to 200 °C/fan 180 °C fan/gas mark 6. Meanwhile, line a 12-hole muffin tin with paper cases.

Melt the butter in a small saucepan over a low heat and set aside.

Place the flour, baking powder, ground almonds and sugar in a large mixing bowl and stir to combine. In a separate bowl, mix together the almond extract, melted butter, eggs and yogurt, then pour into the flour mixture. Stir until combined. Fold in the raspberries and grated apple.

Divide the mixture among the muffin cases and bake for approximately 22–25 minutes until the muffins are risen and golden. Leave them in the tin for a few minutes, then transfer to a wire rack. They will keep in an airtight container (lined with a paper towel) for two days.

> **NUTRITION per muffin:**
> • 186 cals • 5 g protein • 9 g fat (4 g saturates)
> • 22 g carbs (9 g total sugars) • 2 g fibre

Make it vegan

Substitute a non-dairy spread for the butter, use flax or chia instead of eggs (see p. 46) and substitute a non-dairy yogurt alternative.

CHERRY OAT COOKIES

Oat cookies are a firm favourite in my house, so much so that I always have a batch in the biscuit tin. This recipe is made with spelt flour (see 'What is spelt flour?' below), although you can use plain flour equally well. Here, I've included cherries but you can substitute raisins or dried cranberries if you prefer. Whichever you choose, these cookies make a delicious snack that's perfect for refuelling after a workout – or just eating any time!

Preparation time: 10 minutes
Cooking time: 15 minutes

100 g (3½ oz) spelt or plain flour
125 g (4 oz) jumbo oats
100 g (3½ oz) butter
75 g (3 oz) brown sugar
1 tbsp maple syrup or honey
1 tsp vanilla extract
100 g (3½ oz) glacé cherries, cut into quarters
½ egg, beaten

Makes 16

Preheat the oven to 190 °C/fan 170 °C/gas mark 5 and line a baking tray with baking paper.

In a bowl, combine the spelt or plain flour, oats, butter, sugar, maple syrup or honey and vanilla extract and mix well. Stir in the cherries (do this on the lowest speed setting if you're using a food mixer). Add the egg and mix until the mixture clumps together.

Form into walnut-sized balls and place on the baking tray, about 2.5 cm/1 in apart, then flatten lightly with a fork. Bake for 12–14 minutes or until light golden. Cool for a few minutes before transferring to a wire rack.

NUTRITION per cookie:
• 143 cals • 2 g protein • 6 g fat (4 g saturates)
• 20 g carbs (5 g total sugars) • 1 g fibre

Make it vegan

Substitute a non-dairy spread for the butter, omit the egg and add 1–2 tablespoons non-dairy milk.

variations

Cranberry Oat Cookies: **Substitute 50 g (2 oz) dried cranberries for the glacé cherries.**

Raisin Oat Cookies: **Substitute 100 g (3½ oz) raisins for the glacé cherries.**

WHAT IS SPELT FLOUR?

Spelt is a cereal grain in the wheat family that has a nutty and slightly sweet flavour. Some people with wheat intolerance or non-coeliac gluten sensitivity find it easier to digest. Spelt has the same calorie content but slightly more protein than standard wheat flour. It contains gluten (wheat protein) but with a slightly different chemical structure that imparts a crumblier texture to foods. This makes it ideal for making biscuits, cookies and pastry, and it can be substituted for and used in the same way as standard plain flour. However, it's less suitable for bread and cakes, where you need a more aerated texture.

CHOCOLATE CHIP OAT COOKIES

This delicious recipe from my book, *The Vegetarian Athlete's Cookbook* (Bloomsbury, 2017), is one that I return to over and over. Here, I have made a few changes, so it is even tastier. You can substitute broken chocolate pieces or chocolate buttons for the dark chocolate chips. Honey or maple syrup gives the cookies a slightly soft texture.

Preparation time: 10 minutes
Cooking time: 15 minutes

100 g (3½ oz) oats
100 g (3½ oz) spelt or plain white flour (see p. 190)
100 g (3½ oz) brown sugar
100 g (3½ oz) butter
1 tbsp runny honey or maple syrup
½ tsp vanilla extract
1 tsp ground cinnamon
50 g (2 oz) dark chocolate chips
½ egg, beaten

To decorate:
Melted dark chocolate

Makes 16 cookies

Preheat the oven to 190 °C/fan 170 °C/gas mark 5 and line a baking tray with baking paper.

Mix the oats, spelt or plain flour, sugar, butter, honey or maple syrup, vanilla extract and ground cinnamon in a food mixer or large mixing bowl, then process until well combined. When the mixture starts to stick together in clumps, add the chocolate chips and beaten egg and continue mixing together until you have a soft dough.

Using your hands, form the mixture into 16 walnut-sized balls, and place on the baking tray, about 3 cm/1½ in apart. Flatten lightly using the base of a cup (I put a small piece of baking paper between the cookie and cup to prevent it from sticking).

Bake for 12–13 minutes or until light golden. Cool for a few minutes before transferring to a wire rack. Make them showstoppers by drizzling over melted dark chocolate.

NUTRITION per cookie:
• 139 cals • 2 g protein • 7 g fat (4 g saturates)
• 17 g carbs (9 g total sugars) • 1 g fibre

Make it vegan
Use a non-dairy spread instead of butter; substitute 1–2 tbsp non-dairy milk for the egg.

variation
Pecan Cinnamon Oat Cookies:
Substitute 75 g (3 oz) chopped pecans for the chocolate chips.

FIVE-INGREDIENT PEANUT BUTTER COOKIES

This is the easiest cookie recipe you'll ever make! Peanut butter cookies have been a staple in my house since I first created the recipe for *The Vegetarian Athlete's Cookbook* (Bloomsbury, 2017). Since then I've tweaked the recipe, omitting the egg to make it suitable for vegans, so it now contains just five ingredients.

Preparation time: 10 minutes

Cooking time: 15 minutes

125 g (4 oz) peanut butter
75 g (3 oz) dark brown sugar
75 g (3 oz) butter
75 g (3 oz) oats
75 g (3 oz) plain white flour

Makes 16

Preheat the oven to 190 °C /fan 170 °C/gas mark 5 and line a baking tray with baking paper.

Place all of the ingredients in a food processor and process on high speed until you have a smooth, fairly stiff dough, about 1 minute. Alternatively, use a hand blender.

Form the mixture into walnut-sized balls. Place on the baking tray, about 2.5 cm (1 in) apart, then flatten lightly with your palm.

Bake for approximately 12 minutes or until light golden. Cool for a few minutes before transferring to a wire rack.

Make it vegan

Use a non-dairy spread instead of butter.

NUTRITION per cookie:
• 139 cals • 4 g protein • 8 g fat (3 g saturates)
• 12 g carbs (5 g total sugars) • 1 g fibre

BLACK BEAN BROWNIES

I must admit to having been sceptical of 'healthy' brownies made with unconventional ingredients – until recently, when I decided to make my own. Initially, black beans in a cake may sound unappealing but, in fact, they impart no bean flavour at all and give the brownies a wonderful, ultra-fudgy texture (along with tons of fibre, protein and iron), and do away with the requirement for butter. Here, I've added a little olive oil and replaced the usual flour with ground almonds, both of which make the brownies moist and add healthy unsaturated fat. Dark chocolate chips provide polyphenols, which help keep your blood vessels healthy. The resulting brownies are not only good for you, but also taste amazing!

Preparation time: 10 minutes
Cooking time: 20 minutes

400 g (14 oz) can black beans, drained and rinsed
2 tbsp cacao or cocoa powder
50 g (2 oz) ground almonds
65 g (2½ oz) honey
2 tbsp brown sugar
3 tbsp light olive oil
1 tsp vanilla extract
½ tsp baking powder
A pinch of salt
1 egg
100 g (3½ oz) dark chocolate chips

Makes 12

Preheat the oven to 180 °C/fan 160 °C/gas mark 4. Meanwhile, line a 20 x 20-cm (8 x 8-in) tin with baking parchment.

Place all the ingredients except the chocolate chips in a food processor and process until smooth. Stir in the chips, reserving a few for decoration, then pour into the prepared tin. Smooth the surface with a knife and press the reserved chocolate chips on top.

Bake for 18–20 minutes until risen and slightly firm. Leave to cool in the tin – they will firm up as they cool – then cut into 12 squares.

NUTRITION per brownie:
- 161 cals • 4 g protein • 9 g fat (2 g saturates)
- 16 g carbs (12 g total sugars) • 2 g fibre

Make it vegan
Use flax or chia instead of an egg (see p. 46), and maple syrup instead of honey.

CHOCOLATE WALNUT BROWNIES

If, like me, you find traditional brownies overpoweringly sweet and disappointingly unsatisfying, here's a healthier version with less sugar and more fibre. Made with ground almonds, walnuts and olive spread, these brownies are lower in saturated fat and higher in polyphenols and health-promoting unsaturated fats than traditional recipes. Plus, they're light, ultra-moist, infused with intense chocolate flavour and take literally minutes to mix up and get in the oven.

Preparation time: 10 minutes
Cooking time: 20 minutes

100 g (3½ oz) dark chocolate containing 70 per cent cocoa solids
100 ml (3½ fl oz) light olive oil
100 g (3½ oz) brown sugar
2 eggs
1 tsp vanilla extract
100 g (3½ oz) ground almonds
1 tsp baking powder
100 g (3½ oz) self-raising flour
25 g (1 oz) cacao or cocoa powder (see p. 168)
4–5 tbsp milk (any type)
50 g (2 oz) walnuts, roughly chopped

Makes 12

Preheat the oven to 180 °C/fan 160 °C/gas mark 4. Line a 20-cm (8-in) square tin with baking parchment.

Break the chocolate into pieces, place in a small heatproof bowl and melt over a pan of boiling water, stirring occasionally. Alternatively, melt in a microwave on medium-low for 2–3 minutes, stirring every 30 seconds or so.

Place the olive oil, sugar, eggs, vanilla extract, almonds, baking powder, flour, cacao or cocoa powder and half the milk in a large bowl or mixer and mix until well combined. You should have a fairly soft mixture (add a little extra milk if it feels too stiff).

Stir in the melted chocolate and walnuts. Spoon the mixture into the prepared tin, smooth the surface with a knife and bake for 20 minutes until risen and firm and a skewer inserted into the centre comes out clean. Leave to cool in the tin for 10 minutes, then cut into 12 squares and transfer to a wire rack to cool.

> NUTRITION per brownie:
> • 250 cals • 5 g protein • 17 g fat (4 g saturates)
> • 17 g carbs (14 g total sugars) • 2 g fibre

RASPBERRY SCONES

Scones are low in sugar and perfect for refuelling after a workout. The raspberries in this recipe add a burst of tangy, sweet flavour, along with polyphenols for muscle recovery. I like to experiment with adding different kinds of fresh or dried fruit, such as blueberries or dried cherries. Serve with cream or quark and raspberry jam, and extra fresh raspberries.

Preparation time: 15 minutes
Cooking time: 15 minutes

250 g (9oz) self-raising flour, plus extra for dusting
1 tsp baking powder
A pinch of salt
50 g (2 oz) butter
25 g (1 oz) sugar
100 ml (3½ fl oz) milk (any type)
1 egg
1 tsp vanilla extract
75 g (3 oz) fresh raspberries

To serve:
Cream or quark (low-fat soft cheese), raspberry jam and extra raspberries

Makes 8

Preheat the oven to 220 °C/fan 200 °C/gas mark 7. Meanwhile, lightly flour a large baking tray. Place the flour, baking powder and salt in a large mixing bowl and rub in the butter until the mixture resembles breadcrumbs (I use a food mixer, but you can use your fingertips). Stir in the sugar.

In a measuring jug, mix together the milk and egg (reserve 1 tablespoon for brushing), then mix this into the flour until the mixture starts to come together. Add the vanilla extract and raspberries and carefully mix through the dough, trying not to break up the berries too much.

Sprinkle a little flour onto a clean work surface, turn the dough out of the bowl and pat out to a thickness of 2.5 cm (1 in). Using a 6-cm (2½-in) round pastry cutter, cut out the scones and place on the baking sheet. Press the trimmings together, pat out and repeat the process until you have used all the dough.

Brush the tops with the reserved egg-milk mixture and bake for 12–14 minutes until golden and risen. Transfer to a wire rack. Scones are best when they are fresh and warm from the oven, so bake them just before you plan to enjoy them. Leftovers can be stored in a tin for up to 24 hours or frozen for up to three months.

Make it vegan

Replace the butter with a non-dairy spread; use an additional 50 ml (2 fl oz) non-dairy milk instead of the egg.

NUTRITION per scone:
- 188 cals • 4 g protein • 6 g fat (4 g saturates)
- 28 g carbs (4 g total sugars) • 2 g fibre

variation

Blackberry or Blueberry Scones: Substitute 75 g (3 oz) blackberries or blueberries for the raspberries.

Cherry Scones: Replace the raspberries with 75 g (3 oz) chopped glacé cherries.

Raisin Scones: Replace the raspberries with 75 g (3 oz) raisins.

Cinnamon Scones: Omit the vanilla extract and raspberries. Add 2 teaspoons ground cinnamon to the flour mixture before rubbing in the butter.

BLACKBERRY FRANGIPANE TRAYBAKE

Packed with fresh blueberries and almonds, this cake must be one of the tastiest ways to refuel. Made with olive oil and almonds, it has less saturated fat than standard cakes and the berries supply lots of polyphenols. These plant chemicals give berries their vibrant colour but have also been shown to promote recovery and adaptation in muscle cells.

Preparation time: 10 minutes
Cooking time: 20 minutes

100 g (3½ oz) butter
60 ml (2½ fl oz) light olive oil
100 g (3½ oz) sugar
2 eggs
1 tsp almond extract
100 g (3½ oz) ground almonds/almond flour
125 g (4 oz) self-raising flour
1 tsp baking powder
4 tbsp milk (any type)
150 g (5 oz) blackberries
1 tbsp flaked almonds

Makes 12 slices

Preheat the oven to 180 °C/fan 160 °C/gas mark 4. Meanwhile, line a 20-cm (8-in) square baking tray with baking paper.

In a large bowl or mixer, beat together the butter, oil and sugar until well combined and light in colour. Add the eggs, almond extract, ground almonds/almond flour, self-raising flour and baking powder. Mix until well combined, adding enough milk so you have a soft consistency. Fold in the blackberries then spoon into the prepared tin. Scatter over the almonds.

Bake for about 20 minutes or until golden and a skewer inserted in the centre comes out clean. Remove from the oven, allow to cool, then cut into 12 slices.

NUTRITION per slice:
- 195 cals • 3 g protein • 13 g fat (5 g saturates)
- 17 g carbs (9 g total sugars) • 1 g fibre

Make it vegan

Replace the butter with a non-dairy spread; use flax or chia instead of eggs (see p. 46).

COURGETTE CAKE

I've always been reluctant to add vegetables to a cake recipe for fear of ruining its flavour, but when we had a glut of courgettes in our garden, I needed a new way to use them up. Courgettes in a cake may sound slightly unconventional, but, in fact, they create a beautifully moist, light texture and don't impart a vegetable taste at all. Here, I've used olive oil instead of butter as it contains healthy unsaturated fats, and reduced the sugar to a minimal level, so this cake really is good for you! It's not essential, but it tastes even nicer with raisins and pecans.

Preparation time: 10 minutes
Cooking time: 45 minutes

100 ml (3½ fl oz) light olive oil
125 g (3½ oz) brown sugar
2 eggs
175 g (6 oz) self-raising flour
1 tsp baking powder
1 tsp ground cinnamon
2 medium (200 g/7 oz) courgettes, grated
75 g (3 oz) raisins
60 g (2½ oz) pecans, roughly chopped

Makes 10 slices

Preheat the oven to 180 °C/fan 160 °C/gas mark 4. Meanwhile, line a 900-g/2-lb loaf tin with baking paper.

In a large bowl or food mixer, mix together the oil, sugar, eggs, flour, baking powder and cinnamon until well combined. Stir in the courgettes, raisins and pecans, then pour into the tin and level the top with a knife.

Bake for about 45 minutes or until a skewer inserted into the centre of the loaf comes out clean. Leave in the tin for 15 minutes, then turn out onto a wire rack to cool. It will keep for up to three days in an airtight container.

NUTRITION per slice:
• 258 cals • 4 g protein • 13 g fat (2 g saturates)
• 31 g carbs (18 g total sugars) • 2 g fibre

Make it vegan

Use flax or chia
instead of eggs
(see p. 46).

WHOLEWHEAT BANANA BREAD

Banana bread is a classic snack for athletes, multitasking as both pre- and post-workout fuel as well as on-board fuelling during long-distance events. This version is made with wholewheat flour, olive oil and honey. It's higher in fibre, lower in saturated fat and lower in sugar than traditional recipes, plus, it's light, ultra-moist, infused with sweet banana flavour and takes literally 10 minutes to prepare before going in the oven. It takes 60 minutes to bake in a loaf tin, taking you over the 30-minute allowance, but you can shorten the cooking time by dividing the mixture into 10 muffin cases and baking for 20 minutes. Try one of the variations below when you want to change things up a bit.

Preparation time: 10 minutes

Cooking time: 60 minutes

2 ripe bananas, peeled and mashed

75 ml (3 fl oz) light olive oil

100 ml (3½ fl oz) runny honey

2 eggs

1 tsp vanilla extract

200 g (7 oz) wholewheat flour

2 tsp baking powder

½ tsp salt

1 tsp ground cinnamon

60 ml (2 ½ fl oz) milk (any type)

Makes 10 slices

Preheat the oven to 160 °C/fan 140 °C/gas mark 3. Meanwhile, line a 900-g/2-lb loaf tin with baking paper.

In a large bowl or food mixer, mix all the ingredients until well combined (you'll have quite runny batter). Turn into the prepared loaf tin and level the top with a knife.

Bake until a skewer inserted into the centre of the loaf comes out clean, 60 minutes. Leave in the tin for 15 minutes, then turn out onto a wire rack to cool. It will keep in an airtight tin or wrapped in foil for up to five days.

> **NUTRITION per slice:**
> • 182 cals • 4 g protein • 7 g fat (1 g saturates)
> • 25 g carbs (11 g total sugars) • 2 g fibre

Make it vegan

Use sugar instead of honey, and flax or chia instead of eggs (see p. 46).

variation

Chocolate Chip Banana Bread: Add 100 g (3½ oz) dark chocolate chips or dark chocolate (70 per cent cocoa solids), broken into small pieces.

Pecan Banana Bread: Add 100 g (3½ oz) chopped pecans or walnuts.

Date Banana Bread: Add 100 g (3½ oz) chopped dates or any other dried fruit.

Super-speedy Snacks

The recipes on this page take less than 10 minutes to prepare.

PIZZA TOAST

Spread a slice of wholegrain toast with a little pesto, top with a thinly sliced tomato, red pepper slices and mozzarella. Toast under a hot grill until the cheese has melted and is golden.

AVOCADO TOAST

Remove the stone and scoop out the flesh from half an avocado. Mash with a little salt and freshly ground pepper, spread over a slice of toast, then top with any of the following:

o A handful of edamame beans

o A tablespoon of toasted pumpkin seeds (see p. 79)

o A few crushed hazelnuts

o A spoonful of nut butter underneath the avocado

o Some fried mushroom slices

o A few halved cherry tomatoes.

PITTA CRISPS

Slice a wholemeal tortilla wrap into eight triangles, spread out on a baking tray and pop in the oven, heated to 200 °C/fan 180 °C/gas mark 6, for 10 minutes.

LUNCHBOX FRITTATA

Whisk two eggs, mix in a few halved cherry tomatoes, a few torn basil leaves, 25 g (1 oz) crumbled feta (or any other cheese), a few chilli flakes and some salt and pepper. Pour into a hot non-stick pan and cook for 3–4 minutes until the base is set, then pop under a hot grill for 2–3 minutes until cooked through.

FIVE-MINUTE WHOLEMEAL FLATBREADS

These speedy flatbreads are soft and pliable and can be used in the same way as wraps or naan bread to go with curries and hot pots, or filled and rolled up with salad. They don't have to be perfectly round – they look more rustic if you just roll them out. You can freeze any leftover flatbreads. Simply defrost thoroughly, wrap in foil and warm through in the oven, or lightly re-toast them under a grill.

Preparation time: 5 minutes
Cooking time: 15 minutes

225 g (8 oz) wholemeal flour, plus a little extra for dusting
½ tsp salt
2 tsp baking powder
1 tbsp olive oil
200 ml (7 fl oz) plain yogurt

Topping (optional):
1–2 tbsp olive oil
1 tsp za'atar (Middle Eastern herbs available from most supermarkets), thyme or oregano
Sea salt flakes

Makes 4

Put the flour, salt, baking powder and olive oil in a bowl. Pour in the yogurt and mix until you have a smooth, sticky dough.

Dust your work surface and hands with flour (see 'Cook's tip' below), then place the dough onto the work surface. Divide into four pieces and roll each one out into rounds, roughly 5–6 mm (¼ in) thick.

Heat a griddle pan or BBQ until hot, brush the flatbreads with a little oil, then cook for 1–2 minutes each side, until slightly puffy and lightly charred. Brush again with olive oil and scatter over the herbs and salt. Serve warm.

> **NUTRITION per flatbread:**
> • 277 cals • 9 g protein • 7 g fat (1 g saturates)
> • 41 g carbs (4 g total sugars) • 6 g fibre

Make it vegan

Use a non-dairy yogurt alternative.

COOK'S TIP

The dough can be quite sticky, so flour your hands, work surface and rolling pin first to make it easier to roll out.

Hummus and Dips

BASIC HUMMUS

Making your own hummus may seem unnecessary when it's so easy to buy, but homemade is infinitely tastier, contains less oil and is all-round more nutritious. I make a batch every week; it's perfect for dipping crunchy vegetables or Pitta crisps (see p. 202), spreading on toast, as a topping for baked sweet potatoes or adding to a salad. Hummus is made from chickpeas, which are a brilliant source of protein, iron and fructo-oligosaccharides, a type of fibre that feeds the friendly bacteria of the gut and benefits the immune system. This recipe can be whipped up in five minutes and will keep, covered, in the fridge for up to three days.

Preparation time: 5 minutes

400 g (14 oz) can chickpeas, drained and rinsed, or 125 g (4 oz) dried chickpeas, soaked overnight then boiled for 45 minutes
1 garlic clove, crushed
2 tbsp extra virgin olive oil
1 tbsp tahini (sesame seed paste)
Juice of ½ lemon
2–4 tbsp water
Salt and freshly ground black pepper

To serve:
Carrot sticks, cucumber, yellow pepper, celery or toasted pitta triangles or Pitta crisps

Makes 12 tbsp

Reserve 1–2 tablespoons chickpeas. Put the remainder in a food processor or blender with the other ingredients and blend until smooth. Taste to check the seasoning. Stir in the reserved whole chickpeas, then spoon into a shallow dish.

NUTRITION per 1 tbsp (25 g/1 oz) serving:
• 51 cals • 2 g protein • 3 g fat (0 g saturates)
• 3 g carbs (0 g total sugars) • 1 g fibre

variation

Lemon and Coriander Hummus: **Add a handful of fresh coriander to the hummus and pulse briefly until mixed.**

Moroccan Style: **Add ½ teaspoon each of ground cumin, ground coriander and sweet paprika and a few mint leaves and blend together.**

BEETROOT HUMMUS

Preparation time: 5 minutes

400 g (14 oz) can chickpeas, drained and rinsed

150 g (5 oz) cooked beetroot, roughly chopped

1 garlic clove, crushed

2 tbsp extra virgin olive oil

1 tbsp tahini (sesame seed paste)

Juice of ½ lemon

2–4 tbsp water

Salt

A handful of fresh mint, finely chopped

2 tbsp sunflower or pumpkin seeds, toasted (see p. 79)

Makes 20 tbsp

Place the chickpeas, beetroot, garlic, oil, tahini, lemon juice, water and salt in a food processor and blend for 30 seconds until smooth. Add the mint, pulse briefly, then transfer to a bowl. Mix in the seeds. It will keep, covered, in the fridge for up to three days.

NUTRITION per 1 tbsp (25 g/1 oz) serving:
• 46 cals • 2 g protein • 3 g fat (0 g saturates)
• 3 g carbs (1 g total sugars) • 1 g fibre

PEA HUMMUS

Preparation time: 5 minutes

200 g (7 oz) cooked peas

400 g (14 oz) can chickpeas, drained and rinsed

2 tbsp olive oil

1 tbsp tahini (sesame seed paste)

1 garlic clove, crushed

Juice of ½ lemon

2–4 tbsp water

Salt

3 tbsp finely chopped fresh mint

Makes 20 tbsp

Place the peas, chickpeas, oil, tahini, garlic, lemon juice, water and salt in a food processor and blend for 30 seconds, until smooth. Add the mint, pulse briefly, then transfer to a bowl. It will keep, covered, in the fridge for up to three days.

NUTRITION per 1 tbsp (25 g/1 oz) serving:
• 40 cals • 2 g protein • 2 g fat (0 g saturates)
• 3 g carbs (0 g total sugars) • 1 g fibre

AVOCADO HUMMUS

Preparation time: 5 minutes

400 g (14 oz) can chickpeas, drained and rinsed
1 avocado, peeled, pitted and roughly chopped
1 garlic clove, crushed
A pinch of chilli flakes
Juice of 1 lime
2–4 tbsp water
Salt

Makes 16 tbsp

Place the chickpeas, avocado, garlic, chilli flakes, lime juice, water and salt in a food processor and blend for 30 seconds until smooth. Sprinkle a few chilli flakes on top. It will keep, covered, in the fridge for up to three days.

NUTRITION per 1 tbsp (25 g/1 oz) serving:
• 39 cals • 1 g protein • 2 g fat (0 g saturates)
• 3 g carbs (0 g total sugars) • 1 g fibre

CHOCOLATE HUMMUS

Sweet hummus may sound a little far-fetched, but it is unbelievably delicious. It's got that luxurious decadence of chocolate spread but with less than half the calories and sugar. Spread it on toast, rice cakes or crackers, spoon on porridge or plain yogurt, or serve as a dip with Pitta crisps (see p. 202), strawberries, apple slices, banana or whatever you fancy!

Preparation time: 5 minutes

400 g (14 oz) canned chickpeas, drained and rinsed
2 tbsp cacao or cocoa powder (see p. 168)
2 tbsp canned coconut milk (or tahini/sesame seed paste or nut butter)
2–3 tbsp honey, maple syrup or sugar
½ tsp vanilla extract

Makes 12 tbsp

Place all the ingredients in a food processor and pulse until the mixture is smooth and creamy. You may need to stop and scrape the mixture from the sides a couple of times. Add a little extra coconut milk or water if you want a thinner consistency.

Transfer to bowl or jar and store, covered, in the fridge for up to a week.

NUTRITION per 1 tbsp (25 g/1 oz) serving:
• 47 cals • 2 g protein • 2 g fat (1 g saturates)
• 5 g carbs (2 g total sugars) • 2 g fibre

variation

Banoffee: Replace the cacao or cocoa powder and coconut milk with half a banana, 1 tablespoon caramel sauce and 1 teaspoon tahini.

SPICY CHICKPEAS

Chickpeas are packed with protein and fibre, making them a super-healthy savoury snack for any time. Scatter them over colourful salads, hummus, soups or avocado toast for a lovely textural contrast. Make a large batch and keep them, covered, in the fridge for up to a week.

Preparation time: 5 minutes
Cooking time: 25 minutes

400 g (14 oz) can chickpeas, drained and rinsed
1 tbsp olive oil
1 tsp ground cumin
¼ tsp turmeric
½ tsp smoked paprika or cayenne pepper
Salt and freshly ground black pepper

Makes 10 tbsp

Preheat the oven to 190 °C/fan 170 °C/gas mark 5. Meanwhile, line a baking tray with baking paper.

Pat the chickpeas dry with a clean tea towel or paper towel. They should feel dry to the touch. In a medium bowl, combine the chickpeas, oil, cumin, turmeric, paprika or cayenne, salt and pepper until the chickpeas are well coated. Spread them out on the baking tray and roast for 20–25 minutes, or until crispy. After 10 minutes, give the tray a shake to move the chickpeas around. Check they are done with the press of a finger: they should be slightly crisp on the outside but still soft on the inside.

NUTRITION per 2 tbsp (50 g/2 oz) serving:
• 83 cals • 4 g protein • 4 g fat (1 g saturates)
• 8 g carbs (0 g total sugars) • 3 g fibre

variations

• Use 2 teaspoons curry powder instead of the individual spices.

• Replace the spices with 1 teaspoon each of chopped fresh rosemary and fresh thyme.

ROASTED PUMPKIN SEEDS

Roasting transforms pumpkin seeds into a super-tasty, crunchy snack that's perfect for munching on the go, or for sprinkling on salads and dips. Pumpkin seeds are rich in protein, omega-3 oils and zinc, making them brilliant for muscle recovery and healthy immunity.

Preparation time: 5 minutes

Cooking time: 10 minutes

Choose from one of the following mixes:

Salted:

100 g (3½ oz) pumpkin seeds

1 tbsp light olive or rapeseed oil

1 tsp sea salt

Hot Chilli:

100 g (3½ oz) pumpkin seeds

1 tbsp light olive or rapeseed oil

½–1 tsp cayenne pepper, or to taste

½ tsp sweet paprika

½ tsp chilli powder, or to taste

Herby:

100 g (3½ oz) pumpkin seeds

1 tbsp light olive or rapeseed oil

½ tsp dried oregano

½ tsp dried rosemary

½ tsp sea salt

Makes 8 tbsp

Preheat the oven to 200 °C/fan 180 °C/gas mark 6.

Mix all the ingredients together in a bowl, then spread out the seeds on a large baking tray.

Roast in the oven for 9–10 minutes, stirring a couple of times, until toasted and darker. Leave to cool. Store the roasted seeds in an airtight container for up to a week.

> **NUTRITION per 1 tbsp (15 g/½ oz) serving:**
> • 92 cals • 1 g protein • 2 g fat (0 g saturates)
> • 3 g carbs (0 g total sugars) • 1 g fibre

ACKNOWLEDGEMENTS

I want to thank the wonderful team at Bloomsbury for making this book special, especially my publisher Charlotte Croft for her brilliant vision and never-ending support; my editor Holly Jarrald for her clear guidance and consistently positive energy. Also to Jane Donovan for her attention to detail, Louise Turpin for her superb work on the design, and Lizzy, Katherine and Alice for their marketing and publicity expertise.

I'm incredibly grateful to food photographer Clare Winfield for bringing the recipes to life so beautifully, to Jayne Cross for her fantastic food styling, Grant Pritchard for his brilliant photography, and Clare Pinkney MUA, for making me look more glamorous in the kitchen than usual.

But my biggest thanks go to my husband, Simon, and daughters, Chloe and Lucy. They have supported me throughout the writing of this book, provided unending inspiration and served as daily guinea pigs for all the recipes – including the ones that didn't work out! I love you so much.

REFERENCES

Chapter 2

1 Waitrose & Partners. Food & Drink Report 2018–2019. https://www.waitrose.com/content/dam/waitrose/Inspiration/Waitrose%20&%20Partners%20Food%20and%20Drink%20Report%202018.pdf (accessed August 2019).

2 Schwarzenegger, Arnold. 'The Radical Revolution' – Arnold Schwarzenegger on Going Vegan: An excerpt from a Q&A session on Arnold Schwarzenegger's Facebook page: https://www.youtube.com/watch?v=2GkWRe_9WQE (accessed August 2019).

3 World Resources Institute. 'Shifting Diets for a Sustainable Food Future', (2016).

4 Springmann M, Wiebe K, et al. 'Health and nutritional aspects of sustainable diet strategies and their association with environmental impacts: a global modelling analysis with country-level detail', The Lancet Planetary Health (2018) 2(10): e451-e461.

5 Willett, W, Rockstrom, J, Loken, B, et al. 'Food in the Anthropocene: the EAT–*Lancet* Commission on healthy diets from sustainable food systems.' The Lancet Commission, (2019), 393 (10170):447-492.

6 The Intergovernmental Panel on Climate Change (IPCC): 'Global Warming of 1.5 C' (2018).

7 Dinu M, Abbate F, et al. 'Vegetarian, vegan diets and multiple health outcomes: A systematic review with meta-analysis of observational studies,' *Critical Reviews in Food Science and Nutrition* (2017), 57:17, 3640-3649.

8 World Cancer Research Fund. 'Diet, Nutrition, Physical Activity and Cancer: a Global Perspective', (2018).

9 Farvid, M S, Stern, M C, Norat, T, et al. 'Consumption of red and processed meat and breast cancer incidence: A systematic review and meta-analysis of prospective studies.' *International Journal of Cancer* (2018), 143: 2787-2799.

10 NHS: https://www.nhs.uk/live-well/eat-well/red-meat-and-the-risk-of-bowel-cancer (accessed August 2019).

11 Crowe, Francesca L, et al. 'Risk of hospitalization or death from ischemic heart disease among British vegetarians and nonvegetarians: results from the EPIC-Oxford cohort study', *American Journal of Clinical Nutrition* 97/3 (2013), 597–603.

12 Song M, Fung T T, Hu F B, et al. Association of Animal and Plant Protein Intake With All-Cause and Cause-Specific Mortality. *JAMA Internal Medicine* (2016), 176(10):1453–1463.

13 British Dietetic Association. https://www.bda.uk.com/news/view?id=179 (accessed August 2019).

Chapter 3

1 Craddock, J, et al. 'Vegetarian and Omnivorous Nutrition – Comparing Physical Performance', *International Journal of Sport Nutrition and Exercise Metabolism* (2016), 26(3):212–20.

2 Barr, S I, Rideout, C A, 'Nutritional considerations for vegetarian athletes', *Nutrition* 20 (7–8) (2004), 696–703.

3 Lynch, H M, et al. 'Cardiorespiratory Fitness and Peak Torque Differences between Vegetarian and Omnivore Endurance Athletes: A Cross-Sectional Study', *Nutrients* (2016), 8(11), 726.

4 Mangano, K M, et al. 'Dietary protein is associated with musculoskeletal health independently of dietary pattern: The Framingham Third Generation Study', *American Journal of Clinical Nutrition* (2017), 105 (3): 714–722.

Chapter 4

1 Thomas, D T, Erdman, K A, Burke, L M, 'American College of Sports Medicine Joint Position Statement. Nutrition and Athletic Performance', *Medicine & Science in Sports & Exercise* (2016), 48(3):543–68.

2 Moore, D R, Robinson, M J, Fry, J L, et al. 'Ingested protein dose response of muscle and albumin protein synthesis after resistance exercise in young men', *American Journal of Clinical Nutrition* 89 (2009), 161–168.

3 **Schoenfeld, B J, Aragon, A A,** 'How much protein can the body use in a single meal for muscle-building? Implications for daily protein distribution', *Journal of the International Society of Sports Nutrition* (2018)15:10.

4 **Moore, D R,** et al. 'Protein ingestion to stimulate myofibrillar protein synthesis requires greater relative protein intakes in healthy older versus younger men'. *The Journals of Gerontology: Series A, Biological Sciences and Medical Sciences* (2015) vol. 70(1), pp. 57–62.

5 **Hamarsland H, Handegard V, Kåshagen M,** et al. 'No Difference between Spray Dried Milk and Native Whey Supplementation with Strength Training', *Medicine & Science in Sports & Exercise* (2018); 51(1):75-83.

6 **Burke, L M, Ross, M L, Garvican-Lewis, L A,** et al. 'Low carbohydrate, high fat diet impairs exercise economy and negates the performance benefit from intensified training in elite race walkers', *The Journal of Physiology* (2017); 595(9):2785–2807.

7 **Tappy, M D, Mittendorfer, B,** 'Fructose toxicity: is the science ready for public health actions?', *Current Opinion in Clinical Nutrition and Metabolic Care* (2012); 15(4): 357–361.

8 **Khan T A, Sievenpiper J L,** 'Controversies about sugars: results from systematic reviews and meta-analyses on obesity, cardiometabolic disease and diabetes', *European Journal of Nutrition* (2016); 55(Suppl 2):25-43.

9 **World Health Organisation,** 'Sugars intake for adults and children', (2015).

10 **Scientific Advisory Committee on Nutrition,** 'Carbohydrates and Health', (2015). London TSO.

11 **Shing, C M, Peake, J M, Lim, C L,** et al. 'Effects of probiotics supplementation on gastrointestinal permeability, inflammation and exercise performance in the heat', *European Journal of Applied Physiology* (2014) Jan; 114(1):93–103.

12 **McDonald, D, Hyde, E, Debelius, J W, Morton, J T,** et al. 'American Gut: An Open Platform for Citizen Science Microbiome Research', *American Society for Microbiology* (2018) 15;3(3). pii: e00031-18.

13 **Scientific Advisory Committee on Nutrition.** 'Saturated fats and health', (2019).

14 **WHO** Draft Guidelines: 'Saturated fatty acid and *trans*-fatty acid intake for adults and children'. Geneva, World Health Organization (2018).

15 **Sacks, Frank M,** et al. 'Dietary fats and cardiovascular disease: a presidential advisory from the American Heart Association'. *Circulation* 136.3 (2017), e1-e23.

Chapter 5

1 **Ball, M J, Bartlett, M A,** 'Dietary intake and iron status of Australian vegetarian women', *American Journal of Clinical Nutrition* 70 (1999), 353–358.

2 **Alexander, D, Ball, M J, Mann, J,** 'Nutrient intake and haematological status of vegetarians and age-sex matched omnivores', *European Journal of Clinical Nutrition*, 48 (1998), 538–546.

3 **Janelle, K C, Barr, S I,** 'Nutrient intakes and eating behavior scores of vegetarian and nonvegetarian women', *Journal of the American Dietetic Association* 95 (2), (1995), 180–6.

4 **The Vegan Society,** https://www.vegansociety.com/resources/nutrition-and-health/nutrients/vitamin-b12 (accessed August 2019).

5 **Scientific Advisory Committee on Nutrition** 'Vitamin D and Health', (2016).

6 **NHS,** 'Vitamins, supplements and nutrition in pregnancy' https://www.nhs.uk/conditions/pregnancy-and-baby/vitamins-minerals-supplements-pregnant/ (accessed December 2018).

Chapter 7

1 Maughan, R J, Burke, L M, Dvorak, J, et al. 'IOC consensus statement: dietary supplements and the high-performance athlete', *International Journal of Sport Nutrition and Exercise Metabolism* (2018) 28.2: 104–125.

2 Scientific Advisory Committee on Nutrition: 'Vitamin D and Health', (2016).

3 Jouris, K B, McDaniel, J L, Weiss, E P, 'The effect of omega-3 fatty acid supplementation on the inflammatory response to eccentric strength exercise', *Journal of Sports Science & Medicine* 2011;10:432–8.

4 Russell, C, Hall, D, Brown, P, 'European Supplement Contamination Survey', *HFL Sport Science*, (2013).

Chapter 8

1 Prevalence of coeliac disease: https://www.nhs.uk/conditions/coeliac-disease/ (accessed August 2019).

2 Antoni, R, Robertson, T, Robertson, M, et al. 'A pilot feasibility study exploring the effects of a moderate time-restricted feeding intervention on energy intake, adiposity and metabolic physiology in free-living human subjects', *Journal of Nutritional Science* 2018; 7, E22.

3 Trock B J, Hilakivi-Clarke L, Clarke R, 'Meta-analysis of soy intake and breast cancer risk', *Journal of the National Cancer Institute* 2006; 98(7):459-71.

4 Aune D, Giovannucci E, Boffetta P, et al. 'Fruit and vegetable intake and the risk of cardiovascular disease, total cancer and all-cause mortality–a systematic review and dose-response meta-analysis of prospective studies', *International Journal of Epidemiology 2017*; 46(3): 1029–1056.

5 Dimeglio, D, Mattes, R, 'Liquid versus solid carbohydrate: effects on food intake and body weight', *International Journal of Obesity* (2000) 24(6), 794-800.

6 Drouin-Chartier, J P, Côté, JA Labonté, ME et al. 'Comprehensive Review of the Impact of Dairy Foods and Dairy Fat on Cardiometabolic Risk', *Advances in Nutrition*, 2016, 7(6): 1041–1051.

7 Smith-Spangler C, Brandeau M L, Hunter G E, Bavinger J C, Pearson M, Eschbach P J, et al. 'Are Organic Foods Safer or Healthier Than Conventional Alternatives?: A Systematic Review.' *Annals of Internal Medicine* (2012);157:348–366.

8 Baudry J, Assmann K E, Touvier M, et al. 'Association of Frequency of Organic Food Consumption With Cancer Risk Findings From the NutriNet-Santé Prospective Cohort Study', *JAMA Internal Medicine* 2018;178(12):1597–1606.

9 Bradbury K E, Balkwill A, Spencer E A, et al. 'Organic food consumption and the incidence of cancer in a large prospective study of women in the United Kingdom', *British Journal of Cancer* 2014;110(9):2321-6.

Part 2 Recipes

1 Eyres L, Eyres M F, Chisholm A, Brown R C, 'Coconut oil consumption and cardiovascular risk factors in humans', *Nutrition Reviews* 2016; 74(4):267-80.

2 Lockyer, S, Stanner, S, (2016), 'Coconut oil – a nutty idea?' *Nutrition Bulletin*, 41: 42–54.

RESOURCES

www.vegsoc.org The website of the UK Vegetarian Society provides clear information and fact sheets on health and nutrition, animal welfare, sustainability, the environment and recipes.

www.vegansociety.com The website of the UK Vegan Society provides comprehensive resources on the vegan lifestyle, nutrition, food and the environment as well as many recipes.

www.vegetarianliving.co.uk is an online UK magazine featuring news, celebrity interviews and articles on health, nutrition and lifestyle topics, as well as a comprehensive vegetarian and vegan recipe collection.

www.meatfreemondays.com is a not-for-profit campaign launched by Paul, Mary and Stella McCartney. The website includes advice, tips and resources for schools as well as hundreds of vegetarian recipes.

www.vivahealth.org.uk The website of the charity Viva! Health provides well-researched information on vegan nutrition and health topics.

www.vegnews.com is an online US magazine featuring news, health and lifestyle articles, interviews and recipes.

www.ewg.org/meateatersguide The website of the Environmental Working Group and the report, 'The Meat Eater's Guide to Climate Change and Health', provides information about meat consumption and the environment.

www.savvyvegetarian.com This US website provides useful articles and advice on vegetarian and vegan diets and nutrition, health, cooking, environmental issues, green living, sustainability and related issues.

www.vrg.org The US Vegetarian Resource Group provides information on vegetarian and vegan nutrition, recipes, ingredients and vegetarian restaurants, and some useful articles for vegetarian athletes.

www.vegetarianbodybuilding.com This website provides articles and advice on vegetarian and vegan nutrition for athletes and bodybuilders.

INDEX

ALSO BY ANITA BEAN

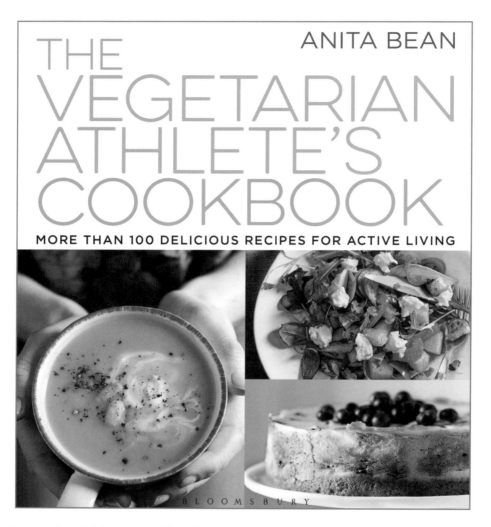

The Vegetarian Athlete's Cookbook: More than 100 delicious recipes for active living
Bloomsbury, £14.99

ALSO BY ANITA BEAN

The Runner's Cookbook: More than 100 delicious recipes to fuel your running
Bloomsbury, £14.99